"Let me go."

To her ears, she sounded breathless and vulnerable. "Now," she said more forcefully when he did not obey.

A chuckle started deep in his chest, the vibration reaching her through the clothing that separated them. The sound escaping him as a low rumble should have been humorous, but was not.

"You have run from me these last ten years. You will run no more—until I am through with you."

The cool of the late-summer night turned cold.

"Let the past go and release me."

Even as she said the words she hoped against hope that they would not apply to him. Once, he had loved her enough to defy her family to have her. She wanted him to love her still.

THE
ROGUE'S
SEDUCTION

Georgina Devon

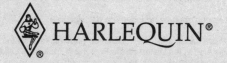

TORONTO • NEW YORK • LONDON
AMSTERDAM • PARIS • SYDNEY • HAMBURG
STOCKHOLM • ATHENS • TOKYO • MILAN • MADRID
PRAGUE • WARSAW • BUDAPEST • AUCKLAND

ISBN 0-373-30459-5

THE ROGUE'S SEDUCTION

First North American Publication 2004

Copyright © 2002 by Alison J. Hentges

www.eHarlequin.com

Printed in U.S.A.

GEORGINA DEVON

began writing fiction in 1985 and has never looked
back. Alongside her prolific writing career, she has led
an interesting life. Her father was in the United States
Air Force, and after Georgina received her B.A. in
social sciences from California State College, she followed her father's footsteps and joined the USAF. She
met her husband, Martin, an A10 fighter pilot, while
she was serving as an aircraft maintenance officer.
Georgina, her husband and their young daughter now
live in Tucson, Arizona.

Chapter One

'Stand and deliver!'

Lillith, Lady de Lisle, recognized the voice instantly.

Jason Beaumair, Earl of Perth.

She did not need to look out the coach's window to picture him. Dark-visaged, with wings of silver at his temples and hair the colour of jet, he haunted her dreams. A scar, received in a duel over another man's wife, ran the length of his right cheek. She was—or had been—that wife.

A shiver of foreboding slid down her spine.

What was he doing, waylaying her carriage here on Hounslow Heath? He certainly did not need her jewels. He was as wealthy as Golden Ball. 'Twas a dangerous game the Earl played.

'You, Coachman,' Perth's imperious baritone ordered, 'descend with your hands empty and in the air. And you—that's right, you,' he added pointedly to the single outrider, 'drop your pistol or the driver will be sorrier for your actions.'

Lillith pulled aside the velvet window curtain in time to see her outrider drop his pistol. Perth sat at his leisure on a magnificent horse, a gun in each hand aimed at the coach. Trust the Earl to know horseflesh and not care who else knew the animal he rode was too fine for a highwayman.

At least the man wore a mask across his face. Should the *ton* get a whiff of this latest escapade of his involving her, all the old scandals would be revisited. She was not sure her reputation could withstand another assault from the Earl. The only thing that had preserved her good name the last time had been her husband's social standing. No one had willingly offended de Lisle; the man had known too many people at court.

However, as a widow, she no longer had her deceased husband's protection. And goodness knew that if her brother sought to preserve her good name both of them would be laughed out of London.

'You inside the vehicle,' Perth's lazy drawl demanded, 'come out where I can get a better look at what my labours have earned.'

He was as disreputable as always. It was his greatest fault and his greatest charm. She had thwarted him only once in her life and lived a long time regretting it.

With a sigh and a tiny smile curving her lips, she pulled her cape tight against the evening air and stepped out. Summer was nearly gone. A chill breeze caught at her silver-blond hair, undoing the intricate curls her maid had spent many hours perfecting. Her slipper-clad feet sank into the damp grass. The fine leather would be stained. No matter. A pair of ruined slippers was nothing. Great wealth was the only benefit she had gained by marrying de Lisle.

She made a mock curtsy, never taking her gaze from Perth's arrogant features. He gave her a feral grin, his strong white teeth flashing in the pale light of the full moon. At one time that look on his face had scared her. Now it excited her. She had been a child the first time she had dealt with him, ignorant and easily led by her family. She was a woman now, ready for him.

His eyes flashed. 'Come here.'

She returned his stare without flinching. 'I think not.'

Using his knees, he urged his mount forward, stopping only when he was close enough that she could smell the animal's musky scent. 'Come here,' he said again, a hint of iron underlying his words.

She shook her head. 'I am on my way home and in no mood for frivolity.'

His eyes narrowed. 'This is no frivolous matter, madam. I mean what I say.'

Without a word, he sent a shot at the feet of her coachman who had climbed down from his seat and gone to the heads of the two horses pulling her carriage. The old servant jumped back as dirt sprayed around his boots.

Anger sent Lillith a step forward. 'You go too far.'

'I don't go far enough,' Perth stated. 'Come here or the next ball will enter his flesh.'

Lillith met his hard look with one of her own. 'You are a rogue, sir, with no scruples.'

He made her a curt bow from the waist. 'You always were observant, as well as ambitious.'

The coolness of his tone set her back up. 'Be done with this and go your way. I tire of this inappropriate jest.'

''Tis no jest, Lady de Lisle. I intend to take you prisoner.'

She gasped. 'Never. Be gone.'

The grin that had been feral turned vicious, and Lillith stepped back without intending to do so. 'What dangerous game do you play now?' she asked, her voice barely a whisper.

He made no reply.

Under the protection of her cape, she searched for the tiny pistol with its mother-of-pearl handle that she always kept ready in her reticule. If he intended to threaten her with ruin and goodness knew what else, then she would protect herself. Before she could think rationally about what she intended to do, she pulled the tiny weapon out and shot.

She missed.

Furious at her own error, she threw the pistol at him. He merely leaned to one side and let it sail past. A grin of anticipation eased the harshness of his jaw, but did nothing to lessen the look of danger in his eye.

'I shall make it a personal goal to teach you how to shoot,' he drawled, that infuriating smile still on his face.

She scowled. 'You shall not be around me long enough to do so, sirruh.'

Her outrider used the fracas to make a lunge for the Earl, only to have Perth's well-trained horse shy away. The animal's action brought Perth's attention back to the servants.

'Enough dallying. Call your lackey off, madam, or I shall be forced to harm him,' Perth said through clenched teeth, the grin gone as though it had never been. His gaze never left her face.

A flush of irritation mounted Lillith's cheeks. 'Move away, Jim.'

When the servant was distant enough to suit him, Perth said, 'This is the last time I tell you to come here. The next time I will come to you.' His voice softened, although it lost none of the threat. 'And I will guarantee that you will not like it if you make me fetch you.'

Her tiny weapon was lost somewhere in the grass behind Perth. Her servants were both unarmed. Still, she did not fear Perth. He was a harsh man with a quick temper, but he would never physically hurt her.

'No.' She notched her chin up and squared her shoulders. 'If you insist on this folly, then you must fetch me. For I will not come to you, not like this.'

'You always were stubborn,' he murmured.

Without warning, he urged the horse forward. Lillith twisted in the damp grass, her foot slipping as she tried to sprint away. He was on her. His right arm swept down and around her waist so that the gun he held bit hard into her side. She took a deep breath to shout at him only to land with a cramping thump, stomach first, in front of him. She sprawled like a sack of grain across his horse's back, all the air knocked out of her lungs. Through the blood thundering in her ears, she heard her servants shouting and moving about.

'I would not if I were you,' Perth drawled seconds before shooting a pistol.

The sound reverberated through her body. If he had truly shot one of her men, she would see to it that the Earl paid.

She tried to wriggle off, determined to escape even if it meant landing face down in the dirt. A large, masculine hand settled firmly on her posterior, holding her securely in place. Heat spread through her hips until it engulfed her entire body. She might just as well be undressed and he with no gloves on, for it felt as though his bare flesh touched hers.

She bit her lower lip. Perth had always had this effect on her. Even after she wed de Lisle, she had responded like a wanton to just a glance from Perth. It was her shame.

De Lisle had called her cold. Thank goodness he had not known the truth.

As though he knew her worries for her servant, Perth said, 'Do not worry, madam, I harmed no one. Something which cannot be said for you.'

The horse lunged forward, scattering her thoughts like clouds before a winter wind. The bones of the animal's neck dug into her gut and made her feel like retching. This was an abominable situation.

'Release me,' she said, trying to shout and hearing her voice come out as a squeak.

'In good time,' Perth said, humour laced through his words.

Drat the man! He was enjoying this.

Her hair, having come completely loose from the topknot her maid had worked so long to achieve, hung in thick strands around her cheeks, providing a cushion from the hard smoothness of his boots. The breeze made by the horse's progress blew up her skirt and chilled her to the bone.

Determined to make this abduction difficult, she wrapped both hands around Perth's ankle and pulled. He lurched to the side.

'Careful, madam,' he thundered. 'You will unseat us both. Plunging from a galloping horse would not be healthy.'

In spite of the truth he spoke, she grinned—momentarily. His powerful hand smacked her rear. She was shocked more than hurt. Her cape and dress buffered any hurt and made it more humiliating than painful.

'How dare you, sirruh,' she said, keeping her grip on his ankle although she no longer pulled. She was becoming foggy-headed from being upside down.

'I dare a great deal,' he said, his voice a low growl of promise.

Her stomach felt as though it rushed to her throat. Surely they would soon be far enough away from her carriage and servants for him to stop so that she could change position. Or better yet, escape.

They came to an abrupt halt, jarring her painfully against the saddle. She released his leg and pushed against the horse's shoulder in an attempt to slip off on to her feet. Perth stopped her by jumping to the ground ahead of her and hauling her off. She landed with her back moulded against his chest, his arm wrapped around her ribs just below her breasts.

Her breath caught in a gulp. His nearness was as heady as the finest French champagne, a drink she enjoyed sparingly for that reason. The scent of musk and cinnamon that clung to him was an aphrodisiac, a strong memory of years before.

Mortification at her weakness made her furious. She twisted, trying to break his hold. Instead of releasing her, he used her momentum to turn her in his arms. Her bosom pressed tightly to his chest. Her loins melded with his. Her face met his. Only inches of cool air separated their lips.

She shuddered and turned her head away.

'Let me go,' she whispered. To her ears, she sounded breathless and vulnerable. 'Now,' she said more forcefully when he did not immediately obey her.

A chuckle started deep in his chest, the vibration reaching her through the clothing that separated them. The sound escaped him as a low rumble that should have been humourous but was not.

'You have run from me these last ten years. You will run no more—until I am through with you.'

The cool of the late summer night turned cold.

'Have you not learned that revenge is best eaten hot? Yours is cold. Let the past go and release me.'

Even as she said the words, she hoped against hope that they not apply to him. Once he had loved her enough to defy her family to have her. She wanted him to love her still.

'You always were intelligent as well as beautiful.'

'Revenge it is then,' she said softly, holding firm to the hard edge of her anger.

He nodded.

Revenge. Something inside her crumbled and died. Hope, perhaps. De Lisle had gone to his maker just over a year ago. Since that time, she had hoped against hope that Perth might still want her. And he did. But he did not love her. By kidnapping her, he showed that he intended to ruin her.

She had to escape him. Before she could think better of it, she stomped on his instep. Her soft leather slipper barely made a dent in his boot, but she took him by surprise. His grip relaxed, and she spun around out of his arms and made a dash for the road they had stopped beside.

He caught her cape and dragged her back, but she slipped the garment from her shoulders and kept going. Her feet slid in the dirt and she gasped for breath but managed to keep running.

Seconds later he had her.

He twirled her around and crushed her to him. One arm wrapped around her waist, the other cupped the back of her head.

He stared down at her, the pale light of a half-moon

glinting off his silver-streaked hair. His features were shadows and angles. She could not see the expression on his face, but there was a tightness to his body that told her more than words.

Lillith sucked air into her lungs. Her palms pressed against him. 'Do not,' she gasped seconds before his mouth took hers.

His lips were firm and sure against hers. His tongue teased her. His teeth nipped her. Hunger and desire beat at her. Shivers chased by flames chased by more shivers coursed through her body. If he released her, she would sink to the ground.

When she felt as though there was no more air left in the world for her to breathe, he let her go. She sagged against him.

The hand that had cupped the back of her head slid to the column of her neck. His fingers glided along her heated flesh and became tangled in the length of her hair. He held her secure.

'I have wanted to do that any time these past ten years,' he said, his voice a rasp.

His grip on her hair chained her to him as surely as the love she had always felt. Lillith pulled herself erect, causing his fingers to tighten their hold, and wondered what had happened to her bravado and determination to escape him. It was an effort to focus her mind on what he said. She licked lips that felt branded. Her fingers strayed to their swollen flesh without her conscious volition.

'Ten years is a long time,' she finally managed.

'I can be a patient man when needs be.'

Exhaustion came fast on the heels of his words. All her hopes and desires combined to crush her emotions. Her shoulders sagged before she realised it. If only this abduction had not happened. As soon wish for Perth's love.

Quickly, defiantly, she straightened to her fullest height. She was tall for a woman, her eyes level with his chin. 'Do you call this act that of a patient man?'

His smile, that devastating slash of teeth, mocked her. 'I call waiting ten years patient.'

He leaned into her and brought a strand of hair to his face. 'Lilac,' he murmured. 'I remember the first time I met you, you smelled of sweet lilac. Everyone else wore rose water or lavender, but not you.'

He let the tress slip through his fingers. The hair slid down her shoulder to curl along her breast where the fine muslin of her evening gown bared her flesh. His gaze followed and sharpened. Desire, hot and hungry, burned in the lines of his face. She saw his reaction and her own body betrayed her. It had always been thus with her.

'I would have forsaken my marriage vows for you,' she whispered, the words coming from a place in her heart she had thought locked away. They spoke aloud the dream she had cherished through the early months of her marriage to a man who cared nothing for her pleasure in the marriage bed. She had thought them long ago forgotten.

The fire died in his face. His eyes became chips of ebony ice. 'I don't dally with married women. Nor do I share what is mine.'

Shame at her words and her weakness goaded her. 'Is that why you fought a duel with my husband, a man many years your senior?'

His hand, which still gripped her nape, tightened. 'You were mine and I intended to have you the only way possible.' Now he shrugged as though sloughing away an unpleasant memory. 'But de Lisle was better with a sword than I. He kept you.'

His grip on her loosened and the temptation to squirm was great. She resisted. He was a strong man, and had he intended to let her go he would have released her completely.

She sighed. 'So what do you mean to do now?'

Clouds scudded across the moon, casting his face into darkness. Lillith could not see him clearly enough to read his emotions. She shivered.

'I intend to make up for the past years. My country retreat is a long ride from here. That is where we are going.'

'No.' The denial was automatic.

His cruel smile returned and he hauled her so close that she could see the night growth of dark hairs shadowing his jaw. 'What happened to your passion, your willingness to deny your marriage vows?'

She flared in anger. ''Tis one thing to give everything to a man who loves you, another to have a man throw your youthful passions in your face and turn them to revenge.'

His mouth thinned into a hard line. 'You are a fool.'

She saw no love or even liking in his eyes. He

watched her with cold determination and it made her hands feel numb with dread.

Revenge, revenge and revenge. Nothing more. He would ruin her for revenge and in the process ruin himself. She would not let him do so.

Her resolve to resist him firmed, and she began to struggle in earnest. She kicked his shin and instantly regretted it as pain shot up her leg. She flung her arms out and at him. He released her waist in time to catch one of her wrists in each hand. He held her effortlessly as she panted from exertion and frustration.

'I won't go with you,' she said between clenched teeth. 'You cannot do this to me. You will ruin me. Us.' Bitterness welled up in her. 'As you very nearly did ten years ago.'

His eyes glinted in what light from the night sky remained. 'And you have no de Lisle to save you this time. And I would wager in Brook's betting book that your brother will not do so.'

She bit her lip and looked away, twisting as far to the side as his continued hold on her wrists would allow. He spoke only the truth, no matter that it hurt. This was a night for long-buried truths and long-remembered pain. She wished to inflict some of her own.

'You are as cruel and self-absorbed as ever. Had you been a different man, my family might have let me wed you.'

She heard his sharp intake of breath and the satisfaction that she had hoped for eluded her. No matter what lay between them, she had never hated him. Far from it.

'Had I been a rich man instead of a distant cousin that no one expected to inherit, things would have been different. Your family sold you to the highest bidder, a shrivelled-up prune of a man who no more knew what to do with you than a youth faced with his first woman.'

Still more truths. He was determined to strip her of the hard-gained pretense in which she had found refuge. He laid bare between them in the cold night air all their past, even as in the doing he laid waste to any possible future they might have had.

Tears stung her eyes, and she could do nothing to stop them or wipe them away. Her fingers were not hers to command.

'Let me go,' she said, trying desperately not to choke and alert him to her turmoil. 'I promise not to run or give you further trouble.'

His hold loosened, but did not release her.

She heard a rumbling in the distance. It sounded as though a carriage came their way, but there was no light as that which would come from outside lanterns. She chided herself. If this were Perth's coach, there would be no light for others to see. Her servants would be looking for her.

The carriage came into view, a darker shadow on the road. Perth released one of her hands and stepped into the path of the oncoming vehicle. The coachman's sharp eyes spotted the Earl and the carriage halted. Without waiting for someone to approach them, Perth thrust her forward, yanked the door open himself and threw her inside.

She landed with a thump and a swirl of skirts that tangled with her legs. The cape that she had lost during her struggle with Perth quickly followed. She tried to get her balance to stand up, only to fall back against the seat when the carriage lurched forward. No sooner had the vehicle started moving than the door opened again and Perth bounded gracefully inside.

Lillith managed to get on to the seat opposite from where Perth deposited himself. Fine leather met her fingertips. Once Perth had been a captain in the Hussars, living only on his army salary. Now he was rich enough to squander money on any toy that took his fancy. Her fingers smoothed over the butter-soft leather. Had he been this rich ten years before, they would not now be sitting here, adversaries, each intent on hurting the other.

She sighed.

No inside lantern was lit, so the interior was too dark for her to see Perth's face. Yet she felt the energy he projected—an energy that excited her as much as it scared her. He would command her attention and her love, and then he would walk away from her without a backward glance.

A chill ran the course of her back. Without taking her attention off him, she leaned forward and groped along what she could reach of the floor in search of her cape. She found it and hauled it up and around her shoulders, as someone might shield themselves from an attack.

'Come here,' he said, his voice soft and dangerous.

Chapter Two

Lillith sat frozen in place.

His command echoed through her mind: *Come here.* She hugged the cape closer until the soft muslin caressed her cheeks and tickled her nose. It did nothing to ease the cold that seeped into her bones. She bit her lower lip.

'I think not,' she managed.

'We have a long ride, Lady de Lisle—Lillith.' His voice was low and thick as sweetest honey when he said her name. 'I think you will come over here sooner rather than later.'

'You always were arrogant and too sure of having things your own way. Your besetting sins.'

He chuckled deep in his chest, a mirthless sound. 'And what are yours, milady? Fickleness and faithlessness? I would rather have my own.'

She reared back as though he had slapped her. In a way he had. 'I do what I must when I must.'

She put all the conviction of her past choices into her words, refusing to let him make her despise herself for what she had had to do. Her family had depended on her. She had saved them. If her own happiness had died because of their need, then it was a price she had been willing to pay, a price she would pay today if need be.

'You do as you are bid to do,' he sneered.

Anger flared in her, setting her chest pounding and her blood rioting. 'You have overstepped the bounds of politeness, sirruh. What I did in the past and what I do in the future is none of your concern. Nor do you have the right to criticise me over something that was no concern of yours.'

'No concern of mine?' He leaned forward until she could feel his warm breath on her face. He smelled of cinnamon and cold night air. 'Who did you leave at the altar?' A harsh laugh tore from his lips. 'My twin?'

'I did my duty to my family. I could do nothing else.'

'You were sold to save your brother from the River Tick and exile to a continent where Napoleon held reign,' he said, disgust and loathing dripping from every word. 'You were nothing but a piece of goods sold to the highest bidder. Unfortunately for me, I was not the highest bidder. I was not even a contender.'

Enough was enough, and she had tired of hearing things that she could not change any more than she could change the position of the stars. She drew herself up and let the cape fall from her shoulders.

'Are you finished insulting me and my family, for I am certainly tired of hearing you?'

His eyes flashed in the dim moonlight that managed

to flicker in through the window, but he said nothing. Instead, he grabbed the cane that lay on the seat beside him and rapped the end on the carriage roof, signalling the coachman to halt. The wheels had barely stopped turning before he was out the door.

Lillith's sense of victory was fleeting at best. Without Perth she was left to her own thoughts and they were not pleasant. Too many things had happened and it seemed worse were to come.

The slowing motion of the coach woke Lillith. She blinked her eyes, trying to see better. She was not at her best upon first waking. The vehicle stopped completely, and she found herself tossed forward and caught by an arm around her waist. Her wits returned in a rush.

Perth. Abducted.

Vaguely, she remembered the carriage stopping once before, but she had fallen into an exhausted sleep, her thoughts and memories twisted into nightmares, and had not roused so much as tossed about. Then warmth and security had enveloped her, and the dreams had eased and she had gone deeper into sleep. She now realised that Perth had entered and had taken her into his arms.

Now he released her before she said a word or even tried to free herself. She nearly tumbled off the seat, but managed to scramble across the vehicle and to sit up, facing him.

The inside was dimly lit from outside light. She guessed it must be some time in the early morning.

They must have travelled some considerable distance since her abduction.

'We are stopping here to change horses and get something to eat.' Perth's voice was deeper than usual. She wondered if he had just woken up. 'Stay here. I will be back shortly.'

Before she could reply, he was gone.

Any lingering tiredness left. If she meant to flee, she had better start now. Grabbing up her cape, she scooted to the door, which she opened and jumped through. The step had not been let down, and it was a long way to the ground. She landed with a thump and twist of her ankle. Pain shot up her right leg. She sank backwards until she sat in the carriage doorway.

She took deep, slow breaths to try to still the pain. Any thought she'd had of escaping seeped away. She could not run and, from the looks of this inn, there was nowhere to run. It was a typical village pub, and a small village at that. From her limited vision, she could see several cottages, a village green and not much else. She had no idea where they were.

She gathered up her courage to try putting weight on her foot when Perth came into view. He moved with a lean looseness that she found intriguing. Dark hair, a little longer than fashionable, swept back from his high forehead. The scar slashing his cheek was pronounced in the dark haze of a face in need of a shave. His full lips were firm, with a hint of sensuality that made her remember how his kiss had felt—punishing, devastating, exciting.

He reached her, dark brows drawn in irritation. 'I told you to stay put.'

She pushed the memory aside and stood. She ignored the shaft of pain streaking from her ankle up her leg. 'I do as I wish. You are not my keeper.'

'I am the keeper of your reputation. What if someone of our circle had been here and recognised you?'

She huffed in indignation. 'And what if someone had? Is it not a little late for you to worry about my good name?'

In the heat of her ire, she stepped forward, intending to face him without hesitation. Immediately, her right leg buckled and a sharp intake of breath caught her unawares. His arms circled her and lifted her up before she could come close to the ground.

'What in Hades have you done?'

She turned her head and glared at him. His eyes met hers. Lillith blinked, and blinked again. He was too close. She shook her head.

'I turned my ankle.'

'Because you defied me. Had you stayed in the carriage this would not have happened.' His face inched closer to hers. His breath stirred a strand of her hair that had fallen over her eyes.

Fresh indignation at his arrogance swept away his appeal. 'How typical. It is all my fault because I did not do as you ordered.' She made an unladylike sound. 'If you had acted like a gentleman and let the step down and helped me out, I would not have had to jump out and thus injure myself.'

It was his turn to shake his head. 'Women. You have no logic.'

'And you have no feeling,' she shot back.

Fury mounted his features, but he did not reply to her taunt. 'Since there is no one of our acquaintance here, I have bespoken a room where you can refresh yourself. Then we can have some breakfast before continuing on.'

She nodded, not sure enough of her voice to answer him.

'I will take you to your room and look at that ankle. The last thing we need is for it to become severe and need a doctor's attention.'

Again she did not answer. Her thoughts were a jumble. Nor did the press of his chest against the side of her bosom or his arms so intimately around her waist and thighs help her concentration. They might as well be naked for the lack of barrier her dress and cape and his greatcoat and jacket provided. To her eternal shame, she had always reacted this carnally to his nearness. When she was young, her feelings for him had scared her. Now only shame mixed with her ardor, and she was not sure that shame was enough to keep her from succumbing to him.

They entered the building to a smiling, bowing innkeeper. The man was young and thin as a whippet. Perth passed him by with a nod. She smiled.

The smells of eggs, ham and freshly baked bread assailed her nostrils. Her stomach growled.

'Soon,' Perth said, a genuine smile tugging at the

side of his mouth for the first time since this adventure
had begun.

He carried her effortlessly up a flight of stairs and
down the hallway, ducking his head as the ceiling got
lower. The building had been built a long time ago.
Thatched roof and timbers spoke of an Elizabethan
birth. The quaintness appealed to her.

Perth stopped before a door and kicked it open with
his toe. He bent forward so that his chin was nearly
in her bosom. Still, his head barely missed the lintel.
But her nerves ran riot. She was sure his jaw had
rested momentarily on the swell of her breast, leaving
a hot brand and swollen flesh behind. He seemed not
to notice anything.

He strode across the small room to the bed that
nearly filled the space and set her carefully down. As
his arms slipped away, she felt instantly bereft and
vulnerable. If anything, she should feel safer without
his body touching hers. Not so.

'Which ankle is it?' He knelt down and cocked his
head up to look at her.

The hair sprang in thick waves from his forehead.
The urge to comb her fingers through the rich mass
was nearly her undoing. With a jolt, she realised what
she was thinking. But it was too late. He had already
seen her response.

His look turned knowing. His eyes took on a smouldering awareness that sent shocks coursing through her
system. His hands slid underneath her skirt and his
long fingers stroked down her left calf.

Her eyes widened as a tiny gasp escaped her.

'Wrong ankle,' she managed to say through the tightness in her chest.

His fingers shifted to her other leg, but not until he had thoroughly stroked the uninjured limb. His gaze never left her face, a face she knew betrayed every emotion she felt, every tremor of desire his touch elicited.

She felt heat mount her neck and flood her cheeks. Still, she watched his long, finely formed fingers skim over her injured ankle. He was gentle yet firm, watching her for every nuance. She winced when he pressed on a tender spot.

His attention shifted to her foot. ''Twould be best if you took off your stocking,' he murmured. 'Fetching as it is, I think there might be bruising with the swelling.'

She stared at his bent head and the proud jut of his jaw. He was a man many women desired. He looked back up at her, one dark brow raised quizzically. She started, caught once more in admiration of him.

'Leave the room, Perth, and I shall do as you request.' Her voice was husky, and she forced her jumping nerves to ease. 'Send a maid to bind the ankle. You have done enough.'

'Have I?'

He rose in one smooth, tightly controlled movement. The muscles in his thighs bunched and flexed, catching her attention as everything about him did. She turned her head away.

'I don't think so,' he said, his voice low and rough. 'I will bandage your ankle.'

Her head jerked back. 'No, you will not. Surely the innkeeper's wife knows better than you.'

'I am more skilled than you think. Wrapping your ankle will take but a few moments.' His eyes narrowed to slits when she opened her mouth to deny him. 'The less contact you have with others, the less likely anyone is to find out what has really happened to you. I am merely thinking of your reputation.'

'Are you?'

He gave her a ruthless smile that did not reach his eyes. 'Yes.'

'Do you honestly think my servants will remain quiet about what has happened? That no one will learn that I was abducted by a man?' She shook her head, wondering how naïve he thought her.

'I think that if they care for your reputation they will confide only in your family. With discretion, no one else need know.' A mocking light in the black depths of his eyes told her what he thought of her brother's ability to keep quiet.

'Mathias is many things, Perth, but he has always been concerned for my well-being.' That much at least was truth.

'As he sees it.' He left without another word.

Lillith instantly felt stranded, alone and vulnerable. She shook her head to clear away the inane thought. Better that she search for a way to escape than that she repine over Perth's departure. He meant her no good.

She slid from the bed, careful not to put her injured foot on the floor. On one leg, she hopped to the single window. From its height, she could see for miles around. Nothing but fields. Nothing that looked familiar. They had travelled a great distance.

With a sigh, she sank into the nearby chair. Its over-stuffed, chintz-covered cushions swallowed her. She leaned her head back and rested it on the well-padded chair, her eyes closing. Even were she uninjured, she would be hard-pressed to get away.

And did she want to?

He would hurt her. He would hurt her badly. Still, a part of her yearned unceasingly for what only he could give her. It had been this way since she first saw him, ten years ago. She feared the longing for him would never cease.

The sound of the door opening jerked her upright. Perth entered, his greatcoat gone and a laden tray in his hands.

'I have brought tea and cold meats and cheese.'

He laid the tray on a nearby table, then shrugged out of his navy jacket and rolled up the sleeves of his fine lawn shirt. From one of his jacket pockets he took a roll of snowy-white cloth.

'You play the servant well,' she said, an edge on the words as she fought to maintain her emotional distance.

The scar on his cheek twitched. 'How proper of you to remind me that, without good providence, I might be one.'

'That was never my intention,' she said, hurt that he thought her capable of trying to inflict pain. 'I merely meant that you do the job well.'

He turned so that his eyes bored into hers. 'My apologies, then. Your brother would not have hesitated to make the comparison and mean every cruel innuendo possible.'

She surged up, forgetting her ankle in her ire. 'My brother is a gentleman and would do no such thing. You may think what you wish of me, but leave my brother out of this. He has nothing to do with what is between us.'

The words were out of her mouth in a rush, followed by a sharp intake of breath as her ankle buckled under her weight. She sank with a moan back into the chair. Lillith squeezed her eyes shut in a futile attempt to stop the tears that sprang to her eyes. He was instantly beside her.

'You always did think your brother a paragon,' he said through clenched teeth as his fingers lifted her skirt enough to reveal her injured leg. 'You have not taken off your stocking.'

'No, I have not.' She forced the tears back even as one escaped to trickle down her cheek.

He reached up and caught the single drop on his forefinger. His touch tugged all the way to her toes. Her heart twisted in knots when he sucked the moisture from his skin, his eyes never leaving hers.

Tension mixed with anger and pain to create a heady sense of invulnerability. 'A maid would do better than you, Perth.'

'I have had plenty of practice wrapping sprains and mending breaks.'

'No doubt you have,' she said with a sardonic curl

on lip. 'Still, I think, for propriety's sake, a maid is better.'

'Propriety is not one of my concerns,' he said, stroking the inner portion of her calf. 'Discretion, yes.'

Tingles shot up her leg, making her catch her breath. 'Do you intend to seduce me? Is that what this is all about?'

The hot leap of desire in his dark eyes told her everything. But why?

'I am not in the habit of abducting women,' he murmured, never taking his gaze from her. 'When I do so, I have a purpose. You have discovered it,' he finished with a hard smile that twisted the white scar crossing his cheek. 'But first, we must make sure that you are capable of the pleasure when it comes.'

'Pleasure?' She raised one pale brow, not surprised by his confidence so much as irritated at his assumption that she would succumb to him.

His hand slipped higher, igniting sparks along her inner leg. His eyes never left hers. When she gasped in surprise and…pleasure…at his touch, his smile hardened. Only then did she jolt into complete realisation of what he did.

Her hand met his face in a loud smack that surprised her. It had been unconscious. His head jerked, the cheek with his scar reddened.

'I…I…' She floundered. 'You go too far, Perth,'

'I don't go far enough. Not yet.' His voice was cold. His hand dropped back to her ankle. 'Remove your stocking or I will do so.'

His change of topic took her breath away. He always had been mercurial.

'Leave the room and I will.'

Disgust twisted his mouth. 'We have been down that road before.'

Without waiting for a reply, he slid both hands up her leg to her knee. His nimble fingers caught hold of her garter and pulled it off. The stocking sagged to her ankle and he rolled the delicate silk covering from her foot. In spite of his gentleness, her ankle was swollen and the removal hurt. Lillith bit her inner cheek and held her breath to keep from crying in pain.

Perth frowned. 'This should have been wrapped immediately.'

'I shall be fine if you will leave me alone and allow me to rest.'

'You will be fine after this is wrapped and you have stayed off it for several days at the least.'

She opened her mouth to retort, but he started wrapping the roll of linen around her ankle and the agony took away all thought of what she had intended to say. For long minutes she alternated holding her breath with shallow breathing. Neither helped. She closed her eyes and tried to think of something different, something pleasant. All she could think about were Perth's eyes when his hands had slid up her leg, his passion riding him like a demon. She gave up.

She opened her eyes and noted that his no longer held emotion. 'That hurt. I am sorry,' he said quietly.

She nodded, not trusting herself to speak without crying.

He opened a flask and poured a thick liquid, then diluted it with a brown liquid and held the mixture to her. 'Drink this. It will help.'

'Laudanum?'

'You should have had it before, but somehow it did not work that way,' he said with a wry twist of full lips.

Still unwilling to speak much, she took the glass and downed the bitter drink in one long gulp. It hit her empty stomach like a bomb.

She gasped and coughed. 'What was that?' she asked when she finally caught her breath.

'Laudanum,' he said, rising in one swift, fluid motion so that his powerful legs were close enough she could run her hands down his flanks.

She shook her head to try and clear it. 'Yes, I know there was laudanum in it. But what else?'

'Scotch whisky,' he said shortly. 'The combination should take care of any lingering discomfort. We have a long way to go today and cannot afford to stay here any longer.' He cast a rueful glance at the tray of food. 'I have ordered a packed lunch and a flask of tea.'

'I shall have to be more suspicious of what you feed me,' she managed to whisper, even though the concoction threatened to spin her head.

'Yes, you shall,' he said, moving to the bed and yanking off the quilt. In several swift strides he was beside her again and threw the cover over her shoulders.

'What are you doing?' she asked, batting ineffectually at the quilt. 'I have a cape, thank you.'

'Yes, you do and it is safely in the coach. Summer is over although autumn is not yet upon us. Later this evening the air will be cool and this will keep you warm for I intend to travel straight through to our destination.'

She tried to push the thing away, but his hands held it secured at her throat as he leaned down so that his face was inches from hers. Without warning, his mouth crushed hers. His lips moved against hers and his tongue swept inside. Lillith's head fell back as he deepened the kiss. Her senses swirled out of control. Her spine arched and to her shame, she would have clasped her hands in his hair had they not been secured under the quilt.

Finally, when she thought that her mind and body were no longer hers to command, he ended the kiss. Her eyelids were heavy as leaded weights, her abdomen was a pool of lava. Yet when she forced her eyes open, his met hers with cool detachment. Her world had spun out of control while he had cold-heartedly seduced her.

Shame flooded her cheeks.

'Bas—' His fingers pressed against her lips, keeping her from saying the only word she knew that adequately described him.

'Careful, Lady de Lisle. You don't want to say things you will regret later.'

'I will regret nothing later,' she stated. *Except that kiss and my response.* She turned away from his knowing look and wished for the strength to resist him.

Before she could think of anything else to say or

try once more to free herself from the heavy folds of cloth, he swept her up into his arms. Her hair, already loose, tumbled down her back. Disgusted by her cowardice and yet unwilling to look at the faces of anyone who would see her in this wanton position, she turned her face against his shoulder and let the length of her hair cover her face.

It was not so easy to shut out the sensations that Perth's closeness ignited in her body. She felt every beat of his heart and every breath he took.

She trembled as he carried her from the room and down the stairs, the food uneaten and forgotten. Even her stocking lay unmissed in the room.

Chills set in, making her shake. Chills that no amount of warmth or covering could abate. He scared her, but her reaction to him scared her even more.

Chapter Three

The inside of the carriage was smaller than Lillith remembered. Perth sat across from her, his knees meeting hers. This had not occurred before. Her nerves jangled.

'Are you hungry?' Perth asked, opening the basket packed by the innkeeper.

Roast beef and fresh baked bread assaulted her nostrils. Belatedly, she remembered the food left uneaten in the inn and her stocking left for someone else to find. Her stomach rumbled. 'That would certainly help ease the effects of your concoction,' she said tartly, wishing something could ease the longing she felt for him.

'Food will help,' he agreed. 'You will need another dose in a couple of hours if you are to keep the pain at bay. You should eat something before then.'

She grimaced. Much as she disliked the mixture, he was right. Her ankle had hurt so badly and now it was a dull throb. She even thought she might be able to escape if the sensation stayed at this level.

He eyed her. 'I am sure you feel much better, but you still are in no shape to stand on that foot.'

Had he read her mind? Or had her face been that transparent? She had never been good at hiding her emotions.

Her much older brother, Mathias, had known instantly ten years before when she'd first fallen in love with Perth. Mathias had told her then that she should never play cards. Her face gave away every thought and feeling she had. De Lisle, on the other hand, had called her a cold fish with a face that showed nothing. Thank goodness for that. However, it seemed that, like Mathias, Perth could read her like a well-marked map.

She sighed as she took the plate of cold beef and buttered bread Perth handed across the too-small space separating them. She was ravenous. The first bites hit with a soothing effect that went a long way to calming her nerves. Several mouthfuls later, Perth handed her a heavy earthenware mug filled with steaming hot tea. She drank it in large gulps.

'Easy,' he muttered. 'You will make yourself ill.'

She continued drinking. 'I was hungry and thirsty. You are less than gracious to your unwilling guests.'

He shrugged, the greatcoat he had put back on emphasising his broad shoulders. 'You had only to ask.'

She made an unladylike face and nearly spilled what little remained of her tea. 'Yes, and you would have told me to wait until we stopped.'

'Probably,' he agreed, finishing off his large helping of food. He took a gold flask out of the side pocket in the coach and took a swig.

Lillith smelled the distinct odour of the brown liquid he had put in with her laudanum. She shuddered. 'How can you drink that barbarous stuff? It is like swallowing liquid fire.'

He eyed her. 'Have you ever swallowed fire?' he asked flatly, a jaundiced look on his face.

'Of course not. That is merely a manner of speech.'

'As are so many other words,' he said harshly. 'I happen to like whisky. It burns going down but I know what I'm drinking. It is honest. Not many things in life are.' He took another swig. 'I always know what to expect from it.'

She set her empty plate and mug beside her on the leather seat before primly folding her hands in her lap. 'Are you talking about something besides whisky?'

'We are talking about whatever you think we are talking about,' he answered.

'I don't play riddle games,' she said on a sniff.

'Neither do I—any more.'

He replaced the flask and turned his attention to the outside. Fields lay fallow. Sheep roamed everywhere. Occasionally they passed a farmhouse. The road itself was dirt and it would be a morass in the rain. Still, they kept a good pace.

'Will we be at your destination soon?' she asked.

'Soon enough.'

He did not even look at her. Frustration made her itch to thump him on the chest and demand that he pay attention to her. But she did nothing. Instead, she took several deep breaths and tried to calm herself. They did no good.

'Why are you doing this?' she finally asked. 'Why now after all this time?'

Still he did not look at her. She thought he did not intend to answer her. She was wrong.

'You are a widow now.'

Long minutes went by. Lillith waited with all the patience at her command for him to continue. She started twiddling with her fingers. Thankfully the gloves she wore kept her from picking at her nails, a bad habit she had developed shortly after marrying de Lisle.

'I have been a widow for just over a year.'

'The proper time of mourning,' he murmured. Without warning he turned and his dark eyes bored into her. 'A year would hardly be time enough to get over someone you truly and deeply loved.'

She felt under attack. She suspected there were things he was not saying. His words hinted at meanings other than those he spoke directly of. He seemed to think she should understand what he really meant and she did not. Her sense of ill usage mounted.

'What are you really talking about?' she demanded.

His countenance darkened. Instead of speaking, he retrieved his cane and used it to bang on the roof again. Within minutes the carriage came to a halt. He flung open the door and jumped out. His greatcoat flapped in the wind and his pale cheeks took on a ruddy hue. He signalled to his groom and was soon mounted on the horse he had ridden while abducting her.

Her sense of ill usage intensified until she wanted

to stick her head out of the window and scream at him. What kind of understanding could they reach when he would not talk to her?

None. Absolutely none.

Time passed and Lillith struggled under its slow hand. Never one to remain idle for even short periods, this enforced inactivity for long hours was trying. A book, her needlework, even mending would be welcome. Anything to occupy her mind and keep her from brooding on Perth and his intentions, which she knew to be dishonourable.

What had been a dull throb in her ankle had increased to nearly the original pain. That did nothing to improve her disposition. Nor did having to admit to herself that Perth's remedy of laudanum and whisky had worked and would very likely work again.

With a sigh of defeat, she picked up the gold-handled cane Perth had discarded on the seat across from her and rapped the roof. The Earl, drat his sense, had been right in that she needed to mend quickly and constant pain did not help achieve that end.

The carriage rolled to a reluctant halt. The wheels had barely stopped when Perth pulled open the door and scowled at her.

'Are you worse?'

His voice was deep and, if she had not known better, she would have said worried. She frowned at him, not wanting to tell him she wanted another draught of his concoction, but knowing it would be for the best.

She had never been good at defeat—no matter who her opponent was.

'Yes.' She watched his black brows raise in sardonic acceptance.

'Do you want another draught?'

Her frown deepened. 'Are you going to stoop so low as to make me beg?'

'I am simply looking for clarification.'

She gripped her hands together. 'You are plainly looking to provoke me, which you are all too ready to do. Yes. Yes, I would like another measure of that swill you call a remedy. Is that clear enough? Are you satisfied?'

He made her a mock bow and entered the carriage and pulled several vials from the leather pocket on his side of the seat. Knowing she could have made the medicine herself had she known where everything was did not make her feel better. Within minutes he handed her the earthenware mug. She took it with ill-concealed ire.

She gulped down the whisky and laudanum in two gulps. Her eyes watered. In spite of her intention to remain stoic while the mixture burned its way down her throat and to her ankle, she ended up coughing.

'Some tea would help,' Perth said almost gently.

She gasped in deep breaths. 'Please.'

He took the mug from her unresisting fingers and filled it. She took it back and sipped at the soothing drink. She had never been one to drink strong alcohol. Her father and brother's examples had been enough for her to see the harm. She was not even fond of ratafia, its sweet almond flavour cloying to her sense of smell and taste. Thus the strong liquor went right to her head.

'That should help the pain and allow you to sleep,' Perth said.

She looked at him with jaundice. 'In a moving carriage?'

'You did once before.'

She could not argue the fact. 'How much longer?' she asked, thinking from a distance cushioned by the alcohol that she sounded much like a child.

He answered her with the obvious patience one would show to a recalcitrant child. 'One more change of horses and then we should arrive by midnight.'

'You planned well,' she muttered. 'Posting spare horses.'

His lips twisted. 'Wealth has its privileges.'

Even in her present haze, she could not mistake the bitterness in his tone. Somehow it hurt her to hear him this way. 'You were not always so jaded.'

'Ten years ago I was young and idealistic. Today I am much more experienced.' His voice was cold as a Scottish winter wind.

'We are back to words within words,' she said. 'Ten years ago I married de Lisle. Is that what you are referring to?'

'Ten years ago you left me waiting.' He leaned his head to one side. A ray of late afternoon sunshine caught the scar on his right cheek and turned it fiery red. 'I waited until evening, thinking you had been unable to escape.'

'Mathias was supposed to meet you and tell you that I was no longer able to wed you against the wishes of my family.'

His laugh was short and hard. 'The family that sold you to a shrivelled-up old man with enough money to pay your brother's gaming debts.' His voice deepened. 'Well, Mathias did not arrive till late.'

Her first inclination was to defend her family. But he was right as far as it went. She had jilted him for an older, wealthy man and for the reason he said. And, if Perth were to be believed, Mathias had not acted as quickly as he had assured her he would.

'I did nothing that is not done every day by members of our class.' Her words slurred slightly and in spite of their argument, her eyelids were heavy. The medicine was making her drowsy despite the acrimony that flowed between them. She wondered if a wish to escape from this hurtful airing of truth was also behind her creeping exhaustion.

'True.' His voice now held no emotion. It was as though, having had his say, all the emotion that might have held sway over him was gone.

'And I did not know that Mathias took so long to reach you. For that I am sorry.'

He continued to scrutinise her. There was an ugly gleam in his eye that made her wonder if she had mistaken his lack of emotion. She wondered if there were things she did not know. Mathias had never told her about that meeting. She had never been brave enough to ask.

'Don't be. It was a salutary lesson in the workings of your family.'

She was the first to look away. Much as she had tried not to think too deeply on it, she knew her family had not treated him well. Leaving him at the altar of the small country church where she had promised to meet him to be married by special licence was not done. Her only balm had been to know that eloping with her lover was not acceptable either. No, she never should have embroiled herself with a penniless young army officer, no matter how much she had loved him. Her family had never made any secret of the need for her to marry well. She had let her emotions rule her for a brief, bitterly regretted period.

Now she was reaping the harvest her rash actions had sown. No, not just now. She had been doing so for the last ten years. De Lisle had never trusted her and had made her life a misery because of that. Nor had the *ton* ever accepted her. A woman who jilts one lover and then has a duel fought over her between that lover and her new husband is never accepted. That taint was still with her. This abduction, when word got out as it inevitably would, would ruin her completely. Perhaps that was Perth's intention. And perhaps it no longer mattered. She preferred the country.

When she glanced back at him, his head was turned away. He lounged back, his beaver hat at an angle that shaded his eyes. His hands rested in his lap. His legs stretched across the space separating their seats. His dusty Hessian boots were scant inches from her slippered feet. Perfectly at his ease, he appeared to have fallen asleep.

All the emotional turmoil of the last minutes seemed to have been sloughed from his shoulders like so much baggage that is disposed of without a second thought. How she wished she might forget the past ten years.

She woke at the sudden cessation of sound. She sat up and looked out. Flambeaux illuminated a small, boxy and symmetrical building made of what appeared to be butter-coloured stone. She wondered if they were in the Cotwolds. They could have reached here in the time they had been travelling.

Perth opened the door before she had the chance to notice much else. He extended his hand to help her down.

For an instant, she thought about resisting, but the firm line of his jaw told her plainly that he was in no mood to countenance defiance. Very likely he would merely reach in and haul her out.

She took his hand and allowed him to help her. A good thing, too. Her head ached from the whisky and laudanum. She told herself that was the reason the feel of her gloved hand in his gloved hand had felt so intimate. But she knew it was only a sop. She had always been attuned to him physically and emotionally.

When he released her, she managed to stand without his help, most of her weight on her good leg. The medicine had not been good for her head, but it had helped her ankle. She took a deep breath and looked around, determined not to feel so acutely Perth's nearness.

Immaculate lawns stretched out like a velvet skirt in the silver light of the moon. Birch trees ringed the circular drive. Roses in their last gasp decorated the borders, their scent perfuming the air.

'Your hunting box?' she asked.

'My retreat,' he countered. 'This is not hunting country.'

That did not tell her much.

Without a word, he went to talk with his coachman. His words drifted to her on the breeze.

'Take the horses and men back to town. I will notify you when I want you to return.'

He was stranding them here. She took a step toward them, intending to tell Perth she had no intention of staying here indefinitely, but her bad leg buckled again. She caught herself with a painful gasp.

'Stubborn,' Perth said, striding to her side and swinging her up into his arms—again.

'I am heartily sick of this position,' she muttered, angling her head so that she did not look at him.

'But I am not,' he said, holding her a little tighter.

She suppressed a moan. Even through the layers of their clothing, it seemed that his body burned into hers. The scent of him assaulted her senses. She remembered the first time she had been this close to him. She had been intoxicated by delight.

They had only just met the night before at Almack's. He had asked her to dance two country dances and then left. Now he was calling on her, along with several other gentlemen. But he was the only one she could remember, the others having vanished into the past. He had leaned over to take a cup of tea from her and the hint of cinnamon had wafted over her. With a quizzical look, she had met his eyes—and been lost.

His warm breath moved over the nape of her neck sending little currents of excitement skidding down her spine and bringing her back to the present in a sensual rush. This compromising position had to end.

She twisted in his hold. 'Let me down. I am perfectly capable of standing on my own.'

He mounted the last steps and entered the house. 'Of course.'

He set her down abruptly. His arm fell away from her legs first, leaving them wobbly. Then he released her back. She was on her own, standing in the elegantly furnished foyer of his house.

'Milord,' a man said, coming hastily in through a side door.

He was short, slim and bandy-legged. His hair was brown peppered with grey. A short beard, neatly trimmed, spoke of independence. It was not fashionable to have a beard. He wore a serviceable country jacket and breeches that had seen newer days. Still, he had an air of dependability about him.

'Fitch, I trust everything is ready?'

The little man drew himself up ramrod straight. 'I should hope so, milord.'

For only the second time since Perth had abducted her, she saw him genuinely smile. 'A manner of speech only, Fitch. I never doubted for a second your ability.'

Only slightly mollified, the servant looked at her. His lively gaze took in everything about her. He nodded as though agreeing with his own assessment.

She held out her hand. It was not the accepted thing to do with servants, but she sensed there was more between this man and Perth than servant and master.

'I am Lillith, Lady de Lisle,' she said.

Fitch took her hand and bowed over it. Very continental. 'I am Fitch. His lordship's batman.' He released her hand.

'Batman?' she asked.

'And general factotum,' Perth said. 'He has been with me since I first entered the army.'

Lillith's smile faded. And he undoubtedly knew exactly what had happened ten years ago. She was to be held prisoner by two men who had no reason to care about what was best for her.

'I have dinner almost done and her ladyship's room ready,' Fitch said, stepping back.

'Roast beef and potatoes,' Perth said.

'If you wanted French food, then you should hire yourself a Frenchie to cook it,' Fitch said. 'I am an honest Englishman and I cook like one.'

'With a Gaelic man's sensibilities,' Perth said, a spark of humour in his grey, nearly black eyes. Changing the subject, he said, 'I will take Lady de Lisle to her room so she can freshen up and then we shall be very glad of supper.'

Lillith edged away, refusing to grimace as her ankle made itself known. 'Lady de Lisle will take herself.'

Both men looked at her. Perth dark and sardonic, Fitch with his brows pinched in worry.

She gritted her teeth and hobbled to the staircase. The solid mahogany wood was a burnished auburn. Taking a deep breath, she leaned on the banister so that it took her weight and hopped up the first step on her good leg. Three stairs later, she stopped to catch her breath. Looking up she nearly groaned. It seemed that the next floor was in the sky. Her stubbornness had gotten her into difficult scrapes before, but none this physically trying.

'Perhaps you would care to lean on me, my lady,' Fitch said from where he stood at the bottom of the staircase.

Three steps and she was winded and her good calf threatened to cramp. 'Perhaps I would, Fitch,' she said, measuring each word for they cost her dearly. At least it would not be Perth helping her.

She glanced at the Earl. He stood where she had left him. His hooded eyes watched her like those of a bird of prey that was keeping in sight its next meal. From somewhere, she found enough energy to toss her head in defiance. Her hair swirled around her shoulders, but when all was done the small act of rebellion did nothing to make her feel better.

Fitch was beside her, his shoulder fitted under her arm, and still Perth did not move or say a word. As she continued up the stairs she felt his gaze on her back. A scorching awareness engulfed her and would not leave no matter how she tried to put him from her mind or how she panted in exhaustion.

'We are nearly there, Lady de Lisle,' Fitch said, his nasal voice pitched to give encouragement. 'Not much more and you will be able to rest. I will prepare a nice hot bath for you. That will help.'

She nodded. There was not enough air in her lungs to speak. Her left leg burned with exhaustion. For a fleeting moment she allowed herself to imagine being carried by Perth. He might excite her and make her unsure of herself, but he never made her so tired she wanted to collapse and cry in frustration.

They reached the first-floor landing long after Lillith had decided she could go no further. And she still had to get to her room. A sigh escaped her clenched lips.

'Enough,' Perth said from right behind her.

Lillith started. She had been so focused on preparing herself for the next ordeal that she had not heard him follow.

'Enough what?' she panted. 'I will say when I have had enough, not you. 'Tis bad enough that I am here against my will.'

She felt Fitch stiffen, but the man said nothing. Just as well. She was rapidly descending into a horrible mood and Perth did not look any merrier. He never had liked having his will thwarted. For that matter, neither did she.

'You will hurt yourself worse if you keep this up.'

'I will do as I please.' She lifted her chin and took a deep breath. She would hop to wherever her room was. 'Where do I go?'

Perth made a sound that she chose to ignore.

'It is this way, Lady de Lisle,' Fitch said, once more extending his arm.

'Don't be any more stupid than you must,' Perth growled. 'Use this.' He thrust the cane from the carriage into her right hand. 'It is not ideal, but it is better than what you intended.'

She suppressed a sigh of relief. Much as she desired to show the Earl that she would do as she pleased, she had not looked forward to more hopping. Her fingers curled around the gold knob. She had large hands for a woman, but the handle of the cane was nearly too big. But then Perth was a tall man.

With Fitch guiding her, Lillith started down the carpeted hallway. Her right shoulder ached abominably from using her right arm so much for support and her left leg felt ready to crumble for the same reason. Somehow she held her back straight. Fortunately, they did not have far to go. This was not a large house by aristocratic standards.

Fitch opened the door with an economy of motion and followed her in. The room was delightful. Mellow yellows and creams graced the walls and curtains. A large bed took up most of one wall. Burl walnut furniture, a table and two cosy chairs, grouped around a cheery fire. Her spirits lifted.

'Here, Lady de Lisle,' Fitch said, moving to her side. 'Let me help you now. His lordship has stalked off to his room. You have no need to further tax yourself.'

This manservant was a knowing one. She slanted him a look. 'Your master is overbearing.'

'He does have that habit, my lady. It comes of being in the army for so many years.' He deposited her in a cream-coloured chair before moving to one of the three doors in the room and opened it. 'This is where your clothes are, my lady. And if you will be so kind as to rest, I will have your bath prepared shortly.'

'A bath?' Just the thought was divine. The pleasure was fleeting as she remembered his other words. 'Clothes? Those are not mine.'

So Perth used this house to entertain women. She should not be surprised or hurt by that. Many men did the same thing. Her brother was one. Still, knowing that Perth considered her no better than one of his lightskirts hurt—hurt badly.

She told herself she was a fool, but that did not ease the tightness in her chest. He had abducted her and kept her with him for nearly an entire day against her will. This latest was nothing. Nothing, she told herself.

'Pardon me, Lady de Lisle,' Fitch said, interrupting her internal tirade. 'But his lordship had them specially made and brought from London for you.' There was a kindness around his brown eyes. 'Lord Perth does not bring women here. This is where he comes to be alone. You are the first woman he has entertained here.'

The vise around her chest seemed to loosen and breathing was just a little bit easier. Once more she was being a ninny where Perth was concerned. When would she learn? Still, she felt better.

Her innate graciousness surfaced. Fitch was not responsible for his master's actions. 'This is a delightful room. And I should be very grateful of a hot bath. It has been a long journey.'

Fitch nodded. 'I know, my lady. I will have everything quickly.'

As soon as the door closed behind Fitch, Lillith let herself completely relax. Her head fell back to rest on the stuffed chair and her eyes drifted shut. Even her ankle seemed to ache less. She dozed off.

Too soon she heard a loud knock. 'Come in.'

Fitch stood in the doorway, wrestling with a hip tub. 'I am sorry that we don't have anything larger, my lady, but this is all I can handle. His lordship has sent away all the servants except me.'

'Whyever for?' she asked. 'This is a great burden on you.'

Fitch pushed the tub across the rug until it sat directly in front of the fire. With the expertise of practice, he draped large towels around the tub.

'His lordship does not want word of your presence to leak out.'

She made a very unladylike noise. 'He should have worried about that before he kidnapped me.'

Fitch did not reply. 'I shall be right back with several buckets of hot water.'

'Your master should be helping you,' Lillith shot back as Fitch closed the door behind himself.

'I intend to do so,' Perth said.

Chapter Four

'Wha—?'

Lillith twisted around to see one of the three doors opened and Perth standing on its threshold. He filled the space and made her nerves jump.

Suspicion raised its ugly head. 'Where does that door go?' she demanded.

He smiled, a brief stretching of firm lips. 'To my room.'

The breath caught in her throat. 'I might have guessed,' she said bitterly. 'You are determined to make this as unpleasant as you can for me.'

His look turned thunderous. 'I don't have to try. You are already doing everything possible towards that end.'

He pushed off from the door jamb and sauntered towards her. His jacket was gone and his cravat missing. The white lawn shirt he wore had the top two buttons undone.

Black hairs curled enticingly over the edges of his shirt. She could imagine how crisp they would feel

against her fingers. Her right hand lifted before she
realised what she was doing. She dropped it to her lap
with a lack of grace that was unusual. A blush suffused
her face.

How many times must she make a fool of herself
over this man? It seemed too many.

'Do you not know how to knock?' she said, putting
all her frustration at herself into the words. Petty as
her demand had sounded, it did stop his progress towards her. That was a great relief to her strained
nerves.

'When it pleases me.' His gaze ran over her. 'You
are exhausted. As soon as your bath is over we will
eat and then you will go to bed.'

Go to bed.

Chills chased up her spine followed closely by lightning. This was the situation she had both dreaded and
desired. For too long, she had wondered what it would
be like to make love with him. But not like this. Not
for revenge.

Before she could think of something to say, there
was a knock on the door to the hall. 'Come in,' she
said, her voice a little too husky.

Fitch entered with two pails of steaming water. He
glanced at Perth on his way to the tub. Just seeing the
hot water and smelling the lilac-scented soap that Fitch
pulled from one pocket momentarily took Lillith's focus off the earl.

Longing must have shown blatantly on her face for
Perth said, 'I will go with you, Fitch. Lady de Lisle

seems ready to dive into the two inches of water and it would be better if she could submerse herself.'

Both men left. Lillith gave herself several deep breaths before forcing her weight up on to her good foot and the cane. She crossed to the hip bath and picked up the soap. She smelled the creamy bar. She had been right. It was lilac. Perth had remembered what she wore.

Her heart did a painful flutter. Such a small thing, and yet to her it spoke of deeper emotions than she could have hoped for. Carefully, she set the soap back onto the special ledge built into the tub and then moved to the door Perth had entered through. She stopped on the threshold.

Her eyes narrowed as she examined the room. This one was masculine to her feminine. Deep forest green and beige curtains covered the window and the same colours lay on the wood floor in a thick carpet. Heavy mahogany furniture—a large bed and chairs and a table—took up most of the room. A toiletry stand was in a corner where the morning light would hit the attached mirror. He spent time here.

His coat, greatcoat and muddy boots were cast aside. Fitch had not been here to tidy.

'Do you find my room interesting?' Perth's deep voice said from directly behind her.

She whirled around, taken by surprise, and the cane twisted from her grasp. She hastily gripped the side of the door and her free hand went to her throat. She had been so engrossed in examining his room that she had not heard him return.

Instantly on the defensive, she demanded, 'Why are we in adjoining rooms?'

He smiled, slow and lazy with a nearly feral gleam. 'For every reason you imagine.'

The pulse at her throat pounded. 'You are fantasising if you think I will participate in anything with you.'

He took a step closer. 'Once you would have done anything I asked.'

She drew herself back, wishing she could disappear because she knew in her heart that what he said was true. She lied. 'You always did think highly of your skills. It seems little has changed.'

He chuckled, but it was not with mirth or with kindness. 'I know you, Lillith. You might have left me at the altar because of your brother's need, but that does not change the fact that you wanted me then and you want me now.'

He took another step towards her. This time she had to edge back. His scent threatened to overpower her as his maleness already overwhelmed her. Somehow, she managed to hold herself high as though she had not just retreated from his assault.

'Right now all I *want* is a bath.' She consciously dropped her hand from her throat. 'If you will move, I will go back to the chair and rest until you and Fitch are done.'

The manservant entered her room just then with more water. For the first time, she noticed that Perth also held two pails. The effect he had on her was not reassuring.

He made her a slight, mocking bow before taking his buckets to the bath and emptying them. Fitch did the same. Steam rose from the little tub.

Longing expanded in her chest. She needed that bath. She felt filthy and tired and utterly exhausted.

Perth must have seen her need. 'We will bring one more round and then it should be ready for you.'

She nodded, not trusting her voice to sound nonchalant. This time when they left, she made her slow, painful way back to the chair. Laying the cane on the floor beside her, she bent over and pulled off her slippers. The delicately embroidered leather was beyond repair. They would do for the present, but she would never be able to wear them in public again. Little matter. She had dozens of shoes, as she had dozens of everything. She had married for money and made sure that she enjoyed what it could provide.

Knowing Perth and Fitch would return soon, she quickly undid her one remaining blue satin garter and then unrolled her silk-knit stocking from her left leg. The stocking was dust-stained and frayed around the top. The last night and day had brought heavy use to her clothing. Next she gingerly unwrapped the linen from her right ankle. The lack of support when she was finished made her ankle start to ache again. Still, the swelling was down and she did not think it looked as bruised.

No sooner had she neatly folded the stocking and wrap and placed them with the garter than Perth returned. This time he said nothing, merely casting a glance at her, before he dumped the water. Fitch followed suit and left.

She raised both silver-blonde brows when Perth remained. 'I intend to thoroughly enjoy this comfort, Perth, but not until you leave.'

He set his buckets down on the fireplace's hearth. 'How do you intend to undress?'

Nonplussed, her mouth dropped. 'Not with your help!'

That knowing, dangerous smile returned. 'You have no lady's maid.'

'I am not a cripple. I can take care of myself.'

'Can you?' He leaned back against the mantel so that his broad shoulders rested comfortably against the creamy marble. 'I did not know you were a contortionist.'

She drew herself ramrod straight, or as straight as the overly-cushioned chair would allow. 'I do not need your assistance. And if I did need help, it would not be you I would turn to.'

'Fitch?'

She glared at him. 'Before you, yes.'

'I see.' He pushed away from the mantel and left the room.

Her eyes widened at his abrupt and unexpected departure. She had routed him too easily. Still, she did not intend to waste any more time.

Without more ado, she twisted her arms up and back and strained her fingers to reach the tiny buttons that held her gown closed. The first three buttons were easy. She swallowed a growl of frustration. Rearranging her arms, she undid the buttons at her waist and below. The ones smack in the middle of her back remained securely closed.

The temptation to rip the gown off was strong. But dirty as it was, she would rather wear it again than anything Perth had bought for her. She willed herself to calm down.

She would stand up and try pulling the gown up enough that the buttons were higher on her back. It worked.

The fine muslin evening dress fell from her body and puddled in a dingy white heap. Only her chemise remained. Fastened with silk ties, it was easily discarded.

Once more using the cane, she hobbled to the tub. Somehow she managed to get in. A sigh of unadulterated pleasure left her as she sank into the steaming hot water. A pillow, another dose of Perth's medicine and she could stay like this all night.

She let the heat soak some of the soreness from her muscles. Even her ankle felt better for the hot water.

With arms gone soft from relaxation, she lifted her hair so that it fell down her back and into the water. Clean hair would add to her comfort. It did not matter that she could not dress her hair afterward. She would braid it.

Quickly she lathered with the lilac soap and rinsed off. When she was done, the room was engulfed in scent. She allowed herself to rest her head on the part of the tub designed for that and closed her eyes. Soon the water would be too cool for comfort, but for the moment it was bliss. Later she would have to wrestle with getting out.

She dozed, only to waken with a mouthful of soapy water. Taken unawares, she flailed at the water, sending sprays onto the surrounding towels. Coughing assailed her.

Strong hands hooked under her arms and pulled her up and out of the tub. A large drying sheet fell on her shoulders and hung to her bare feet. Water dripped unheeded on to the floor.

Still coughing, she pushed back a strand of damp hair with one hand and held the sheet at her neck with the other. Only one person would be in here. Cinnamon assailed her even as intense awareness made the hair at her nape stand up.

Perth.

The urge to turn so that she found herself in his arms was great. She felt the heat of his body, so close to hers that any movement would cause them to touch. She was so weak where he was concerned.

She did not turn around. 'Please go.'

His hands caught her shoulders and gently turned her, the way she had just wished to move. She lifted her chin in defiance of him and of her reactions to him. His mouth was close enough that she could touch it with hers by standing on tiptoe.

Her ankle started throbbing again. She shifted her weight to her good leg.

'Go away,' she said, unable to keep her petulance out of her voice. Things with him were so incredibly difficult. 'I do not feel well.'

He did not budge. 'You need more medicine. And food.'

'What I need is for you to leave me alone.' She sighed, gripping the sheet around her as though it were the only thing that kept her safe. 'If you truly want to help me, then let me eat alone and give me another draught of your concoction and then let me be.'

The sharp blackness of his unfathomable eyes clouded. His gaze lowered and his face took on a tension that sharpened the angle of his jaw. She looked down and saw that the sheet was damp and clung to her like a second skin, leaving nothing to his imagination. He took a deep breath that shuddered through his body and released her so suddenly that she stumbled.

'Not now. Not yet,' he said in a voice uneven from suppressed longing. He dragged his attention from her body. 'I will bring you food and medicine, but I will not leave you alone. Not yet.'

She gripped the edge of the tub and started to shiver. He mistook it for cold. He went to the fireplace and stirred the coals into a blazing heat. Several swift strides later and he was in the room with the clothing. He returned with a royal purple robe made of brocaded silk. He laid it on the nearby chair and left without another word.

Lillith gaped. His departure had been too easy to be permanent. She quickly dried and donned the robe. It fit as though it had been made to her measurement. She belted it securely. Only then did she look around for a brush, knowing there would be one. Perth had thought of everything so far, she did not think he would fail here.

She was right. A gold-embossed brush with matching comb and mirror reposed on a woman's dresser. She hobbled to it and then back to the chair. She was beginning to think of the overstuffed seat as an old friend that welcomed her with cushioned arms. She sank into it and began to carefully untangle her fair hair.

She had barely finished one strand before Perth returned with a laden tray. He set the food and beverage on the table and moved everything closer to her. The aroma of mutton and mint sauce made her stomach growl.

Serviceable plates, flatware and mugs made place settings. Simple and sturdy like a man would use if he did not care what others thought of the table he set. Nothing was monogrammed with his coat of arms.

She watched him like a mouse watches the cat before it springs. The brush slipped from her fingers and fell to the carpet where it lay ignored. The urge to jump up and pace the room made her fingers knot into the folds of the robe. The inability to release some of her tension tightened her mouth.

'Drink this.'

Perth held out a mug she knew contained his cure-all. The strong, musty smell of Scotch assaulted her. The drink would ease some of her anxiety as well as help her ankle. She took it and swallowed quickly, only to nearly cough the liquid up.

'Wha-what did you do? Double the dose?' she gasped.

The mug dangled from her forgotten grip and Perth caught it just before it fell. 'I decided that you need a good night's sleep more than I need what I brought you here to have.'

She gulped hard and her eyes watered. She felt as though someone had ignited a bomb inside her ribs. But there was more. Tendrils of excitement twisted through her limbs. Her mouth turned suddenly dry.

She took several more deep breaths and pushed her palms against her stomach in an attempt to stop it from somersaulting. She picked her words carefully.

'You intend to spare me your attentions?'

That was not what she had meant to say. The last thing she needed to do was provoke him, yet here she was doing that exact thing. What had got into her? But she knew. Desire. Desire for him. Only for him.

His mouth thinned into a sword-sharp line. 'For to-night.' He spun on his heel and went to the door that separated their rooms. 'But this is a respite only.'

All she could do was stare. A sense of bereavement moved over her like a reluctant breeze. No matter what she told herself or told him, she wanted him. She always had and always would. Still, before she slept, the door between their beds would be locked and a chair wedged under the handle. She would do the same thing under the knob for the door to the hallway.

Whether the precautions were to keep him out or keep her in, she would not even consider.

Chapter Five

Light streamed onto her face, waking Lillith and giving her a blinding headache. Her ankle added its complaint before she struggled to sit up. With blurred vision, she looked around the unfamiliar room and wondered where she was. Her sight finally focused on a man lounging at his ease in an overstuffed chair.

Perth.

Memory rushed back.

'How did you get in here?' she demanded, pushing thick strands of nearly white hair back from her face.

He eyed her steadily with no softening of his expression. 'Do not again attempt to lock me out of a room in my house.'

He did not raise his voice, but the total lack of inflection was like a whip. Instead of intimidating her, his order infuriated her.

'It is rather early for you to act the high-handed lord and master.'

Instead of having the effect she had hoped for, Perth's gaze lowered. The coldness that had made him

look formidable quickly became heated desire. She
blanched. Belatedly, she realised that the night rail she
wore was fine muslin, so fine that it was nearly trans-
lucent, and that the sheets were around her waist. She
yanked the covers to her chin.

His eyes met hers. Hot, liquid and nearly overpowering need forced her to an awareness of him that she
had tried so hard to ignore throughout the long night.

She licked lips gone dry. One hand gripped the
sheets until her knuckles turned white. The other rose
to the rapidly beating pulse at the base of her neck.

'Why?' she asked, the cry torn from her. 'Why are
you doing this?'

He rose in one lithe motion. Before she could blink,
he was on the bed, his hip a hot brand against her side,
his mouth too close to hers.

'Because I must,' he said.

She closed her eyes to the desire in his that went
beyond need to obsession. Every emotion she saw in
his face she knew to be a mirror of that in her own.
A soft moan escaped her just as his lips took hers in
a kiss that punished even as it rewarded.

His fingers tangled in her curls, holding her head
for his plunder. His tongue demanded a response. She
could not resist. They met in a battle of sensation that
set her body afire.

Her back arched and before she knew it, her fingers
dug into the thick waves of his hair, holding him as
he held her. Her mouth moved beneath his, an open
invitation to anything he asked.

Nothing mattered but the feel of him against her and in her. Nothing. She had waited too long.

She heard him groan as his mouth slipped from hers to trail down her jaw to the place where her neck and earlobe met. His tongue slicked along her skin, leaving shock and delight in its trail. Her hands fell to his shoulders where her fingers kneaded at the hard muscles. Sensation after sensation buffeted her. Desire rode her.

He shifted so that he lay lengthwise beside her. Her head fell back, giving him full access to the gentle swell of her neck and bosom, the sheet once more at her waist.

With mouth, tongue and teeth, he traced the line of her gown, never going beneath its gossamer protection. He teased her with skill and passion. She responded like a woman starved. Her body was beyond her conscious control. Instinct drove her.

Unable to withstand his assault without completion, she gripped him and pushed his mouth where she needed it. His lips closed over one breast and pulled. His teeth nipped lightly, followed by his tongue. Sharp stabs of excruciating delight shot to her gut and lower.

'Jason.' She breathed his Christian name as passion consumed all else.

He lifted his head so that his eyes, black with hunger, met hers. His nimble fingers undid the laces of her nightgown as he watched her face. With stroking movements that sent thrills along her skin, he skimmed the material from her bosom. His thumbs plucked at her nipples. Her eyes shut.

Nothing separated her flesh from him. His mouth closed over one aching breast as a hand slid down her rib cage to her thighs.

She gasped, then moaned as ecstasy caught her in its talons until a scream was torn from her lips. Not until she lay limp and replete did he stop.

Reality came back to her slowly and shamefully. Unable to meet his gaze, she flung an arm over her eyes and turned her head to the side.

'Go away,' she finally managed through lips swollen and sensitive from his kisses. 'Have you not done enough? Proven your mastery over me? Must you stay and gloat as well?'

'Look at me, Lillith.' His voice was low and harsh and full of dissatisfaction. 'I am in too much discomfort to gloat. I want you too badly, and not in the way we just shared. I want to be inside you. I want to have what you just experienced, but I want to be buried in you when I do and to feel you as you reach your pleasure with me.'

Heat that she had thought dissipated through release and shame rushed back, tightening her belly. The ache he had only just appeased started anew, stronger and more demanding. How could this be? How could she be so wanton, so…so…

'You make me your harlot,' she whispered, the words barely audible.

'No,' he denied her. 'I make you my woman. As you should have been ten years ago. I intend to claim you, to brand you with my body and my passion until no other man can satisfy you. Only then will I release you. Only then.'

Not looking at him, she did not see him move. His hand caught her wrist and pulled her arm down. His other hand threw the covers aside. No gentleness this time.

He ripped the gown from her and pillaged her. He was a pirate, raiding every secret she possessed. She rose up to meet him: passion for passion, need for need, pleasure for pleasure.

When he finally entered her, it was one powerful surge that brought them together in a meeting of male and female that took her breath away. He moved forcefully, filling her and overwhelming her. What had gone before was nothing compared to the contractions ripping her apart now.

Her back arched, her pulse pounded and a scream ripped from her. He increased his motions and covered her mouth with his, his tongue imitating their other joining. She went up and over, her release sending him to his.

Only later, as the late morning sun entered the room where they lay covered in sweat, their legs joined, did she come back to sanity. Now that he no longer made love to her.

Never had she experienced such a total and complete surfeit of physical desire. Just knowing that he could bring her such an experience again, in moments, made her desire him once more.

Her shame was tenfold. The anger she had felt upon

first awakening and realising that he had somehow
broken into her room resurfaced. Only this time it was
aimed at herself for her weakness, but she lashed out
at him for what he had done to her and for what she
had begged him to do.

'You are a rutting beast.'

The warmth that had heated his eyes turned to the
sharp coldness of obsidian. 'And you are better?'

His mocking question infuriated her more. 'Get
out.'

With lithe grace that took no note of his nudity, he
rose from the bed and gathered his clothing. He gave
her not a backward glance.

In spite of her anger and her need to have him gone,
she watched him hungrily. Their passion had been
white hot, with no time to savour one another. Now
she drank her fill of his tall, broad-shouldered form,
his lean well-muscled hips. His legs were shaped so
that many a woman would sigh at the sight of them.

The only mar to his physical beauty was a series of
scars criss-crossing his back. At some time he had
been badly whipped. Probably while he was in the
army.

The urge to go to him and run her fingers in soothing strokes over the scars was nearly irresistible. Only
the knowledge that such action would end in more
lovemaking stopped her.

He pulled the chair from beneath the doorknob and
disappeared into his room. She felt cold and alone. No
satisfaction accompanied her privacy.

She rolled to her side and curled into a tight ball.

If she squeezed herself hard enough and long enough, she might find comfort or, lacking that, the strength she needed to resist him. He had vowed to make her desire him above all else, and she already did so. Now she had to keep that from him.

Knocking, knocking, knocking. In her dream she knocked on Perth's door, demanding that he let her in. Her need for him was something she could not resist.

Knocking…

Lillith roused. This time she came instantly awake. Someone knocked on the door from the hallway. It had to be Fitch.

She pushed up in bed. Instantly, the aches from her morning activity assailed her. She was long unaccustomed to the acts she and Perth had performed.

The sheets twisted around her naked body. Her torn nightgown lay on the floor like a discarded rag. And her ankle began to throb.

'Come back later,' she managed to get out through a throat that felt swollen and sore. 'I do not feel well.'

The knocking stopped. 'I will be back, my lady, with some food and a posset.'

'Thank you, Fitch, but there is no need. I just need rest.' Exhaustion ate at her, brought about by physical exhaustion and mental dismay.

'His lordship will not agree, my lady.'

'His lordship can go—' *to hell*, she finished in her mind.

There was no answer so she assumed Fitch had left. She collapsed back on to the pillows. She needed

Perth's concoction for her ankle, a cup of strong hot tea and another bath. She needed the moon.

She forced herself to sit on the edge of the bed. The cane was propped against the wall where she had left it after climbing into bed the night before. She gripped the golden handle and gingerly lowered herself to the floor. The pain that shot up her ankle was like a slap across the face. If she had been even slightly dazed from exhaustion, she was now very much aware.

The curtains billowed into the room, the breeze from outside filling them like a ship's sails. She had closed the window before going to sleep.

She hobbled to the window and looked out. A large, old oak tree grew up the side of the house, its branches reaching close enough that an agile man could gain entrance to her room. So that was how Perth had entered. Tonight she would make sure and latch the window so that it could not be opened from the outside.

If she did not get away before then.

Moving more steadily, but no less painfully, she returned to the bed and used the cane to hook up the torn nightgown. With a snarl, she wadded it into a tight ball and stuffed it into a drawer that was filled with silk stockings and ribbon-encrusted chemises. Last night she had marvelled at all the gowns for bed, each one as gossamer as a butterfly's wing. She had wondered if Perth intended to keep her captive long enough to wear each of them. Now she wondered if one would even last a night if he gained access to her room.

A shiver of desire coursed through her. She deliberately stepped on her bad foot. The excruciating agony sent all thought of the Earl and what he might do from her mind. Biting her lip, she collapsed on to the bed. That had been a very stupid thing to do.

She fought back tears.

If only she had married him. Things would not be like this. But that was not what had happened. Long ago she had schooled herself not to look back. It only brought regret.

A knock heralded Fitch's return.

Lillith took a deep breath and pulled on the dressing gown that also lay near the bed. She was naked underneath, but there was no helping that. The way she felt right now, she could not dress herself.

'Just a minute,' she managed. Getting to the door was torture. Her abused ankle screamed at her. Before she moved the chair and unlocked the door, she asked, 'Are you alone?'

'Yes, my lady. The Earl has gone for a ride. He will not be back for some time.'

She breathed a sigh of relief.

But not until she had taken the whisky and laudanum mix and had several strong cups of tea did she relax. Fitch brought her food and she ate. He brought hot water and she washed. He found a gown she could don without help and she did so.

The situation tempted her anger to resurface. It would be so easy to become furious again, but it would accomplish nothing. She had to heal and she had to get away from Perth before he stole all her strength from her.

* * *

Perth rode like the Wild Hunt chased him. And if regret and anger and passion made up the Hunt, then it did hound him.

He had accomplished what he had set out to do. He had made her desire him, and he had made her beg for him. But that was no longer enough. He wanted more. He wanted everything she had to give. And then he wanted it to never end.

He groaned. His body was in no condition to be riding. His desire was unquenchable and though she was not near, he reacted as though she lay naked in front of him.

He laughed harshly, the sound mingling with the wind that tore at his hair and blew his coat out behind him. His gelding responded by running faster. A fence loomed ahead. They took the obstacle in one jump and continued their reckless, headstrong rush.

Only once before had Perth ridden this passionately with such disregard for his or his mount's safety. That had been ten years ago. He cursed himself for his weakness where *she* was concerned. But it did him no good.

His desire for her rode him like he rode this horse, unrelenting and without thought for the consequences. He wanted her more than he had ten years before. Ten years before he had not made love to her, felt her surround him and take him inside her body. Ten years before he had lost his heart. Today he had lost his soul.

He had to have her.

*   *   *

He found her sitting on a bench in his garden. The fish pond was at her feet and rabbits hopped through the grass that surrounded her. Rose bushes shaded her, the last of their flowers scenting the air.

Lillith watched him stride towards her. His hair was windblown and there was a wild glint in his dark eyes. The scar that ran the length of his right cheek stood out white and fierce.

'What are you doing here?' he demanded, sitting beside her without asking permission.

The narrow bench was barely large enough for both of them—it certainly provided no distance between them. Still, Lillith edged away until she was nearly unbalanced. It was not far enough. He radiated heat, and the smells of horse and the outdoors mingled with his cinnamon and musk.

She looked away, focusing on the distance. 'Who landscaped the grounds?'

It was an inane question, but she dared not let him pick a topic of conversation. The dark hunger in his gaze told her all too well what he would pursue.

'Capability Brown.'

A curt answer. She waited for more, sensing that nothing would be forthcoming. She licked her lips and still did not look at him. 'He achieved a fine result.'

'I think so.'

She sighed. 'I think I will go in now. It is becoming hot.' She took up the cane she had used to walk out here and levered herself to a standing position.

'How is your ankle?' he asked, standing with her.

'Better,' she answered as curtly as he had.

'Look at me,' he ordered, his voice low and demanding.

'I think not,' she said, wishing her voice did not sound so breathless.

She tried to move around him, but he gripped her wrist. His free hand cupped her chin and before she could do anything, he angled her face so that she had to look at him or close her eyes. She looked at him.

His gaze roved over her, devoured her with his intensity. She felt a flush rise up her bosom to her neck and mount her cheeks. Still, she would not relent before his onslaught and look away.

'Once is not enough,' he said, his voice low and raspy. 'I have waited too long to let you go now.'

She did not pretend to misunderstand him. 'So, you intend to continue keeping me against my will. I had thought better of you now that you have got what you set out to get.'

He flinched as though she had hit him. 'That sharp tongue of yours. I like better what you did with it this morning.'

The blush that had suffused her deepened, and once more she spoke to hurt. 'A gentleman would not mention that.'

His face whitened. 'I am not a gentleman, as we both know too well.'

Was there pain in his words? Looking at the hardness of his face, she thought she was mistaken.

'What do you intend to do, then?' she asked.

He still held her wrist. His eyes still held her captive. 'I intend to make love to you until we both can stand no more.'

His bold statement hit her like a flood and filled every empty part of her body and heart with desire for him. Somehow she managed not to fall into his arms.

She took a deep breath and shook herself as though trying to rid herself of a sensation too great to bear. 'I am hungry. Fitch said he would have dinner ready by the time you returned from your ride.'

His eyes narrowed and bitterness tinged his words. 'Nothing I have said means a thing to you.'

She glanced away from him and forced the lie to her lips. 'Nothing.'

He released her and she hobbled away, refusing to look back at him. If she did such a weak thing, he would know instantly that she had not spoken the truth.

Fitch waited inside the French doors that opened into the library. He had lit a fire that took the chill out of the air. Books lined every wall and where the shelves did not go to the ceiling, portraits filled the spaces. Warm woods and rich reds made the room cozy.

'If it pleases your ladyship, I shall serve dinner here. It is only a cold collation.'

'That will be perfect,' she said, making her way to one of the couches that flanked the fireplace. She sank deep into the burnt-red brocade cushions. 'And tea, please.'

Fitch drew himself up. 'Of course, my lady.'

She smiled. Her butler had much the same way

about him. His dignity was every bit as great as any duke's, and if the truth was told, the servant probably held himself more upright.

Fitch was barely out of the room when Perth entered. 'I take it that this is where we will be eating.'

He did not wait for an answer but moved a large table so that it stood between the two couches. Next he pulled up a straight-backed leather wing chair and sat down. Silence fell.

Outside a bird chirped. Inside the fire crackled and the mantle clock ticked. She looked everywhere but at Perth. Several books lay on the side table near her: Cicero, Scott and Byron.

'Have you read these?' she asked, attempting to ease the silent tension that engulfed them.

He glanced at the books. 'When I cannot sleep or the weather is too nasty to go out.'

'I have read Scott and Byron,' she replied.

'Everyone has read them,' he said. 'Both are lionised.'

Fitch returned with the food, putting an end to a conversation that was fast running out of steam. Perth thanked him and then waved him away.

'I will serve Lady de Lisle and myself. Go do something you would enjoy.'

Fitch looked at both of them then thought better of protesting. 'As you wish, my lord.'

Perth quirked one dark brow. 'I am not going to devour her.'

'As you say, my lord.'

Lillith studied the servant's bland face. She wondered if he meant to be as impertinent as he sounded.

'Be gone,' Perth said.

Fitch bowed himself out, but there was an air of defiance about him. He might have done as ordered, but Lillith sensed that the servant did not approve of what was going on.

They ate in silence. The hunger she had felt earlier had long passed. Nerves always affected her thusly.

Instead of ringing for Fitch when they were through, Perth cleared the table himself. He would not be gone long and Lillith decided to wait. If she went to her room, she did not doubt that he would follow. That was the last place she wanted to be with him.

When he returned, he was scowling as though he had been through something unpleasant, but he made no mention of it and she did not ask. He sat down in the same chair and stared at the fire.

'Do you play chess?' he asked without looking at her.

'Occasionally,' she answered, gratified when he gave her an irritated look.

'Will you play against me now?' he asked, his tone mocking.

''Tis better than some games we might play,' she said, striving to keep her own tone as cool as his.

He rose and fetched a chessboard and a satinwood box that held marble pieces. She watched him set up the game. His long fingers moved with a sure deftness that brought back memories of them moving over her skin. The nails were clean and well kept, as was all of him. His skin was smooth yet without softness. He was not a dandy.

When her body screamed to be touched as he touched the chess pieces, she forced her attention elsewhere. 'Twould do her no good to continue desiring him. There had to be more between them than their bodies.

'You may start.'

His deep voice startled her. She had been too intent on her emotions and had lost track of what he did.

'Oh, yes,' she muttered, reaching for a pawn and moving it recklessly.

He looked from the pawn to her face. 'You must not play much.'

Within three moves he had that pawn and a knight. Not long after he had two more pieces. She was going to lose without ever having given him a fight. Their chess was like their lovemaking. Her hackles rose at this idea. Somehow, some way, she had to resist him. He checkmated her easily.

'I will play you another game,' she said fiercely. This time she would concentrate and consider each move.

He eyed her with surprise. 'You want to be bested again? I have never taken you for a woman who likes to lose.'

She sat up straighter and scowled at him. 'I don't. I intend to win the next game.'

His smile was a lazy act that lent a slumberous slant to his eyes. The breath caught in her throat.

Without a word, he set the pieces in order once

more. This time she refused to watch him. She had no intention of being distracted.

He rose and went to a side table where a decanter of liquor sat with two glasses. 'Would you care for a drink?'

'No,' she said curtly, wrinkling her nose.

He sauntered back to his seat. ''Tis just as well.'

She glared at him. 'For once you are right. My brother drinks enough for ten men, as did my father. I know what too much alcohol can do.'

He saluted her with a finger to brow and took a sip. 'We both know.'

His words were a knife. Her face blanched and she looked down at the chessboard. Too much drinking and too much gambling had put her brother into the type of debt that had forced her to marry de Lisle in order to get a settlement to bail Mathias out of the River Tick. Perth was never going to let her forget that she had chosen another man over him and why. Never.

She took a deep breath and moved her first piece.

Two hours later she had him in check, but not mate. He leaned back in his chair and took a sip of his third glass. He studied the board.

'You have improved vastly,' he drawled. 'Somehow I thought you might.'

She gave him a tight, cool smile.

'Still,' he said softly, 'I think that I win.' He moved a piece. 'Checkmate.'

She frowned and her fists tightened. A low growl escaped her clenched teeth. 'Drat. I did not see that.'

He finished the drink and leaned back in his chair. 'It is getting late.'

His words and all that they implied sent a shiver up her spine. She looked at the French doors and was surprised to see that it was dusk outside. It would be dark soon.

'Let us play cards,' she said hastily. Anything to keep them in this room and away from their connecting bed chambers.

A predatory grin slashed his face showing strong white teeth, teeth that could nip her skin with great tenderness or with tantalizing provocation. Her fingers went involuntarily to her throat where the breath seemed to be trapped.

'A game of whist,' he said, gathering the chess pieces and returning them to their box.

She stared at his hands and then at nothing since everything about him roused her senses. 'That would be fine.'

He rose and put the chessboard and pieces away. Then he lighted a branch of candles and set them on the table between them before fetching a pack of cards. He sat down and shuffled them.

'Shall we play for straws?' she asked, thinking that was a safe wager.

'Scared?' he taunted her.

'I have played cards nearly since I could crawl,' she retorted. She felt much safer playing whist than she had chess. She had a chance to beat him at this game.

His heart-stopping grin returned. 'I think the stakes should be higher.'

'A shilling a point.'

His eyes became heavy-lidded. 'A piece of clothing.'

Chapter Six

'What?' She gasped, not sure she had heard him correctly. 'I won't play you for your clothing. Nothing of the kind. A shilling or I will…'

She did not want to say go to her room. She knew from the look on his face that he would follow her without a qualm, whether she wished it or not. A repeat of this morning's activities was not what she wanted, or at least not what she felt was best, regardless of what her heart and body desired.

His grin turned wicked. 'I will make it easy on you, Lillith.' Her name on his lips was seductive and made her pulse pound. 'You may play for shillings. I shall play for clothing.'

She gaped at him. The urge to beat him that had driven her all afternoon as she lost at chess faltered. She knew she could not keep him from removing his clothes one piece at a time as she won. The only way to keep him dressed was to lose. Her pride rebelled, but her head knew what she must do.

She nodded.

With fingers that shook in spite of her determination that they should not, Lillith picked up her cards and fanned them. She suppressed a groan. They were better than good.

'You should not play cards when there is a wager you don't want to lose,' Perth said. 'Your face is transparent.'

Her brother had often told her the same thing so she had no doubt that she had given away the truth. She would win this hand by the strength of her cards. And she did. She closed her eyes when his fingers went to his throat.

'Don't worry,' he drawled. 'I am only going to take off my cravat this time.'

Under the lazy words was the hint of sensuality. He knew she was attracted to him against her will. He had proved that this morning. She heard the slide of material as he pulled the long cloth from his neck.

'You can look,' he said.

She told herself that what he had done was nothing. He was still fully clothed. She opened her eyes to see that he had undone the first button of his shirt. Dark, wiry hairs curled around the fine white lawn. She knew they were crisp to the touch and, if wound around her finger, would cling like a lover's kiss. Her gaze rose to his face where she saw that he knew exactly what was going through her mind. His eyes were dark as the night and as filled with flames as the fireplace. With hands that shook worse than before, she picked up the cards and shuffled. Somehow she had to lose.

Two hands later, he murmured, 'You win again. Try as you might, you cannot lose every hand.'

She averted her eyes and shuffled the cards until her fingers ached. A solitary shilling lay on his side of the table. A shilling she had borrowed from him and insisted that he fetch so there was tangible proof that he had won a hand.

The fire had burned low and the candles were a third gone. The room was cooling off in the night air. Yet, Lillith felt as though she sat on burning coals.

Against her will, her gaze returned to Perth. He watched her like a predator watches its prey. Slowly and deftly, his fingers worked down the front of his shirt, undoing buttons with ease. The fine material opened to show a V of sun-browned skin with dark hairs trailing down his chest. With the grace of a cat, he stood and stripped the shirt off.

His shoulders were as broad as she remembered. His stomach as flat and hard as the floor that suddenly seemed more inviting than a bed. The flames from the fire played along his muscles, seeming to make them ripple as though he moved. She shook her head and made herself look away from his male perfection.

Instead of sitting down, he moved to the table that held the alcohol and poured another glass. With his back to her, she watched him with a hungry intensity that made her ache. Heaven help her, she wanted him—just as he had planned.

To ease some of her need and to satisfy her curiosity, she asked, 'What happened to your back?'

He stiffened and did not turn towards her. 'Nothing.'

His curt reply told her not to pursue the topic. Whatever had happened must have hurt him greatly if he still would not discuss it. She despaired of ever reaching him emotionally.

He angled around. 'We can stop this stupid game any time you wish,' he said, his voice rasping like a man deprived of air.

She grasped at his offer of respite. 'Good. I would like to read one of your books.'

He lifted one brow in a sardonic statement. 'I did not mean that you could escape the inevitable. Merely that we would forgo this particular brand of foreplay.'

She stopped in her attempt to stand. Anger at her cowardice flared. 'Then the next time you lose, take off your boots instead of your breeches.'

He laughed outright. 'That is more like the girl I once knew and the woman I first abducted. I had thought that the injury to your ankle had taken away all your spirit. I am glad to be mistaken.'

His words said one thing, but the smouldering heat in his eyes said something altogether different. There was no humour in his gaze, only desire and need. She sank back into her chair, all her bravado fading away under the intensity of his study.

'Another hand, then,' she finally said. 'I cannot let it be said that I feared to finish what we have started.'

Even as she agreed, she wondered what she was doing. She knew where they were headed. It was inevitable, much as she tried to deny her reaction. He wanted her and he was determined to have her. Unfortunately for her peace of mind, she wanted him just as badly.

They played the next hand without speaking. Perth sipped his drink and Lillith wished for some strong hot tea. The tension between them made her crazy.

Perth played his last card. 'I believe you have won again,' he drawled.

She stared helplessly at her boss card. 'It takes greater skill to play badly than to win.'

He shrugged, the flicker of fire and candles glimmering across the expanse of his chest. 'Perhaps I am more motivated than you.'

She gave him a jaundiced look. 'Most definitely.'

He bent over and tried to pull one of his boots off and could not. One black brow raised. 'You will have to help if this is the item of clothing you intend me to remove.'

'I *intend* for you to take nothing else off. You are the one determined to undress.'

Her words dripped like acid. He ignored them.

'If you refuse to help, then I will take off something else.'

'No.'

He stood and undid the button at his breeches. She jumped up, knocking the table and nearly overturning the candles. Like lightning, he grabbed the candelabra and set it straight.

'You are too late,' he drawled, undoing the last button so that the front fell open.

'Wicked. You are wicked,' she accused, flushing

from her bosom to the roots of her hair. 'Isn't it enough that I desire you before all else, even my honour? Must you bedevil me until I can think of nothing but you and what you do to me?'

'I will do whatever I must to have you, Lillith.' His eyes were darker than hell.

He rounded the table and grabbed her. She gasped and took a step back. Her heel hit the grate in front of the fire. Heat scorched her as he grabbed her shoulders and pulled her to him. His scar stood out in livid relief against his skin. Then he bent his face to hers.

She cried out, whether in denial or a plea, she did not know.

He covered her mouth with his and she melted into the all-consuming heat of his passion. Nothing else mattered.

Desire, hot and unquenchable, drove him through the night. He could not get enough of her. Need whipped him until he drowned in his passion, her passion, their passion. No sooner were they done and lying limply entangled than his need rose again, an insatiable heat that engulfed him—them. He entered her, devoured her and was consumed by her.

It was late the following morning when he finally left her. She curled into a tight ball as his body moved away from her. The urge to stroke his palm down her flank and rejoin her was nearly impossible to ignore. Clenching his fist, he turned sharply and left without a backward glance. He knew that if he looked at her, he would never leave her.

He entered his room and shut the door quietly behind him, keeping under tight rein all the emotion that boiled inside him. Someone cleared his throat.

'Pardon me, my lord,' Fitch said. At least the servant had the grace to flush on seeing his master standing naked.

'Damn it, Fitch. If I need you, I will call,' Perth growled.

He felt no embarrassment at his lack of clothing. Fitch had seen him in worse situations. What did discommode him was the emotion he knew had been on his face when he entered the room. A naked body was nothing. A naked heart was altogether too vulnerable.

Scowling, Perth crossed the room and took the robe Fitch had picked up in spite of being told to leave. He belted the heavy silk robe about his waist.

'Well?' he finally said.

'Pardon my saying so, my lord—'

'But you are going to say so anyway,' Perth said sardonically. 'As you did last night.'

'Yes, my lord. We have been together too long and gone through too much for me to stand by and watch you do this deed without trying to stop you. The lady deserves better than you are giving her.'

Perth's scowl deepened into an angry flush. The scar running his cheek stood out like a streak of white lightning.

'You go too far.'

Fitch said nothing, just watched the Earl.

'I intend to offer her marriage.' Perth crossed the room and threw open the window. The fragrant morning air washed over him. He turned back to the manservant. 'That will take care of any wagging tongues should word of this get out.'

Seeing the harsh line of the Earl's jaw and the way the scar blazed, Fitch knew that to continue arguing would be fruitless. 'As you say, my lord.'

Fitch could not keep the disappointment from his voice. With a curt bow, he left the room.

Perth watched his manservant leave. As Fitch had said, they had been through much. And now this.

He ran his fingers through his hair, remembering against his will how Lillith's fingers had clutched hanks of his hair in order to hold his mouth to hers. Her scent still clung to him, lilacs and woman. He groaned.

Frustration was an emotion he had great experience with, but why should he suffer it now? She was in the next room and he knew that if he went to her, caressed her, she would open to him. He knew that with a certainty that threatened to send him to her.

'Damnation.'

He slammed his fist against the wall. This was not how it was supposed to be happening. This was not supposed to be tearing his gut out. She wanted him and admitted it. He intended to offer her marriage. She would accept. She would be his, to have and do with as he wished.

Nothing more. Nothing less.

* * *

Lillith sat down at the small table and wondered why she had come downstairs. Fitch would have brought her breakfast up to her. But Fitch had to do everything because all the other servants were gone. Perth had done what he could to see that none of this leaked to a member of their set.

The hunger that had brought her downstairs dissipated. She had never been concerned about acceptance. Vouchers for Almack's, invitations to all the proper balls and routs, all of that had never interested her. She attended as a matter of course. Everyone of her acquaintance attended.

She heard the door open and turned. Perth stood in the doorway, looking as though he had not kept her awake most of the night, looking as though nothing had happened between them.

She forced herself to take a sip of the tea she had prepared along with a slice of toast. 'What do you want?'

She kept her voice flat and hoped he would leave without saying anything. She did not think she could bear to hear anything he might say to her after what they had done.

He remained where he was, his stance easy. He wore a green jacket over a shirt that was open at the neck. Buckskin breeches accentuated the muscles in his thighs, thighs that had rippled under her fingers just hours before. She shook her head.

'I want to marry you.'

She dropped the cup. The fragile china shattered, sending tea splattering. She knew the hot liquid hit her hand, but it did not hurt. Nothing could hurt like the words he had just spoken. He only wanted to marry her to possess her, to continue his revenge by breaking her heart. He did not love her.

'Marry *you*?' She put her palms on the table and pushed herself into a standing position. 'After what you have done? Never.'

A stillness came over him. If she did not know just how little she really meant to him, she would have thought that her words pained him.

'What other choice do you have?'

She blanched before anger came to her rescue. 'I am a widow. I have any choice I choose to make.'

His mouth curled. 'What if word of this spreads? I have done everything I can to prevent that, but you may after all have to doubt your servant.'

Her anger turned bitter. 'Nor did you do anything to disguise the fact that you were a nobleman abducting me.'

'True. I intended to marry you when we were through.'

'When we were through?' she asked, incredulous at his assumption. 'You thought I would marry you after what you have done? Dragged me here with no consideration for my wishes, my needs. You are more arrogant than I thought.'

He shrugged and moved into the room, closing the door behind himself. 'What if you have a child from this? Have you considered that possibility?'

Because she had not, the question set her back. She

sank to the chair with a thud. A cold lump settled in her throat, but she met his look squarely.

'After nine years of marriage and no children, I don't think I need worry about that. And if I do, then it will be my problem.'

Fury twisted his face. He lunged forward and caught her shoulders with his hands before she realised what he was doing.

'You will not. Should you bear a child, it will be mine as well as yours. I will have as much to say about what happens to it as you do.'

She stared up at him, surprised by his vehemence but determined that she would do as she felt best. 'You say that now, but we will not be wed. You will not even know should that come to pass.'

He shook her, not hard, but enough that she knew her words had increased his anger. 'I will know.'

They stayed like that for long minutes, eyes locked, mouths hard lines of stubborn rejection. Her heart beat painfully and she could see his scar whiten until it stood out harshly on his cheek. Meeting him glare for glare after what they had just said was one of the hardest things she had ever done.

After an eternity, his hands fell away and he stepped back. 'I will have a carriage pick you up in one hour. It will be a hired one from the nearby village. It will take you wherever you want and no one need know you have even been here.'

'Like that?' she asked, taken aback by his abrupt change of focus. 'You are freeing me without another word?'

He nodded. 'If you will not marry me, then there is no more need for you to stay under my roof.'

Her mouth was dry and a lump had lodged in her throat, making breathing difficult. This was what she had wanted, her freedom. But this suddenly, this abruptly, after being asked to marry him and talking of a child that she knew would never exist, made her head spin.

Dazed, she watched him leave, his boots cracking against the wooded floor. The door slammed behind him. Silence reverberated through the room. She slumped into her chair.

He had asked her to marry him, and she had told him no.

Her hands shook when she tried to pour herself more tea. Somehow she managed to get cream and sugar in the cup and got the drink to her lips. The scalding heat helped ease some of the ice that seemed lodged in her chest. A tear escaped her eye and slid down her cheek.

If only he had spoken of love.

Exactly one hour later, Perth caught her hand, knowing she did not want him to touch her and unwilling to do as she wanted. He helped her into the rented carriage where she sat with ill grace. He leaned in so that whatever he said to her would not be overheard by the hired driver.

She tugged, trying to free her hand from his. He tightened his grip. 'Look at me, Lillith,' he demanded, angered by her determination to ignore him.

'Why should I do that?' she demanded. 'You will only use it to say something I don't want to hear or to take liberties I don't want to give.'

She was leaving him and the pain of that loss strengthened his resolve. 'I do what I must.' He caught her chin with his free hand and turned her face to his. 'I have treated you abominably, but I have also given you pleasure. Things would not be easy between us, but I believe we could make a go of marriage.'

She glared at him. 'I have had one marriage of convenience, I will not willingly enter another.'

His pulse quickened. 'So you want a love match.' Something tightened his chest and twisted his gut. She had hurt him too much, he would never give her that power over him again even if it meant losing her. 'Then you had best be on your way, Lady de Lisle, for I have no intention of marrying anyone for love. Lust, yes. Mutual satisfaction, absolutely. Love, never. I suffered from that malady once and have vowed never to do so again.'

Still, determined as he was to keep her from his heart, he could not resist the closeness of her. Her scent invaded his mind and the thought of making love to her very nearly had him climbing in the carriage and shutting out the world.

Instead, he held her chin steady while he took what he wanted. His mouth plundered hers. He kissed her with an intensity that surprised even him. When he finally released her, he breathed hard as though he had run a great distance. He noted that her bosom rose and fell in deep gasps. Her cheeks burned crimson. Her eyes were wide and haunted.

She did not say a word to him, but her now free hand rose to her mouth and pressed hard.

He stepped back and signaled the coachman to start. 'If you change your mind,' he said softly, 'you know where I am.'

She turned away as the carriage moved forward. He did not expect to hear from her. But did he want her enough to follow her? He feared that he might.

Chapter Seven

Lillith limped into the foyer of her dower house. An Elizabethan manor home that had once been the county seat of the Lords de Lisle, her deceased husband had bequeathed it to her until her death or remarriage. Her mouth twisted bitterly. She would die here.

'My lady.' Her impeccable butler, Simmons, hastened to meet her. 'We did not expect you. We have been worried. You have been gone for several days.' He ran to a stop, his face suffused with red at his unaccustomed outburst.

'I was...I was staying with a friend. She was in need of companionship.'

She saw by his eyes that Simmons knew she lied, but he nodded. That was the story she would tell and if her servants had not gossiped—she nearly laughed in bitterness for she knew they had—no one would be the wiser. However, she would never acknowledge anything. The *ton* would talk about her behind her back, and some of the doors previously open would close, but within a fortnight her escapade would be stale as yesterday's bread. Someone else's escapade would be the latest *on dit*.

'I will have Cook prepare you tea,' Simmons said, studiously ignoring her lack of luggage.

She took pity on him. 'My things are on the front steps.' The clothes Perth had ordered for her were packed in several trunks sitting outside. She would distribute them to the poor tomorrow or the day after. She wanted nothing to remind her of the past week.

The butler's normally passive countenance lost its tension, and the twitch at his left eye stopped. He was very protective of her. He had been with her the entire ten years since her marriage and had elected to come to the Dower House with her.

'Thank you, Simmons. I could use some very hot tea,' she said, untying the green ribbons on her chip bonnet. 'Please have it served in my rooms.'

'My lady.' He bowed. The tick at his left eye was back. 'Mr Wentworth is in the drawing room. He has been here for several days.' Lillith blanched. Mathias had travelled far.

'Have the tea served in the drawing room and include biscuits and cake.' Still clutching the ribbons of her bonnet, she went to meet her brother.

She opened the door herself and waved Simmons away. Mathias stood with his back to her; his gaze focused on something in the rear gardens. A deer paused in the act of eating one of the last roses of the season.

Mathias turned. 'My dear, you are finally home. I was beginning to worry. You left no word.'

His tone was mild with just a hint of censure. His mouth was a puckered Cupid's bow. Lillith's palms began to sweat in their fine kid gloves. Mathias was half a dozen inches taller than she was and he shared her thick, nearly silver hair. That was the only trait they shared. He had a robust figure, held in check by a girdle much like that worn by the Prince of Wales.

He also gambled with the Prince and the Prince's cronies. He was welcomed everywhere in spite of his excessive gaming because his tailor might never be paid, but his gambling debts always were. They were considered a debt of honour and not a vice by England's aristocracy.

Lillith tossed her hat on to a nearby Chippendale chair in a forced effort at nonchalance. Under the best of circumstances, Mathias had an awful ability to see right through her. This was the worst of circumstances, and she could not afford for even her brother to know where she had really been. He would challenge Perth to a duel and one of them would surely die. She could not chance losing one of the two men that meant the most to her.

Somehow, she managed to fluff her hair as though she had not another thought in the world. 'I have been with a friend. Now, before you start, Mathias, I cannot—absolutely cannot—tell you who she is. That would be a betrayal. She was in need and I did what I could.'

She hoped with all her heart that one of the ladies

of the *ton* had been in the country this last week. Better yet if the woman was married and had left her husband in Town.

'I would never ask you to betray a confidence, my dear. You know that.'

Yes, she did know that. It was similar to a gambling debt. One always paid one's debts, no matter what it cost oneself or one's family.

She closed the distance between them for the hug they always exchanged. Instead of releasing her afterwards, Mathias held her and studied her face.

'You look different, Lillith. Tired. You are not getting sick, I hope.'

She pulled her hands from his and put distance between them. He was always too perceptive. Always.

She forced a laugh. 'I am tired, as you say. Nothing else. We spent long nights talking and getting little rest. I shall spend the next week catching up.'

Simmons entered with refreshments and Lillith took the opportunity to pick a seat that put her back to the light coming in from the window. Shadows would serve her best.

She prepared the strong tea liberally laced with cream and sugar as Mathias liked. 'A biscuit? Some cake?' Her goal was to keep the rest of their conversation neutral.

'Thank you, my dear. I have been too worried about you to eat properly. As soon as your servants reported your abduction, I came here.' He watched her like a hawk.

She nearly cried out in frustration. Of course her

servants had gone straight to Mathias. Why she had thought she could get away with Perth's charade, she did not now know. Still, she had to try.

'My friend had me abducted as an exciting game. You know how life becomes so boring after the Season ends.' She waved her hand in imitation of languid disregard. 'Why, the late Duke of Richmond held up his own wife and a pompous cleric. Why should we be any less intrepid today?'

Mathias sighed. 'Ah, yes, the late Duke. But that was many years ago, my dear. No one's reputation was at risk, and you are not normally so full of spirit.' He took a large sip of tea and a hearty bite of cake. Pleasure eased some of the edginess that had crept into his blue eyes. 'However, Mrs Russell says she did have you abducted as a lark.'

Lillith's mouth dropped before she could gain control of the surprise at her friend's timely ingenuity that took her, which was quickly followed by anger with Mathias. 'Why did you go to someone else looking for me, Brother? And why did you not say so at the start?' But she knew why. He had been testing her as both he and her father always had. She let go of her anger. This was just Mathias. 'Did *you* care so little for my reputation that it did not matter if word of my disappearance got out?'

He scowled, his pleasure in food momentarily forgotten. 'I feared for your safety and went to the one person I knew I could trust with news of your disappearance. But not until I had given you several days to return. Mrs Russell assured me that it was a lark, you were safe and she would tell no one.' He sipped his tea and eyed her. 'As to informing you at the beginning, I wanted to hear if you would prevaricate.'

She set her teacup down with a click and took a deep, fortifying breath. She never stood up to Mathias. He had been too much older than she. But she would take no more of his meddling. 'Twas bad enough that Perth had abducted her and kept her against her will. Her only family should not also be so cavalier towards her.

'Mathias, what I do is no concern of yours. I am a widow. In the eyes of the world, our world, I am free to come and go as I please.' That was stretching the point, but to seem weak now would only make him more inquisitive.

There was a sceptical gleam in Mathias's eyes. 'Even a widow—a respectable widow—has limitations on her freedom.' He took a large, determined bite of his cake and got back to his point. 'Mrs Russell said that she had her husband kidnap you.' After an almost imperceptible pause, he added, 'If you truly were abducted by your friend.'

'Yes, Nathan Russell played a highwayman to perfection.' The lie fell from her lips, and the urge to stand up and leave the room, ending the inquisition here and now was strong, so strong, she put weight on her feet in anticipation. Her ankle twinged and she winced.

Mathias put his cup down and rose. 'You are hurt. How did this happen when you were in the safety of friends?'

He towered over her. Once she had felt protected by his massive size; now she felt overwhelmed. All this deception that led from one lie to another. If only he would stop this interrogation and let her alone. But she knew he would not, so she had to.

She used her ankle as an excuse to escape. 'It is merely my ankle. I twisted it getting out of a carriage. Nothing more, but I should like to go to my rooms and rest.'

Not letting him nay say her, Lillith stood. This time her ankle truly protested. She gasped and reached for the back of her chair.

'Perhaps I should have continued to use the cane,' she said with a wry twist of her lips. 'But I was too vain. Now I shall pay the piper.'

Mathias scowled as he put an arm around her waist and helped her to the door. They climbed the stairs slowly, neither saying what they thought. All Lillith wanted was to reach the privacy of her rooms. With luck, Mathias would return to London now that she was home. She could only hope.

He escorted her into her rooms where her lady's maid, Agatha, waited. He waved the woman from the room.

Not releasing Lillith, he said quietly, 'I know there is more to this story than you will tell. All of London knows of the abduction—or will shortly. Servants talk. If this woman is truly your friend, she has done you no good having a man carry out her lark.' His arm tightened so that she could not ease away.

'She meant no harm. Please let me go so that I can sit down and rest my ankle.'

'Of course,' he said, abruptly releasing her.

Thankfully she stumbled on to a settee. He was furious or he would never have treated her so cavalierly.

'I shall be returning to Town tomorrow,' Mathias said, picking a piece of lint from his otherwise immaculate sleeve. 'The Prince has need of my company. I suggest that you remain here in the country for a lengthy period.'

'I fully intend to, Brother.' She lifted her chin. 'Until the Little Season begins, Town is so boring.'

His eyes narrowed, but he left without another word. She watched him with a heavy heart. They had not done well together since her marriage. Once she had thought everything of him. Now he was close to being an adversary.

Agatha's return made her focus on undressing and getting into a hot bath. She wished for some of Perth's concoction. Not only would it help her ankle, it might ease some of her emotional turmoil. But she did not truly need it for her ankle and she did not drink alcohol. Her brother and father had shown her only too well what drunkenness could do.

Only when she was completely alone did she allow herself to think of Perth's last words, said as the carriage pulled away. *If you change your mind, you know where I am.* If she changed her mind, she should be put in Bedlam, for that is where she would eventually end up if she married Perth without his love.

He would use her as he saw fit and then toss her aside. He would break her heart and then her soul.

Lillith gazed at the sheet of paper lying in front of her on her rosewood desk. Her eyesight was not strong and writing was always a strain, but today she had been sitting here an hour trying to think of what to say. Madeline Russell deserved to know what had happened between her and Mathias. The task was beyond her concentration today. 'Twas just as well. What she had to tell Madeline should not be trusted to paper.

Sighing, she stood and went to the window. Snow dusted the trees and lay on the ground in a patchwork quilt. This morning the sun shone brutally cold.

Two months had passed since her abduction. She had heard nothing of Perth. Her fingers knotted at her waist.

The Little Season would begin soon. Parliament would sit before the Christmas season and all the political hostesses would accompany their husbands to London. Perth always attended Parliament.

She watched a doe leave the safety of the nearby woods and enter her garden. Hunger drove the animal. She was much like that doe. Her hunger to see Perth, hear his voice, urged her to abandon caution. She would never contact him, but she would go to Town in the hope of meeting him.

She turned away to give the doe privacy and perhaps a measure of comfort. Lillith feared her body had betrayed her. She would never tell Perth, but the need to be near him was too great for her to resist.

She had three more baskets of food and warm clothing to prepare for her tenants and deliver. Then she would journey to London and whatever future awaited her there.

Several days later, Lillith's carriage drew up in front of the small London town house that her friend Madeline Russell shared with her husband of nearly four years, Nathan Russell. Nathan came from a minor branch of a noble family. The couple was comfortable, but far from wealthy, and their tiny home was not in the fashionable West End. But it was cosy and welcoming and the Russells were accepted everywhere.

When the butler announced her, Lillith rushed across the small sitting room that separated her from Madeline. Madeline had been her dearest friend since infancy. Their fathers' property marched side by side and the two girls were like sisters.

'I have missed you dreadfully,' Madeline said, rising and enfolding Lillith in her arms.

Lillith stood a head taller than her auburn-haired friend, the difference a source of good-natured banter and true chagrin on Madeline's part. The role of Pocket Venus had not been one Madeline enjoyed.

'And I you,' Lillith said with heartfelt truth. 'So much has happened. And I must thank you for the Banbury tale you gave Mathias.'

'Pshaw.' Madeline waved the thanks aside. 'You would have done the same for me.' Her hazel eyes lit up. 'But now you owe me the true story, for I am sure that it is juicier than anything I might have made up.'

Lillith sank into one of the overstuffed chintz cushions that Madeline loved so well and gratefully took a cup of steaming tea. She took a long swallow before staring into the milky mirror. 'Where to start? 'Tis a long story that started ten years ago.'

'Ah.' Madeline sighed. 'The Earl of Perth. I knew he still cared for you.'

Lillith's laugh was harsh. 'He desires me.'

'That is a good start,' Madeline said with a surge of the practicality that so often seemed at odds with her otherwise whimsical nature.

'De Lisle desired me,' Lillith said flatly.

Madeline shuddered and took a dainty bite out of a cake. 'That is entirely different. De Lisle was old enough to be your grandfather. Perth is a man in his prime and, if rumour tells the truth, as good in bed as he is with swords. And I don't know any man who would willingly cross him in a duel. At least not any more. Ten years of practice have made him an expert, or so Nathan says.'

Lillith's mouth twisted. Honour and reticence kept her from confirming Madeline's words. But her face must have given away her thoughts.

'He is,' Madeline crowed. 'I knew it. He abducted you and then seduced you. How absolutely delicious.'

Lillith set her empty cup down. 'This is not a fairy tale, Madeline. It is my life.'

Madeline sobered. 'I am sorry for making light of it, but not for what happened. You belong with Perth. I have thought so from the minute I first saw you together.'

'That was years ago. Even you cannot be that sentimental,' Lillith said.

'Hah. The way the two of you looked at each other that night at Almack's set my blood boiling and at that time I had no idea what a man and woman did together.' She took another bite of her cake and smiled dreamily. 'Now I do and I would not forgo that delight for anything.'

Now Lillith laughed. 'You and Nathan have a very unusual marriage.'

'True,' Madeline said, coming back to reality. 'A love match.'

'Exactly,' Lillith said drily. 'That is not what Perth offered me.'

Madeline watched her friend closely and saw the pain and disillusionment. 'Ah, he still smarts from being jilted. But surely you explained to him that you left him for the good of your family.'

Lillith's mouth twisted. 'Nothing I said mattered. He does not care why I chose de Lisle over him. He wants…he wants revenge. Nothing more.' Her fingers twisted in her lap, pleating and unpleating the linen napkin Madeline had given her with the tea. 'He offered me marriage. One of convenience. Nothing more.'

'Then take it,' Madeline said stoutly. 'Many a marriage of convenience has become one of love.'

Shame at her weakness paled Lillith's face. 'I could not survive. I want too much from him. As God is my witness, I would go insane married to Perth, knowing that he did not care for me the same. Every time he left the house, I would wonder where he went and whom he went with. He would make love to me one time and then leave my bed for his mistress's. That is what a marriage of convenience is. I could not live that life.'

Madeline sighed and reached out to take one of Lillith's busy hands. She held tight until Lillith's fingers stilled.

'Then you must not marry him, if he will make you so miserable. And there is no reason you should. You are wealthy enough from what de Lisle left you that you need never consider marrying again. You can do whatever you want and answer to no one.'

Lillith gave her friend a watery smile. 'That sounds very convenient.'

Inside, she wished that it were that easy. Her emotions threatened to drown her in their intensity and there seemed to be nothing she could do to escape them. But she knew that talking of this to Madeline only made the situation seem more immediate.

She took a deep, shuddering breath and vowed to change the subject. 'Are you going to Sally Jersey's tonight?'

Madeline, ever willing to do what she could to help Lillith, tacitly agreed to change the subject. 'But of course. Everyone who has come to Town for the Little Season will be there.'

'I had thought of not going,' Lillith said quietly, realising that even this new topic must lead back to Perth.

Madeline sat straight up and frowned. 'You most

certainly will go. No one knows what happened to you except me, Perth and you. That is, unless that brother of yours told others.'

Lillith smiled gently. 'Servants, even the best, will talk and before you know it the talk has spread to another house and to another master or mistress. Even if Mathias has managed to keep this to himself, it will be known by others.'

Madeline sat back, her auburn brows drawn in worry. 'You are right, unfortunately. However, you must on no account shun Society. As soon as you do that, everyone will know that whatever scandalous thing they have heard about you is true. Meet them face to face and spit in their eye if you must.'

For the first time in many weeks, Lillith's laughter was genuine. 'You are such a fierce little thing when you are bent on protecting your own. And you are right. The *ton* likes nothing more than gossiping about someone's mistakes. 'Tis much less fun for them if the person they are waiting to devour fights back. I will go.'

'And I will be there to stand by your side,' Madeline said, handing Lillith another cup of tea. 'Let us drink to that.'

Both laughing, they lifted their cups.

That night, Lillith entered Sally Jersey's London town house with her head held high. The soft lavender muslin gown she wore helped. She knew it was the perfect foil for her pale complexion and willowy fig-ure. In the world in which she moved clothes did make the woman. Just as attending functions such as this assured one's place in Society. Thankfully, Sally was an old friend and would no more ostracise her than she would fail to provide Lillith with the much-coveted vouchers for Almack's.

The rooms were crowded, but with winter in the air they were not hot. Parliament was back in session and only the diehard socialisers were in Town along with the politicians.

Several women looked her way, but avoided eye contact. She had expected nothing else. Others would accept her.

She made her way around small groups, smiling and nodding to those she knew. Most acknowledged her. Madeline, present as she had vowed, saw her and broke away from her companions.

'Lillith, see how easy it was to come tonight? Although I had begun to despair that you would not.' Her laughing eyes held a hint of compassion. 'Ignore anyone rude enough to stare.'

Lillith took Madeline's outstretched fingers and squeezed them warmly. 'I have already refused to see at least half-a-dozen dowagers.' She smiled for her friend. ''Tis so much easier to stay in the country and let the London tabbies do as they please. And less tiring.'

What she did not say was that Perth had drawn her back. She could not bring herself to tell even Madeline that secret of her heart.

'Tsk. You have more energy than a full nursery—and no one rusticates all year.' She linked her arm in

Lillith's and drew her into a slow promenade around the room. 'Smile and nod like there is nothing on your mind but this moment.' Madeline followed her own advice.

It was difficult at first, but Lillith found that the more she smiled and laughed, the more she nodded to acquaintances and friends, the easier the entire charade became. 'Careful, Madeline. Before you know it I shall become a social butterfly.'

'Become?' Madeline teased. 'You are one already. Even Mrs Drummond Burrell cannot cut you after this outing. Sally will not allow it.'

'Are the rumours that vicious?'

'So I have heard,' Madeline said *sotto voce*, keeping a smile on her face. 'But, of course, no one has dared mention them to my face.'

They continued their walk and Lillith even managed to smile and nod graciously at an older woman whom she knew would be telling the worst tales about her. Unfortunately, they were very close to the truth. The only element missing was the name of the man with whom she had spent a sinful few nights. In the *ton* one could do anything, defy any propriety, ignore any convention so long as one was discreet and did not get caught. She had been as good as caught.

'Still,' Madeline said, her voice perking up, 'if you brazen this out, there will be another tale to occupy them within a fortnight.'

'Quite true,' Lillith murmured, resisting the urge to spit at the woman who had just given her the cut direct. She could not hide her flinch.

'Grace Lovejoy is poisonous, Lillith. Pay her no heed. Her mind is always in the gutter and every word she utters confirms that.'

Surprise at her friend's vehemence lightened Lillith's heart. 'Madeline, that is not at all like you.'

Madeline shrugged. 'You are my friend.'

Simple words, but from a true friend and full of support. 'Thank you. I know I can depend on you.'

Madeline hugged her close. 'Never mind. There is Nathan. He is so unfashionable. He thinks I should spend every minute with him.' Her voice held ennui, but her eyes held love.

'Two children and four years has not lessened his *unfashionable* love,' Lillith said with gently mocking humour. 'Every woman should be as lucky as you, my dear.'

Despite her liveliness, Madeline was very perceptive and caring, the trait that had first drawn Lillith. She caught Lillith's unspoken desire. 'You will find someone. You did not choose de Lisle. Some day you will have with a man what I have with Nathan, trust me on this.'

'Perhaps,' Lillith said, releasing her friend. 'Now you must go or Nathan will surely come to fetch you.'

'It would not be the first time,' Madeline said with just a touch of chagrin.

Madeline had barely left when a deep baritone said, 'Lady de Lisle, so nice to see you returned to Town.'

Lillith whirled around. She had been concentrating on Madeline and had not heard the Earl of Ravensford approach. He was a good friend of Perth's. Instantly, her fair complexion suffused with pink.

'How nice of you to say so,' she managed.

Ravensford was as tall as Perth, but there the similarities ended. Ravensford's hair was auburn and his eyes green. He was easy going and had a manner about him that could charm the chemise off a doxy— or more likely his new wife. Theirs was said to be a love match.

The smile left his handsome face and he studied her openly. 'Perth is here.'

Her eyes widened before she had control of herself. 'Really? How…interesting.'

'It could be,' he agreed. 'He is in a foul mood.'

'When is he not?'

'Where you are concerned, not often, unfortunately. He is in the room set aside for cards.'

It was her turn to study him. 'Why are you telling me this?'

He met her scrutiny calmly. 'Because he is my friend, and I do not want to see the two of you make a hash of everything. Nor do I want to see either of you do something that will add to the unsavory gossip circulating about you.'

'You are nearly as blunt as he, but I thank you.'

He nodded. She turned away. Perhaps it was time she left. There were too many pitfalls here.

She cast a glance towards the door leading to the card room and froze. Perth lounged against the frame, watching her like a panther watches a long-desired prey. Her muscles tightened and her right hand crept

to her throat. She could not look away. Heaven help
her, she could not ignore him.

He pushed off and moved towards her, his pace a
slow saunter that drew her attention to his lean hips
and strong thighs. She looked back up in time to see
ardor darken his eyes and hunger sharpen the angles
of his face. She took an unconscious step back.

'Lady de Lisle,' he said, taking the hand that had
rested on her throat and bringing it to his lips. His
eyes never left hers as he pressed his mouth to her
fingertips. 'I had hoped you would be here.'

Gloves were no barriers to the passion his kiss con-
veyed. She gulped and pulled her hand away. 'I am
just leaving.'

'Allow me to get your wrap and call for your carriage.'

'No.' The word came out like a shot. She took a
deep breath. 'No, thank you. That is the footman's job,
my lord Earl.'

'How kind of you to remind me,' he murmured,
stepping away, his eyes gone hard and cold. 'I mistook
my welcome—once again.'

He twisted on his heel and was gone before she
could catch her wits that had gone begging. Lillith
ignored the audience his approach had attracted. Looking straight ahead and with her shoulders back, she
left. But she knew that the encounter would add more
conjecture to her disappearance. By tomorrow everyone would remember the old scandal.

Later, when she was alone and safe from prying

eyes, she would allow herself to remember the feel of his lips and the sound of his voice.

She loved him so much it was an ache in her chest that refused to go away.

Chapter Eight

Perth lounged at his leisure. Ravensford sat across from him and both drank from glasses filled with Brook's finest burgundy. When Ravensford had called to invite him to Brooks, Perth had been more than happy to quit the solitude of his own house.

Lillith's snub last night at Sally Jersey's rout had not improved his mood. He had been in London exactly two days, having left his country retreat as soon as the servant he bribed at Lillith's country estate told him she had left. He still was not sure why he had come, but that was how he felt about everything involving the beautiful Lady de Lisle.

'Town is scarce of people,' Ravensford drawled.

Perth forced himself to set aside thoughts of Lillith and eyed his friend from beneath heavy lids made heavier by several bottles. 'Since when did you care about Society? I thought you considered it well gone since your marriage to the delightful Mary Margaret.'

Ravensford grimaced. 'Sarcasm always was your forte. Mixed with just enough truth to make it bite.'

Perth raised his glass. 'To a direct hit.'

Both drank.

'And what of you?' Ravensford asked, a sly grin bringing a sparkle to his eyes. 'I see that you are squirming on the end of Cupid's arrow.'

Perth studied the dregs of wine in his glass. 'Not me, my friend. Women are like wine—to be enjoyed while being consumed and then forgotten.'

'Ha!' Ravensford finished his glass and, instead of pouring another, rose. 'Let us go see what the Betting Book says about you.'

Perth raised one black brow, but stood and followed his friend. The infamous book was easily found.

Ravensford opened it to the last page and ran a finger down the print. 'Nothing. Damme, Perth, there is not a single thing about you and the elusive Lady de Lisle.'

'And why should there be?' Perth queried with an uninterest he was far from feeling.

Ravensford shot him an irritated glance. 'Because there is definitely something between the two of you. Always has been and always will be.'

He paged back and still found nothing.

'Enough of this nonsense,' Perth said. 'There are better things to do with this afternoon. I hear there is some prime horseflesh to be gotten at Tattersall's.'

'Nothing,' Ravensford said in ire. 'Both Brabourne and I were subjected to having our amorous adventures written about and bet on, but not you.' He gave Perth a suspicious look. 'But not you.'

Perth shrugged. 'With you and Brabourne there was fire with the smoke. With me there is neither.'

'Really?' A mocking grin showed Ravensford's very white teeth. 'Then instead of visiting Tattersall's you will be delighted to accompany me on an afternoon visit to Lady de Lisle.'

Only for an instant did Perth hesitate. Another man would not have noticed, but Ravensford did and grinned.

Perth scowled. 'Of course. I am sure that both she and her brother will be delighted to see us.'

'Wentworth is staying with his sister?'

'He is being dunned,' Perth said flatly, knowing that explained all.

'The man is a leech. Always has been,' Ravensford said, setting his glass down. 'But come along, old man. We have a visit.'

Refusal passed through Perth's mind but, much as he detested his weakness, he wanted to see her. At least with Ravensford along he could not seduce her or challenge her brother—or could not do so without Ravensford trying to intervene.

He set his empty glass down. 'A tame way to spend a perfectly good afternoon, but come along or we shall be past the acceptable hours for visiting.'

Lillith listened to her brother discuss his latest coat with one of her male callers while she poured tea and offered cakes to Madeline, who had come hoping for a quiet talk. Lillith was not sure whether she was glad of Mathias's company so she could not satisfy

Madeline's curiosity or not. Her horrible suspicion was fast becoming a certainty and part of her wanted to discuss the situation with Madeline. Another part of her did not want anyone to know. What to do?

For now, nothing.

She turned to answer a question from Mathias about the cut of his coat and missed Perth's entrance. His voice made her jerk around even as it shot through her entire being like lightning striking a tree and setting it afire.

'Lady de Lisle, Mrs Russell, Wentworth, Peters.' Perth's unmistakable voice greeted everyone.

There was dead silence.

'Hello, all.' Ravensford broke the silence, a look of unholy enjoyment on his handsome features. 'We told the butler not to stand on ceremony and announce us. The poor fellow was devastated, but what could he do?'

With a quick, questioning glance at Lillith, Madeline held her hands out first for Ravensford's quick kiss and then Perth's. 'Ravensford, Perth, how delightful to see you. Things were getting deadly dull here.'

'So we thought,' Ravensford said, taking an empty seat where he could watch everyone at the same time. Such diverting entertainment was not to be wasted. It was too bad Brabourne was not here to enjoy this, for the Duke had a wicked sense of humour. But he and his new bride were on the Continent.

Perth looked at Lillith. 'Lady de Lisle.' She nodded coolly at him, but did not offer her hand.

Mathias scowled at both men in turn. 'What brings

you two to call? There is nothing here that would interest rakes of your stamp.'

Madeline's gasp of surprise was the only sound. Lillith gave her brother a warning frown but Mathias ignored her.

Desperate to keep the situation from getting worse,
Lillith dropped the cup of tea she had just poured. The
liquid spattered the pale lavender of her gown and the
fine bone-china cup shattered on the floor.

'Oh,' she gasped. 'I can be so clumsy. Mathias,
please ring for Simmons.'

With ill grace, Mathias crossed to the fireplace and
pulled the ribbon to summon the butler. He stayed
standing where he was.

Sensing that her brother was not going to let the
small matter of a broken cup and spilled tea alter his
course, Lillith jumped to her feet. 'I am so sorry to
end this delightful gathering—' she sent a pointed look
at Perth '—and so soon after you and Ravensford have
joined us, but I simply must change my gown.'

She stood and individually stared each guest down
until, one by one, they rose and took their leave.

Madeline pressed her fingers and murmured, 'Do
not let this distress you. Men can be such boors.'

Lillith smiled weakly.

Ravensford tossed off a casual farewell.

Perth moved forward and took the hands that Lillith
had not extended. Shocks of desire and need flooded
her, moving from the tips of her fingers to the tips of
her toes. She straightened her shoulders, intent on resisting his pull.

'Lady de Lisle, I hope to see you again.' He lifted her right hand for the touch of his lips.

The breath caught in her throat as his skin touched her. If his touch had been electric, his kiss was a lightning storm out of control. She yanked both her hands free in a movement that lacked grace.

'My lord Perth,' she said, her voice much too husky for her liking. 'As we move in the same circles, our seeing each other from a distance is inevitable.'

A sardonic smile curved his mouth. 'I shall endeavour to do everything in my power to ensure that we not only see each other from a distance, but that we see each other much closer.'

Her blush was hot and instant, beyond her control. His smile turned knowing as he made her a curt bow.

She watched him saunter from the room. Slowly, her blush receded to be replaced by cold dread. Mathias had stood his ground as the others left.

'He is not the man for you, Lillith. He will never offer marriage.'

Her brother's cold words chilled her. Unconsciously, she lifted her hands to rub the gooseflesh that broke out on her arms. The urge to tell Mathias that Perth had already offered marriage was strong. She resisted. Perth offered a marriage she could not, would not, accept. She had married without love once. She would not do so again.

'I am the judge of who is right for me,' she said, 'and if it is Perth, then so be it.' Shock held her motionless. She had intended to agree with Mathias, not confront him and—worse yet—tell him that if she wanted Perth then she would take him. This was not like her.

Mathias crossed the room in several swift strides and gripped her elbow. 'He was not right for you all those years ago. He is not right today. See that you remember that.'

She looked defiantly up at her brother who towered over her. 'I am no longer a child, Mathias. I will choose whom I see.'

'And whom you consort with?' He sneered. 'For, make no mistake, that is all you will do with a man of Perth's ilk. He will not offer marriage. Not now. He is known throughout the *ton* as a womanising rogue who dallies where he pleases and leaves without a backward glance. Will you become his next doxy?'

The blush she had lost returned in a rush. Only this time the reason was anger, not desire. And fear. For his words came too close to reality.

'Let me go,' she gasped, yanking away from his punishing grip.

He released her and stepped back, surprise flashing momentarily across his fleshy face. 'Perhaps I spoke too harshly, but only out of concern for you.'

'Perhaps you spoke too harshly? Perhaps?' Her voice rose before she could control her fury. 'How dare you call me a doxy, or even hint that I might be one! How dare you do that to me. And *you* my brother.'

'I am only worried about you, Lillith.' His voice took a more conciliatory tone. 'Perth is a scoundrel and, while he intends you no honour, it is obvious that he still desires you. I wish only to help you stay out of his clutches.'

How many more truths would her brother utter? They were like darts that pierced her skin and left poison in their path.

She took a deep breath. 'I am fully aware of Perth's intentions. I do not plan on succumbing to him. I am a woman now, not a young girl—as I told you before.' She turned away from him so that he would not see the sparkle in her eye that hinted of tears to come. Things were so complicated.

'Please go now. I must change and then rest. This evening I am promised to Lord and Lady Holland for dinner.'

'As you wish,' he said.

She heard the door close behind her brother, but sensed that this was not the end of his objections. He would watch her closely. And he would do everything in his power to see that she and Perth were kept apart. She was not sure whether that knowledge gladdened her or made her ineffably sad.

That evening, to Lillith's chagrin, she sat across the table from Perth. Lord and Lady Holland, as usual, had invited a mixture of politicians and wits. She wondered where she fitted in. Probably as a single woman. Other hostesses were always in need of single men; Lady Holland never was.

'Do you not agree, Lady de Lisle?' Perth's deep voice asked.

Politics were not a great interest of hers and she had

no desire to become a political hostess, yet she did keep up with the trends. Even she knew that Perth's plan would not do well.

'I think your idea is honourable, but I fear you will find opposition in executing it.'

Interest sparked in his eyes, making them snap. He was so devastatingly handsome, she wondered how she could continue to resist his advances.

Lord Holland interjected. 'The returning troops are in sore need of jobs, else they will become lawbreakers and a worse burden on the country. But you are right, Lady de Lisle, Perth will face opposition in Parliament, just as Lord Alastair St Simon has.'

'Honour is not always a matter of paying one's gaming debts,' Perth said harshly. 'We, and all of Europe, owe these men a chance to find fit employment and the means to feed and clothe themselves and their families.'

She listened to him speak with conviction about the needs of the returning army. Now that Napoleon was finally defeated, men were being let go from the army and navy. Many of them had no other skills and could find no work. Many became beggars, others thieves.

The man on her right made a comment that demanded her response, and she reluctantly let Perth's words fall away from her attention. Her first duty as a guest was to entertain the people seated beside her.

To Lillith, it seemed an eternity before Lady Holland rose, signalling that it was time for the women to leave the dinner table. She rose with the other women and followed them to the drawing room, while the men

stayed behind to drink port and smoke cigars or cig-
arillos as the inclination took them.

One of the married women, Constance Montford,
sat beside Lillith. She was older and considered one
of the forthcoming London hostesses. She was also a
gossipmonger.

She gave Lillith a large smile. 'My dear Lady de
Lisle, so delightful to see you back in Town.'

Lillith returned her smile with a nod. 'Thank you,
Mrs Montford. I am delighted to be here.' She was
not going to give the woman anything to bandy about.

Mrs Montford tittered, a trait that would not do well
in a political hostess. 'One hears such malicious rumours.' If she had a fan, Lillith thought the woman
would be fluttering it. 'But of course, one knows not
to believe all of them.'

'A very wise choice,' Lillith murmured, wondering
when the woman would get to the point and mention
the *on dit* circulating about Lillith's disappearance.

'Titbits are like spice,' Mrs Montford continued.
'They enliven an otherwise dull evening.'

Lillith gave the woman a tiny smile. 'I thought you
enjoyed politics over all else, Mrs Montford. Are you
not trying to set up a saloon to rival Lady Holland's?'

It was a bold thing to say in this company, but Lillith was determined that Mrs Montford should get as
good as she gave. The woman was determined to drag
Lillith's potential scandal into the open, so Lillith
would make sure that Mrs Montford's ambitions were
discussed as openly.

Mrs Montford's eyes narrowed and her voice lowered to a sibilant whisper. 'I had heard that you flaunted convention, Lady de Lisle, even to letting yourself be kidnapped by a gentleman and then staying with him for a length of time unbecoming to a respectable lady.'

Lillith's smile thinned. 'Ah, the gloves are off. One should not believe everything one hears, my dear Mrs Montford. The *ton* is notorious for rumours that ruin a person's reputation.'

'Yes, is it not?' the other woman murmured.

A retort rose to Lillith's tongue only to be swallowed by Perth saying, 'Lady de Lisle, Mrs Montford, such beauty in one spot. May I join you?'

He sat down in a chair close by without waiting for them to invite him. Mrs Montford simpered at him. Lillith glared at him. With the *on dit* of her abduction making the rounds of the London drawing rooms, she did not need Perth's proximity. She was not sure she could hide the emotions he engendered in her. Someone would be sure to notice and talk would eventually link him to her disappearance. Their past would only hasten that conclusion.

'Lord Perth,' Mrs Montford said, 'you must come and call on us. I am holding a small gathering tomorrow. I am sure you will find many of your acquaintances there.'

'You honour me, Mrs Montford.'

Lillith noticed that he neither accepted nor declined the invitation. He had charm when he chose to use it.

'And what of you, Lady de Lisle?' he asked, turning

his dark gaze on her. 'Will you have a small gathering tomorrow?'

He was baiting her. 'I think not, my lord.'

His smile became predatory. 'A shame. The one you had this afternoon was so interesting.'

Her fingers stilled in her lap. As soon as she realised that she had reacted, she sought to dissemble. 'My brother is staying with me. His friends are always about.'

Mrs Montford's sharp gaze went from one to the other. 'Ah, yes, I had forgotten you two are acquainted.'

Perth turned back to her. 'A long-standing acquaintance.' He rose gracefully. 'If you will excuse me, ladies. Lord Holland seems to want me.'

Lillith seethed. He'd added wood to Mrs Montford's budding fire and then he left her to put it out. There was nothing else she could say to sidetrack the woman so she decided to leave.

'If you will excuse me as well,' Lillith said.

Before the woman could answer, Lillith used the arm on her chair to help lever herself up. Her ankle was much better, but it was still difficult at times to rise up after sitting for a while.

She made her way to Lady Holland and made her excuse. 'My ankle is acting up again, I am afraid,' Lillith said.

'By all means, don't think you must stay here when you are uncomfortable.' Lady Holland accompanied Lillith to the foyer. 'I see that Mrs Montford had you cornered. The woman is thoroughly unlikable. I don't blame you for wanting to get away.'

Lillith smiled and nodded. She had no intention of slandering any person to another, not even someone such as Mrs Montford. She knew only too well how harmful that could be. Her carriage arrived shortly after and she escaped gratefully.

Perth watched Lillith leave. No doubt she and Mrs Montford had come to an agreement that their dislike for one another was mutual. By tomorrow there would be fresh meat for the gossip mill.

'Be done with it, man,' Lord Holland said. 'Marry the woman.'

Perth refocused his attention. 'I beg your pardon?'

Lord Holland shook his head. 'Lady de Lisle. Marry her and get this over with. Watching you watch her is like seeing a rabid wolf eyeing a sheep. 'Tis painful.'

Perth felt himself flush. 'My apologies. I did not know I was making you uncomfortable.'

Lord Holland gave him a rueful grin. 'She feels the same about you, you know. Written all over her.'

'I see,' Perth said for lack of anything else.

'Then do something.' Lord Holland slapped Perth on the back.

'Perhaps. If you will excuse me.' Perth made his bow and his escape.

Outside his carriage waited, the horses pawing impatiently at the ground. He leapt inside and they were off before he even sat.

It was the small hours of the morning and he did

not want to go home. He was not sleepy and he would do nothing but brood about Lillith. He would go to Brook's instead.

The exclusive club was filled with gentlemen gambling, drinking and talking. Perth made his way to one of the card tables and took an empty seat. Viscount Chillings, a tall, elegantly lean man with thick silver hair, was already there. They were shortly joined by Lord Alastair St Simon, who had married Lizabeth Stone, Lady Worth, just a year ago. The three men were old friends.

'All we lack is Brabourne,' Chillings said, 'but he is on the Continent with his lovely bride. Shall we cut for deal?' He fanned the cards across the table.

'We are short,' Lord Alastair said, 'but we might as well.'

While they did that, a fourth man sat down in the last empty chair. Perth glanced up to see Mathias Wentworth. The man was as self-satisfied as ever. His silver-blond hair, so similar to his sister's, fell over grey eyes that were as red-shot as the setting sun.

Perth resisted the urge to tell Wentworth to go and instead said, 'You are just in time to draw. But I doubt that we play the stakes you are used to.'

Wentworth's mouth split into the parody of a grin. 'I think that tonight you will.'

Chillings lounged back in his chair as he flipped over his card, the ace of spades. 'I am not in the habit of wagering my inheritance.'

Perth glanced at his friend from the corner of his

eye. Was Chillings trying to provoke Wentworth? He turned his card over, the two of hearts.

'It seems I am not to start this game.'

Lord Alastair St Simon turned his over to show the ten of diamonds. 'Nor I.'

Wentworth, with the smirk still on his face, showed his card, the queen of spades. 'It seems that neither am I.'

Chillings gathered the cards and expertly shuffled them. He then offered them to Perth to cut before dealing. The play began, the stakes relatively low for men of their wealth. Lord Alastair never played for great sums since his wife's young brother had killed himself after losing a large amount of money to Lord Alastair in this very room. Perth was actually surprised to see him here.

'Where is Lady Worth?' Perth asked, knowing Lord Alastair would not be here if his wife wanted him by her.

Lord Alastair played a card before answering. 'She is with my mother. It seems they think my country house needs refurbishing.' He shuddered. 'And I am not the man to tell them they are wrong. But I don't intend to be there when they rip it apart.'

Chillings nodded. 'I know exactly. My wife did the same thing. Made no difference that the place had been good enough for my family for the last four hundred years.' He also shrugged. 'Now it does not matter.'

No one said anything. The Viscount's wife had died

two years ago during childbirth. The babe had died as well.

The game continued. The stakes mounted. Wentworth continued to throw his vouchers on to the growing pile of wagers. No one thought him capable of coming up with the amount should he lose, but no one said anything either. It was for Wentworth and his own sense of honour to know when he needed to stop.

They broke their sixth bottle of port when Perth won the last hand. Everyone drank to him, even Wentworth.

'I think it is time I left,' Chillings said, finishing his wine and standing. 'I will be by tomorrow with a bank draft.'

Perth nodded, never having expected differently.

'The same,' Lord Alastair said, leaving his port unfinished as he stood to leave.

When they were gone, Wentworth still sat across from Perth. His eyes were feverishly bright, an addicted gambler to the core. 'I will play you another hand,' he said, his voice high and excited. 'All or nothing.'

'You will?' Perth drawled, wondering what the man was about. 'You already owe me around ten thousand pounds.'

'So I do. So I do.' He rubbed his hands together. 'But I have a better prize for you, one you have coveted for many years.'

Perth's eyes narrowed, but he resisted the urge to lunge across the table and grab the repellent man by the neck. 'Do you?' he drawled. 'Somehow I doubt that it is yours to give.'

'Oh, never doubt that the prize goes where I bid it go. You of all people should know that.'

Wentworth's knowing grin and sly words were nearly Perth's undoing. Under cover of the table, his hands fisted until the knuckles turned white, but he maintained his outward pose of indifference.

'We wagered money, not lives,' he said softly.

'So we did,' Wentworth said. 'I did not know you were so fastidious. Particularly since you have been panting after her for years. Why, just this afternoon you came sniffing around.'

The urge to knack the man's teeth into the back of his throat was nearly overpowering. But that would create only more scandal than his actions toward Lillith had already started brewing.

'Apparently, I am more interested in allowing people to do as they wish than you are.' Perth paused and took a long drink of wine. 'But then we already knew that.'

Wentworth bared his teeth. 'Yes, we did. A pity. Of all the possible suitors for Lillith's hand, you would be the easiest to land and the wealthiest.'

Wentworth's crude words ignited the embers of anger that Perth had so far kept in check. 'You intend to try and sell your sister to the highest bidder—again?'

Wentworth's smirk widened. 'Plainly put, yes. Do you care to enter the fray?'

Perth's eyes narrowed to dangerous slits. 'If you

haven't the blunt to pay me,' he said slowly so that every insulting word would sink in, 'then I will pretend that we never met tonight.' He flicked a contemptuous glance over the other man as he rose. 'But I will not take your sister's life in trade.'

Wentworth poured himself another glass of wine and gulped it down. 'You want my sister and I am willing to give her to you. So why all this fuss? Why not make things easy?'

'You always were willing to give her to the highest bidder.' Perth's lip curled in contempt. 'Is that why you sat down here tonight, so that you could gamble away Lady de Lisle's freedom once again? And did you pick me because you thought I would make the trade? You are a despicable worm.'

Wentworth sneered as he poured himself still another glass of wine and gulped it down, bringing a hectic flush to his cherubic cheeks. 'You are no different from de Lisle, only younger. After that, you want exactly what he wanted. He had the money. Now you do.'

A low growl started deep in Perth's throat. It would be so easy and so satisfying to rip Wentworth to shreds. And it would accomplish nothing.

'I am not interested in playing your game. Don't pay me what you owe—or have your sister pay it. She is wealthy enough to support you for some years to come.'

Wentworth's heavy brows knitted for an instant before the man realised his features gave him away. Suspicion flared in Perth.

'What have you done, Wentworth? Are you selling her to the highest bidder because you must in order to maintain your gambling obsession?'

Lillith's brother downed his wine and stood. The creak of his stays was loud in the silence.

Perth stood as well. 'It was a mistake for de Lisle to leave her inheritance under your management. But then, I imagine that you made that deal with him long before he passed on.' In a show of indifference he did not feel, Perth poured himself another glass of wine and downed it in one gulp. 'Have you paupered her already?'

Wentworth turned away without comment. His corpulent figure weaved its way from the room. There was a horrible sinking feeling in Perth's gut. Lillith was back up for sale to the highest bidder.

Damned if he would lose her a second time.

The next day Perth received a draft on Mathias Wentworth's bank for ten thousand pounds. He stood in front of the fire and stared at the piece of paper. He was tempted to throw it into the flames. Wentworth did not have this kind of blunt, he must have got it from his sister.

But if his fears were true, Lillith did not have this kind of money either. The man was playing a dangerous game with Lillith's future.

Chapter Nine

Perth raised his quizzing glass and surveyed the crowd at the Covent Garden Opera House. Anyone who was anyone in Society was present. The Duke of Wellington sat in his box with friends. The Prince of Wales held court in his private box. And—his perusal stopped. Lillith sat with Madeline and Nathan Russell.

'Found her at last,' Ravensford drawled.

'Andrew,' Mary Margaret, Lady Ravensford, chided in a husky voice that sounded as though she had just risen from making love. Her voice had first caught and held Ravensford's interest. 'Leave the man alone.'

Ravensford took his bride's fingers and raised them for a kiss, all the while giving her a devastating smile. 'He would feel uncared for if I did not tease him.'

Mary Margaret snorted. She was a beautiful woman although not in the current vogue. She was dark where blonde was fashionable. Her figure was full-busted and slim-hipped. But her eyes were her best feature, brilliant as finest emeralds; they showed compassion and depth. Ravensford doted on her.

'Ignore him, Perth,' she said.

'Always,' Perth said, suiting action to word by rising and leaving.

On stage the dance continued. In the pit, those who could not afford seats or boxes watched for any sight of delicately turned ankles. Perth ignored it all as he made his way to the Russells' box.

His knock was curt and he entered before permission was granted. He scowled.

'Perth,' Madeline Russell trilled. 'Do join us. We are become quite a party.'

Chillings, sitting at his ease beside Lillith, waved languidly. 'All the world's a stage, as the Bard said,' he drawled.

'So it would seem,' Perth replied, pulling a chair up to Lillith's other side.

He nodded at Madeline Russell, who watched everything with an avid gleam in her eye while her husband had a more sanguine look. Perth nodded to him.

'Been following your bill in the House of Commons,' Russell said. 'Heavy going. Let me know if there is anything I can do to help.' Nathan Russell had influence in the Lower House and would be a valuable ally.

'Thank you, I will.' He turned his attention to Lillith, who laughed at something Chillings had said. 'I did not know you like the opera.'

She turned a cool gaze to him. 'There are many things you do not know about me.'

'And many things I do,' he said low, his voice a husk as memory caught his gut and twisted it.

Chillings watched the interaction between them. 'I believe I must be going.' He bowed to Lillith and looked pointedly at Perth. 'I will be at Brook's later.'

Perth nodded.

No sooner than Chillings was gone than another knock sounded on the door. The Prince of Wales entered with Wentworth in his wake. Everyone stood before the men bowed and the ladies curtsied. Behind the Prince's back, Lillith's brother smirked.

'Mrs Russell, Lady de Lisle.' The Prince took a hand of each of them. 'I could not resist such beauty.' He slanted a glance at his friend. 'And Mathias here insisted on visiting with his sister.'

Perth said cynically, 'It seems that living with her is not enough.'

Silence fell and tension mounted. Lillith, resenting the fact that once more she must play peacemaker between her brother and the man who had been her lover, said, 'Mathias has joined me in London because he knows how I hate to stay alone in a house as large as mine.'

No one said a word.

Madeline jumped into the fray. 'We are delighted to have you, your Highness. Can we offer you some wine?' She gestured to the opened bottle and empty glasses.

The Prince, never one to deny himself pleasure, accepted. When he sat down, Mathias held his arm out to Lillith.

'Come walk a moment with me, Lillith,' he said, his tone an order.

Lillith's hackles rose but, with Perth so close and ready to pounce on Mathias for any reason, she stood. Better to keep the two men apart. They had never got on well, but lately it seemed as though something had happened to make everything worse.

She laid her hand on Mathias's arm and allowed him to escort her from the box. She heard a chair scrape behind her and turned to see Perth getting to his feet. She frowned at him and shook her head. His eyes narrowed, but he did not follow and she breathed a sigh of relief.

Out in the corridors it was colder than the box. She released Mathias's arm to pull her shawl closer.

'What do you wish to discuss?' she asked, impatient with him because she knew he meant to scold her.

'You should not encourage Perth. I have told you before, he offers nothing honourable.'

Lillith's mouth thinned. Perth was more honourable than her brother allowed. It was love the Earl did not offer.

'We have been down this road before and it goes nowhere,' she said testily. 'Should I pursue Viscount Chillings? It seems that he left your party to join mine tonight. Did you suggest it?'

A gloating smile made Mathias's cheeks puff out. 'You have been widowed a year. It is time you looked to remarry. Chillings would make a good match. He is a widower, so the two of you would have something in common. And a man, once married, tends to marry again.'

A young woman carrying oranges passed them,

casting a curious glance their way. Her presence reminded Lillith that they were not private.

'This is not the place to discuss this, Mathias.'

He shrugged. 'There is never a good time to discuss matrimony.'

Still, he turned them back toward the Russells' box. He opened the door without knocking and angled Lillith in ahead of him. The Prince had already left, but Perth sat where she had left him, a brooding darkness on his face.

The Earl stood abruptly. 'Lady de Lisle, Mrs Russell, I would be delighted if you would join me for a ride in Rotten Row tomorrow. It will be cold, but invigorating.' His words included everyone, but his eyes held Lillith's.

She shivered and opened her mouth to refuse but Madeline beat her. 'Why, Perth, we would be delighted. Wouldn't we, Nathan? Lillith?' She shot Lillith a quelling glance that said louder than words that they were going on this outing.

Lillith turned away. Madeline was an inveterate matchmaker no matter who the couple was. Earlier she had tried as blatantly to put Chillings with Lillith.

'Lillith is already engaged to me,' Mathias said, his face dark with irritation.

In spite of trying to keep her face impassive, Lillith's muscles tightened in rebellion. Mathias was only trying to keep her from Perth's company, which was no bad thing. She said nothing.

'It seems that Lady de Lisle dances to your tune

once more,' Perth said, his tone dangerously close to insulting.

Silence reigned as everyone watched Mathias, wondering if he would take offence or let the tone go. He was known as a man who avoided duels. He stiffened and his hands squeezed Lillith's arm. Then he released her and stepped away.

'You would do well to remember that, Perth,' Mathias said before turning and leaving with poor grace.

Perth, a knowing look on his face, took his leave, saying, 'I shall look forward to seeing you another time, Lady de Lisle.'

Madeline, vastly enjoying herself, held out her hand for Perth to kiss in the Continental way. The Earl obliged her while Nathan Russell looked on with amusement at his wife's antics. Then, before Lillith realised what Perth was about, he took her fingers and raised them to his lips. This contact had to stop. Most Englishmen did not greet women this way. But she could no more find it in herself to deny herself this pleasure than she could root out the love she felt for him.

His eyes held hers as his mouth touched the fine leather of her gloves. The intimacy of his look intensified her unreasonable desire. She knew only too well how his mouth felt on her bare flesh. She flushed and pulled her hand away.

Perth nodded and left.

'He is devilishly handsome,' Madeline said. 'Any woman would be beside herself to receive such marked attention from him.'

Lillith frowned as she surreptitiously wiped her hand down her skirts. Somehow she had to forget the feel of his flesh on hers. 'I am not any woman,' she said acerbically.

Madeline became comforting. 'And nor should you be. He would not be so interested if you were.'

Lillith turned away from her friend's knowing eyes. If she had not wanted Perth's attentions then she should not have come to Town for she had known this would happen. She had, in fact, longed for it. Now the intensity of their meetings scared her more than when he had abducted her. She began to think that perhaps he truly cared for her since he pursued her so diligently. But no. He wanted revenge.

It was painful to remind herself that he wanted revenge for what had happened so long ago, but she had to remember. Otherwise she would fall into his arms and be miserable for the rest of her life, always loving him and wanting him to love her. For she knew him well enough to know that, where he did not love, he would not be faithful. It would kill her to be married to him and have him turn to another woman.

She sighed. That was not the life she wanted.

As soon as Perth exited the Russells' box, he left the opera. Ravensford would wonder, but he would not worry. Outside, the weather was cold and wet. Fog blanketed the streets so that not even the light from a linkboy's flambeau could provide more than ten feet of visibility. Brook's was a distance from here but, the mood he was in, Perth knew the walk would do him good. He was balked of his goal, and he was too active for this sedentary London life.

He set out with long strides, his cane swinging at his side. The night air was brisk and he needed that to ease some of the heat his meeting with Lillith had created. No matter how many times he saw her, or how he tried to win her, she resisted him.

He hit the cane against the street in frustration. She wanted things he could not, would not, give. He had loved her once, he would not make that mistake again.

He increased his pace until he turned the corner of the street where Brook's stood. Inside the exclusive club it was warm, smoky and dimly lit.

Perth shrugged out of his greatcoat and gave it to the nearby footman. Somewhere here, Chillings waited for him, if he had not misunderstood the Viscount. Rather than ask a servant for the Viscount's whereabouts, Perth set out on his own. He found Chillings ensconced in a leather wing chair in a dark corner with a decanter of amber liquid and two glasses on the table beside him. Another chair sat opposite. Perth took it.

'Whisky?' Chillings asked by way of hello. 'I had it brought specially.'

'Thank you,' Perth said, accepting the offered glass.

For long minutes, neither spoke. Each drank a glass of whisky and poured another. Someone smoked cheroots across the room. Someone else smoked a pipe. The haze curled around the chandelier and the branches of candles. A roaring fire added its particular scent and fuzz to the air.

Chillings pulled a snuffbox from his jacket pocket,

flicked open the lid and offered some to Perth. 'It is the Beau's own mix.'

Chillings had been a particular friend of Beau Brummell's and had stuck by the man even after Brummell had his falling-out with the Prince of Wales. If talk was true, Chillings had also lent quite a sum of money to the Beau and never gotten it back. He was not the only one.

'No, thank you,' Perth said. 'I am not a snuff taker.' He finished his second glass while the Viscount took a pinch of snuff and with a flick of his wrist sniffed the concoction. Never a patient man, Perth broke the carefully created calm between them. 'Why did you ask me here?'

Chillings raised one coal-black brow so that it nearly met the premature grey of his hair that hung in one rakish lock over his high forehead. 'I thought that was obvious—the lovely Lady de Lisle.'

The muscles in Perth's shoulders tightened into painful knots. His voice, however, was non-committal. 'I was not aware that we had something to discuss pertaining to her.'

'Enough prevaricating,' Chillings said. 'Life is too short to allow misunderstanding to ruin a friendship or to let pride keep one from going after what one wants.' He put the delicately enamelled snuffbox back in his pocket and took a swig of whisky. 'Believe me, I know.'

Perth set his empty glass down and waited.

'Lady de Lisle is an extraordinary woman and not at all in the common way. Any man would be interested in her—if he were not already engaged else-where.' Chillings met Perth eye to eye. 'I enjoy her company, but that is as far as it goes. I was in her box because her brother asked me to pay attention to her as a favour. It seems she lacks for male company.' He said the last blandly.

'Or the kind Wentworth deems appropriate,' Perth said.

'That too.' Chillings finished his drink and stood. He held out his hand. 'Friends?'

Perth rose and took the other's hand. 'I wish you the best of luck with the lady who *has* caught your fancy.'

Chillings laughed ruefully. 'I shall need all the luck I can get. She is a high-flyer, new to Town, and not at all interested in becoming a cyprian. I hope to convince her otherwise.'

'You will succeed. But, in the meantime, how about a hand of cards?'

In charity with one another, they moved to a room where groups played all manner of gambling games. Before they could settle at a table, Chillings walked to where the Betting Book was kept. He flipped it open to the last page and motioned Perth over.

'I saw you in here with Ravensford several days ago. Were you checking to see if someone had written anything about you and Lady de Lisle?'

Perth eyed the Viscount. 'Ravensford insisted.'

'But you knew there would be nothing,' Chillings said.

'What do you mean by that?' Perth asked, careful to keep any hint of suspicion from his voice.

'Oh, I think you know exactly what I mean.' Instead of pursuing the topic, Chillings turned away. 'Are you up to faro tonight, Perth? I feel like taking a risk.'

Perth laughed. 'If I can be guaranteed a turn at being the bank, I will be more than happy to indulge your desire.'

The two made their way to the table where a game of faro was in action. Perth knew Chillings was done speaking of the Betting Book, but he still wondered how much the Viscount knew. If he knew everything, he had been very discreet throughout the past months. And if that were so, he knew he could trust the man when Chillings said he was not interested in Lillith.

But Perth knew Wentworth would stop at nothing to ensure that he married Lillith off to the highest bidder once more, a man who would be willing to pay Wentworth's debts. He intended to have her for himself, but he'd be damned if he would pay Wentworth's gambling debts in the bargain.

Days later, Lillith paced her bedchamber. The large airy room, done in shades of lavender and blue, normally eased her nerves. This morning she knew nothing would help. Her stomach roiled and she had already lost what little breakfast she had managed to eat. Each passing day made it harder to deny what her body told her.

'My lady,' Agatha said, 'your guests will be here shortly. I still need to fix your hair.'

Lillith sighed. She and Madeline and Nathan were going for a picnic in the country. Madeline had said she would invite some others to go with them, but it was Lillith's gathering and they would all be meeting here. At the time she had proposed it, it had seemed a delightful diversion and a good effort to do something that might, if only for a couple hours, keep her mind from Perth. Now she was tired and grumpy with a digestive system that refused to cooperate. She wished she might claim sickness, but dared not.

She pressed her hand to her abdomen as she sat for Agatha's ministration. She had been waking up sick for the last three weeks. She was also more tired than usual.

'Ouch,' she said, tears springing to her eyes. 'Do be careful, Agatha.' It seemed the maid was less gentle than normal.

'Pardon, my lady. I did not mean to hurt you.'

Lillith sighed. 'I know you did not.'

Her thoughts whirled around. What if her fear was true? What if she was carrying Perth's child? No. It was impossible. Nine years of marriage had never ended in this—surely three nights could not?

'Bring me the green shawl,' she said, forcing her thoughts to her toilet. 'And the bonnet trimmed in green satin and apple blossoms.'

'Yes, my lady.'

Agatha rushed to do her bidding. Lillith stood and started pacing before she caught herself. Enough of this.

She donned the clothing and swept from the room,

intent on ignoring the rumblings of her stomach, though she knew from experience that it would be lunchtime before she got relief. Right now she needed to make sure that Cook had everything packed and that the coach was ready. That would take her mind off the other things.

Agatha ran after her with the apple-green pelisse.

Thirty minutes later, Lillith was assured that everything was as complete as she could possibly make them. And not a minute too soon. She heard the knocker and the sound of the door opening.

'Mr and Mrs Russell,' the butler announced just as the knocker went again.

Lillith moved to take Madeline's outstretched hands. Nathan stepped aside and smiled as the two of them hugged.

'You are positively glowing,' Madeline gushed, moving back.

'Thank you,' Lillith said, grinning and making a short curtsy. 'You are delightful as well. Going on a picnic suits you.'

'A perfect idea,' Madeline said, releasing her light, trilling laughter. 'To go at this time of year is even more enticing. Town can be so boring during the Little Season, with so many staying in the country, that a picnic in questionable weather adds spice.' She laughed again. 'You always were one for doing the unexpected.'

Lillith laughed as well, enjoying her friend's pleasure in this unusual adventure. 'Let us hope it does not snow. Who else did you manage to coerce into taking this risk with us?' Lillith asked.

Madeline glanced at her husband and some of the laughter left her face. 'Well, you see…Nathan ran into Lord Ravensford and his wife riding in Rotten Row. Yesterday. And…'

She trailed off as the butler opened the door again and announced, 'Lord and Lady Ravensford and Lord Perth.'

Lillith blanched and her eyes held such a look of reproach that Madeline flushed bright red. 'I am terribly sorry, Lillith, I did not… Oh, dear, I have made a muddle of everything.'

Lillith's good manners rose to the fore. She forced a smile to her face and turned to her new guests. 'Ravensford, Lady Ravensford, Perth, how delightful to have you join us.'

Ravensford's eyes sparkled. 'I cannot tell you how delighted we are to be here. A rare bit of luck to run into Russell in Hyde Park yesterday.'

Lady Ravensford's eyes held sympathy. 'I hope we are not too many. Men often don't think of that sort of thing when they plan an outing, particularly when it is not their outing to plan.'

Lillith's smile turned genuine. 'Do not worry, Lady Ravensford. I asked Madeline to find some others to go with us. I am glad she found you.'

Some of the tension in the room eased.

Then Lillith shifted to greet Perth. His eyes were stark. She raised a hand to him, the pulse beating at the base of her throat.

'Perth.'

'Lady de Lisle.'

She forced a weak smile. 'We must be leaving if we hope to have any time in the country,' she said breathlessly, wishing she could resist him and knowing once again that she could not.

Without waiting for a reply, she swept from the room. The sooner she put some distance between her and Perth the better for her peace of mind—and heart.

She stood in the foyer, donning the heavy cape Simmons held when a sense of foreboding came over her. Looking up, she saw Mathias on the first-floor landing. He was watching her like a ferret watches a mouse.

He had spent the night. She thought that he was being dunned and could no longer afford his fashionable set of rooms in the Albany. But she did not know for sure. She did not ask and he did not tell.

'Going out, Sister?' For a man as heavy as he was, he moved lightly on his feet as he descended the stairs. 'Did I hear Perth?'

Just then the rest of her party spilled into the foyer. Madeline and Lady Ravensford laughed at something Nathan was saying. Lord Ravensford, one auburn brow raised, looked at Mathias while Perth ignored her brother.

In a rush, Lillith said, 'We are going for a picnic, Mathias. As you can see, we are a group.'

Instantly she regretted the last words. They sounded as though she sought to impress upon him the innocence of the situation, something that was no concern of his. At worst her words implied that there was a need for innocence, which then implied that there was more between her and Perth than she wished anyone to ever realise—especially Mathias.

Mathias stopped halfway down the stairs. His gaze swept over them and a sneer marred his face.

Perth's heavy-lidded eyes were cold and deadly.

Apprehension chewed at Lillith. Something more had happened since the incident in her drawing room several days ago. She would have to find out from Mathias when she returned. Right now, she wanted to get her party out of here before the situation became ugly.

She rushed forward and took Madeline's arm and pulled her out the door, hoping the others would follow. Outside, her coach waited. The Russells' carriage, a high-perch phaeton done in hunter green, stood behind hers. Behind them was another phaeton done in ebony and bearing the Earl of Ravensford's coat of arms. No other vehicles waited.

The tension created inside changed focus but remained. She turned and spoke without thinking. 'Where is your carriage, Perth?'

His eyes caught hers. 'I walked.'

'What? I find that hard to believe.'

He shrugged and settled his curly-brimmed beaver on his head. 'I find that after so long in Town, I need exercise. I walk a lot in the country. Besides, I live only a few streets away.'

'How do you intend to accompany us? You have no carriage and both Nathan and Ravensford have phaetons that will only hold two.'

His eyes held hers. 'I had hoped you would offer me transportation.'

'No, no, that cannot be,' Madeline said, stepping between them. 'You must ride with Nathan, Perth. I will go with Lillith.'

Relief warred with disappointment. But what Madeline said was best. She might be a widow, but that did not give her carte blanche to be alone in a carriage with a man who was not her relative. It could be done, but should not be done with the rumour circulating about them, for his name was now being linked with hers.

Perth cast her one last smouldering glance before joining Nathan Russell in the phaeton. She and Madeline got into her carriage and the coachman whipped the horses into motion.

They passed quickly through London, the cobbles sounding loud through the West End and out into the country, Richmond their destination. Soon the phaetons passed them by.

'I am so terribly sorry,' Madeline said. 'I did not know until it was too late that Nathan had invited Ravensford. Then for Ravensford to bring Perth.' She reached for Lillith, only to withdraw her hand. 'I am so sorry. I know you find his presence uncomfortable.'

Lillith smiled ruefully. 'It does not matter, Madeline. I must learn to deal better with his company, but it is hard.'

She gazed at the countryside they passed. The trees had lost their leaves and the furrows in the fields were brown. November was here and the earth was going to sleep.

Many members of the aristocracy had homes in Richmond. It was an easy travelling distance if one went by water. De Lisle had a house there, which had gone to his heir, a distant nephew, who was not much older than Lillith. The new Lord de Lisle did not care much for her, having been against the marriage from the start. Still, they managed to maintain a distant relationship of tolerance.

'Well, then,' Madeline said, her voice perkier, 'I can hope for the best. I still think you should accept his offer. 'Tis time you remarried.'

Lillith listened to her friend's ramble, nearly choking on the last. 'You would have me marry the Earl of Perth? A man who does not love me?'

Madeline shrugged, looking not a whit chastened. 'He obviously cares for you. And there is the rumour already linking you to him. A marriage would soon scotch that.'

Lillith sighed. 'Yes, there is the rumour,' she said softly. 'Somehow my disappearance has been linked to Perth and I don't know why.'

'Don't you?' Madeline raised one auburn brow. 'Surely you dissemble, something you need not do with me.'

'Why should my absence from my country house be instantly linked to Perth's absence from Town? Either one of us could have been gone for any number of reasons not related to the other.'

'You could. I agree. But no one believes it.'

'Why?' Lillith turned a puzzled face to her friend.

Madeline shook her head as though such a question had such an obvious answer that it was ridiculous that Lillith did not see it. 'Because the two of you look at each other as though you are one another's most coveted treasure. Everyone has seen it, and everyone has commented on it at one time or another. Many wonder when you will marry. Or, barring that, begin an affair. The disappearance is taken as the start of the affair.'

A soft gasp escaped Lillith. 'Why have I not heard any of this?'

'How should I know? Perhaps you have refused to hear what is being said.' Her voice softened and she added, 'But none of that really matters. You love him, you should marry him and be done with it.'

'Perhaps,' Lillith replied. There was much to consider here. 'He does not love me,' she added softly.

Madeline barely heard her friend's last words and could not suppress a comment. 'Vastly dramatic, but I think far from true.'

Hope surged in Lillith's heart only to be ruthlessly suppressed. 'He desires me,' she murmured.

'Oh, yes, he does that,' Madeline said with a delightful shiver. 'It must be infinitely exciting to have a man of his ilk want you. *I* would be ecstatic.'

Lillith laughed. 'Now I know you jest. You are madly in love with Nathan. No other man even catches your eye.'

Madeline shrugged. 'As to that, no woman can *totally* ignore the Earl of Perth. He is so dangerous looking. One can imagine him abducting one and carrying one off without a thought for what anyone else might think. A rogue.'

'Yes,' Lillith said, 'he is all of that and more. But as I have already told you, he does not love me.' When Madeline opened her mouth to speak, Lillith held up her hand to stall her. 'Desire is not enough. Not for me. I have had that before and it is a cold bedfellow.'

'Oh, dear,' Madeline breathed. She took Lillith's unresisting hand in hers. 'I am sorry. I did not think of that, only that where there is such burning desire surely love will follow.'

'But not always,' Lillith said bitterly. 'Not always.'

The carriage slowed down and both stopped speaking. They were pulling on to a dirt side road and would soon be at their destination, a small hillside on Lillith's late husband's property. It was a charming respite from the buildings and the dirt and the soot of London. Lillith had often come here for peace. Today would be vastly different.

She said to Madeline, 'We are here.'

Madeline nodded and let the previous subject die.

Soon they were all climbing out of their carriages and the servants were unloading the baskets of food. Blankets flapped in the wind and soon covered the dying November grass. No wildflowers greeted them, but a view of rolling countryside rewarded them for the journey. By evening it would be unbearably cold. As it was, Lillith's adventure was truly that. The weak November sun warmed no one. They had come more for the company than the weather. Thankfully it was not raining, or worse, snowing.

Chapter Ten

Lillith found Perth sitting beside her on the blanket, her acute awareness of him warming her despite the day being cold and the sun weak. He poured her a cup of tea, even though a footman hovered nearby ready to serve. She took the cup, her fingers brushing his, and memories of the first time he had poured her tea flooded her senses. It had been during that coach ride. She flushed hotly as her mind continued to remember the rest of her abduction.

He seemed to know her thoughts. 'We can have that again,' he murmured, his voice husky.

She lowered her eyes from the intensity in his. 'No, we cannot. And please…' she lifted her free hand to keep him from speaking '…say no more. If for no other reason than that there are others around us.'

A grim smile twisted his mouth. His scar looked pinched. He rose and went to speak with Nathan Russell, who stood some distance away looking out at the surrounding fields.

Mary Margaret, Lady Ravensford, sat where Perth had. 'He is a passionate man,' she commented mildly.

Lillith gave her a bland look.

'Sometimes you must do what your heart tells you, not what your head cautions,' Mary Margaret said gently. 'Believe me, I know that is not easy.'

'Thank you,' Lillith said. But she did not want to talk about this with her. 'Have you been here before?'

Lady Ravensford took the hint and followed. Madeline soon joined them and the three discussed the latest *on dits* with relish. Shortly the gentlemen joined them and organised pandemonium set in as the footmen served the food on specially packed china and silver. Crystal goblets filled with champagne. Laughter filled the chilled air.

'To Lady de Lisle and her fantastic entertainments,' Ravensford said, raising his glass.

'Yes,' everyone else added, following his lead.

Lillith laughed with delight, only to feel Perth's gaze on her. Drawn inexorably, she looked at him. He raised his glass to his lips and drank, his attention never wavering from her.

'To Lady de Lisle,' he finally said, his glass empty.

There was an expectant pause, almost as though the others felt momentary embarrassment at witnessing something too private. Shivers chased down Lillith's spine.

Against all sense of self-preservation, she was drawn to Perth as a moth to the flame that would destroy it. She gathered all her strength of will and looked away from him. She must return to the country soon or she would be lost.

The next afternoon Lillith found herself riding in Hyde Park in spite of the cold weather and her own exhaustion. Somehow she had allowed Mathias to talk her into this outing. They had argued when she had questioned him about the increased hostility between him and Perth. Mathias said it was nothing. She knew better.

Today, they were in a small group of three men, another woman and Lillith. The other female was Lady Annabelle Fenwick-Clyde, the twin sister of Viscount Chillings. Lillith had just met her this day.

Like her brother, who also rode with them, Lady Annabelle had prematurely grey hair and eyebrows dark as the night. She was elegantly slim in a hunter-green riding habit and dashingly fashionable in a matching military-style hat. Her blue eyes sparkled and her wit was acerbic. Lillith found her very entertaining.

'Oh, look,' Lady Annabelle said, 'the Earl of Perth. I have heard he is a devil with the ladies and a military hero.' She prodded her brother with her riding crop. 'Do call him over here, Chillings, for I don't doubt that you are acquainted with him.'

The Viscount gave a long-suffering sigh. 'There are times like now when I wish you had not returned from Cairo, Belle.'

The lady laughed heartily and winked at Lillith. 'I am such a trial to him.' She slanted a glance at Mathias's portly figure and frowning face. 'Something I am sure you are never to Mr Wentworth.'

Lillith looked at Mathias and fought the urge to tell him he looked like he had swallowed a lemon whole. After all, this outing and the people they were with had been his plan. Instead, she said demurely, 'I try not to be a bother. There are always repercussions I would rather not face.'

Lady Annabelle gave Lillith a sharp look but said nothing.

The third man of the party, Mr Carstairs, moved closer to Lillith and said, 'I cannot believe that you are ever trouble.'

Lillith smiled graciously and hoped that Perth noted the ruggedly handsome man who sat his horse so well. It would do Perth good to know that other men found her attractive. It would do her more good if she found someone attractive besides the Earl. This longing for someone she could not have for anything more than a surcease of passion had to stop.

Mr Thomas Carstairs was an East India Company nabob recently returned to England. His hair was bleached blond by the Indian sun and his face was burned a swarthy golden brown. His teeth shone blindingly white when he smiled, and the skin around his piercing blue eyes crinkled. A very handsome man.

Lillith sighed internally. Too bad he did not make her blood boil and her pulse pound. A hint of cinnamon floated on the cold November air. Perth was near.

She turned her head in his direction as nonchalantly as she could, when the urge to feast her eyes on him was nearly overpowering. It seemed that she had not seen him for longer than she could bear, although she had last been with him yesterday.

'Did I see you summon me over, Chillings?' Perth asked with cool composure.

The Viscount laughed. 'My sister wants to make your acquaintance. Englishmen are a novelty where she has been the last two years and so far she cannot get enough of meeting her countrymen.'

Perth looked at Lady Annabelle and his eyes lit with appreciation. 'My pleasure to help a lady in distress. I am Perth.'

The lady held out her gloved hand and smiled so that a dimple showed in her left cheek. 'I am Annabelle Fenwick-Clyde, Chillings's twin sister.'

Lillith watched the exchange with distress. Lady Annabelle was a handsome woman with intelligence and wit; qualities Perth admired. The lady also did nothing to hide her interest in the Earl. Lillith bit the inside of her cheek to keep from saying something, anything, to break the awareness between the two. She was spared further discomfort.

'Lady de Lisle, would you care to race to that large tree by the Serpentine?' Mr Carstairs asked.

Fearful that she could not keep her sense of gratitude out of her voice, she nodded and spurred her mare forward. It was not something she would have normally agreed to, but for the instant the freezing wind in her face was like a much-needed slap of cold common sense. Perth's flirting with Lady Annabelle was to be expected and another reason she would not marry for convenience.

She and Mr Carstairs arrived at the tree breathless. Her black velvet hat with its white ostrich plume had tilted too far back during her dash and threatened to fall. She steadied her mount and reached up to better secure the hat.

'Let me,' Mr Carstairs said. 'After all, I am the cause for its precarious position.'

It was an offer she had not expected and was not prepared for. Mr Carstairs edged his large grey gelding close to her mare and leaned towards her, his hands reaching for her head. He smelled of sandalwood and the cold, both pleasant but neither exciting. When his shoulder brushed hers, she felt nothing, neither discomfort nor anticipation. Nothing.

She thought he might have lingered longer than absolutely necessary on straightening her hat, but she was not sure. 'Thank you,' she murmured, smiling at him as she backed her mare away.

He grinned, his strong white teeth so appealing. 'My pleasure. Any time.'

The look in his blue, blue eyes and the inflection of his voice hinted that many things would be his pleasure to do with her and for her. Still she felt no excitement. She did not even blush.

She had barely put distance between them before the rest of the party caught up. She ignored Perth's obvious irritation at something, probably her, and turned to Mathias. 'Is it not time for us to return home? I believe you have a meeting later this afternoon.'

Her brother scowled at her. 'We have time enough for another canter around the park.'

She thought about arguing, but the set of her brother's shoulders told her that he would be obstinate. Her reluctance would only cause a scene. 'As you wish,' she murmured, angling her horse away from Mr Carstairs.

Unhappy with the entire situation, she urged her mare into a canter, hoping to leave the others behind. Disappointment pierced her as she heard the clop of another horse's hooves.

'You are free with your favors,' Perth said, his voice rough.

He caught up with her and for a moment she thought he intended to reach for her reins. He obviously thought better of it, but his hands clenched on his own reins.

She glanced sideways at him. 'As are you. Lady Annabelle is a very interesting woman.'

'That she is,' he murmured. 'But I have not made love to her.'

The blush that would not come for Mr Carstairs flared into existence. Heat scorched Lillith. 'Be quiet,' she ordered. 'Someone will hear.'

He glanced back. 'They are too far away. Besides,' he scowled at her, 'Carstairs might as well know now that his chances are non-existent.'

Her hands jerked on the reins, causing her mount to

prance. She leaned forward and soothed the mare with strokes along its neck. 'That is not your decision.'

The scar running the length of Perth's right cheek whitened. 'By heavens it is. You are mine, Lillith, whether you admit it or not.'

Her brows snapped together. 'I am no one's plaything, sirruh. And most definitely not yours.'

Anger turned Perth's eyes black.

'I thought I told you to stay away from my sister?' Mathias's voice separated them.

Lillith jumped. She had been so involved in her fight with Perth that she had not heard her brother approach. Anyone else from the party might have interrupted them and neither of them would have known it until the other person had overheard everything.

What was happening to her? Not even her sense of self-preservation worked when Perth was near. Heaven help her.

Perth cast Mathias a contemptuous glance. 'I do as I please, Wentworth. You should know that by now.'

'Then go and flirt with Lady Annabelle,' Mathias said with a nasty twist of his mouth. 'That seemed to please you well enough, and leave my sister alone.'

Perth's lips thinned. He nodded to Lillith. 'We shall discuss this later.'

He turned his horse and cantered back to join the other three where he positioned himself beside Lady Annabelle. Anger at Mathias mixed badly with the anger she felt toward Perth and the jealousy Lady Annabelle generated.

'Stay out of my affairs, Mathias,' she said flatly.

His face red enough to cause an apoplexy, he retorted, 'You act like a harlot around that man. How many times must I tell you he is not for you? You need to remarry and Perth will not do.'

Her hands clenched the reins. 'What I do with Perth is my concern, not yours. Nor do I need to remarry.' Her mouth twisted bitterly. 'My marriage was not so enjoyable that I am anxious to repeat the experience. And I don't have to. De Lisle left me a wealthy woman, as you should know since he appointed you the trustee of my estate.'

For a second his eyes shifted from hers before he returned his gaze to her and said, 'You are a headstrong woman, Lillith, and it will bring you nothing but trouble. Already everyone is talking about you and Perth. Will you have them decide the two of you are having an affair? Do you intend to be one of those widows who become the acknowledged mistress of a wealthy man? For that is where you are headed.'

She said nothing. There was too much truth in his words. Her fury turned inwards.

'Besides,' Mathias continued in a more reasonable tone, 'it has been over a year since de Lisle's death. 'Tis past time you remarried. Carstairs or Chillings would be perfect.'

She stared straight ahead and, even through her irritation, suspicion began to show. 'Why are you so intent on my remarrying, Mathias? I have plenty of money from de Lisle's settlement. And a new husband might not be so eager to have you live with us as has been your wont the past six months.'

It was long moments before Mathias answered, as though he considered his words carefully. 'A woman who has enjoyed the marriage bed once is more likely to seek such pleasure elsewhere if she is not wed again. And you need a man's hand and guidance. You are far too attracted to Perth for your own good. Another man would keep him from your thoughts and your side. I am only thinking of you.'

'You are saying that you think I am a trollop and too weak to manage on my own.' She gave him a hard look. 'You are insulting me.'

'No, no.' He raised one gloved hand in protest.

She studied him. He was her only living relative. Her brother. But there were times when she wondered if she was the only one of them to care that their relationship was all the family they had left. When she managed to think about Mathias with her head and not her emotions, she realised that he treated her like an object that was his to dispose of as he willed. It was not a pleasant thought and she tried to keep herself from it. Unfortunately, since Perth had re-entered her life, the knowledge had been forced upon her that she was always the one to reach out to Mathias—unless her brother had need of money. Then he came to her.

Whatever else Mathias might have said, and what she might have replied, never happened. The rest of their party caught up with them and this time she was very much aware of their coming close.

She gave everyone a false smile. 'My brother has decided to continue on his ride by himself or with the rest of you if you so please. My apologies, but I have matters to attend to at home.'

She glanced at their faces. Surprise on Lady Annabelle's, disappointment on Mr Carstairs's, consideration on Chillings's and, of course, sardonic acceptance on Perth's. Her brother she ignored. She left without another word.

Perth watched her go, noting the stiffness of her ramrod back. Whatever Wentworth had been prattling about, it had infuriated Lillith. He considered that a good thing. She was too controlled by her brother and it would do her good to stand up to him. Particularly since he had an instinct that Wentworth had gone beyond the bounds of what even a loving sister could accept—or so he hoped.

Lillith lifted her aching head from the chamber pot. Her bleeding was three months late. She could no longer deny the truth. She carried Perth's child.

She rocked back on her heels and fell backwards so she sat on the floor. One hand slipped to her still flat belly. All these years of thinking herself barren, listening to de Lisle berate her for her inability to conceive.

She was not sure if she felt joy or despair. She had always wanted children, but over the last years she had finally reached a sort of dispassionate acceptance that she would never have any. Her second hand strayed to her waist.

In six months she would have a child.

Wonder held her for long minutes. Would she have a boy or a girl? It did not matter.

But what about Perth?

If Perth learned of her condition, he would force marriage on her. He would feel it his duty and to do less would besmirch his honour. She had no doubt that the abduction of months ago would be as nothing compared to what he would do this time. She would not put it past him to hire a minister to join them against her protests. A powerful nobleman could do many things.

That was not what she wanted.

She levered herself to a standing position and crossed to the window. Outside night was descending. In what light was left, she could make out a cold drizzle. A carriage rumbled by, the inside a golden glow. Someone headed to a dinner party, and then perhaps to the opera or the theatre.

She sighed and her warm breath left a cloud on the glass. She rubbed the fog away, noting the chill that came through.

She did not want another marriage of convenience. And especially not with Perth. It would be the end of too many girlish dreams that she had cherished in spite of all the facts that said her chances for a love match with him were gone.

But what of her child? Could she condemn it to be a bastard because of her own cowardice?

She turned from the window and went to sink in a chair in front of the roaring fire. Warmth eased away some of the chill that still held her. Her hands fluttered listlessly before setting once more on her stomach.

She could go to the Continent, have the child and leave it with a couple who would care for it. She knew of women who did that. Her heart wrenched. No, she could never do that.

She closed her eyes and wished life was easier, but it was not. This child she carried was hers, and she would keep it and raise it with all the love she had to give.

But she would not go to Perth with this news.

She would go to her Dower House and wait for the birth. She would lie, tell everyone that she met and married the babe's father during the time she disappeared. If need be, she would go to the Continent in the spring, have the child and return. No one would believe her, but it did not matter. Other noble families raised bastards and the children were accepted into Society. Hers would be too.

Her decision made, she stood. 'Agatha.'

The maid looked in from the dressing room where she had been making minor repairs to some of Lillith's dresses. 'Yes, my lady?'

'We are leaving first thing in the morning for the Dower House.'

The maid nodded. It was normal for her mistress to return to the country at this time of year.

The decision made and the order to pack understood by her maid, Lillith felt a weight lift from her heart. She would go to the country, bear her child and raise that child on her own. She would not look back with regret to this choice. The child would be enough for the rest of her life.

She could not have Perth. She would have his child.

Chapter Eleven

Perth stared morosely at the fire.

A month after coming to Town, he was no nearer his goal for the returning army veterans or his pursuit of Lillith. Bitter frustration soured his mood. As did Fitch's reproachful looks. The manservant chose that moment to enter the library.

Caught in regret and guilt, Perth said testily, 'I have asked her a dozen times to marry me. Does that satisfy your pinched idea of responsibility?'

'Pardon me, my lord,' Fitch said with a voice that would have curdled milk, 'but have you told her that you love her?'

Perth drew himself up. 'I do not lie, no matter what the cost.'

Fitch made a noise under his breath. 'You have been doing a pretty good job of it for the last ten years.'

'You go too far.'

Perth's voice would have frozen another person. Fitch had been with the Earl too long and gone through too much. War had a way of forging relationships.

'I believe you have done that on your own, my lord.'

'Get out.'

Fitch did so without a qualm.

Perth rose and went to a table where a decanter full of good Scotch whisky awaited his pleasure. He poured a glassful and downed it in several gulps. The alcohol burned down his throat and exploded in his stomach. It changed nothing.

'Damnation!'

He threw the glass at the fireplace where it shattered against the brick. There was only one thing to do.

Less than an hour later, Perth stood in front of Lillith's door. The night air rifled through his greatcoat and whispered down his neck. The flambeau held by the linkboy he had hired to light his way blew out. It did not matter. He had already seen all he needed. The knocker was gone. She had left Town.

He banged on the door anyway. With luck she had left a couple of servants to care for the empty house. He had only to rouse them.

'My lord,' the boy said hesitantly.

Never one to take his anger out on someone less fortunate than himself, Perth reached in his pocket and tossed the youth a Golden boy. 'You may go.'

The youth had managed to relight his flambeau and in its flickering light he saw what he held. 'Thank you. Thank you much, my lord,' he said, his joy in such

bounty showing on his face. He bowed and hurried
away as though fearing Perth would realise how much
he had given and demand it back.

Perth hardly noticed that the boy had left. He
pounded harder. Someone had to be here. He would
find them if he had to go around to the back and beat
on every door there. He would break in through a window if he must.

Although, once he stopped and thought, he knew
where she had to be, or where he hoped she had gone
to—her Dower House. If she had gone to the Continent instead, he would be hard pressed to find her. But
it was a strong possibility. Since Napoleon's final defeat, all of the *ton* was flocking to Europe. If she had
gone there, her servants would know where and getting that information from them would save him weeks
of time. For he would find her.

When no one answered he swore under his breath
and headed for the back. All the windows were dark,
making him fear that she had not left anyone here. He
banged on the door and looked in all the windows.
Not a glimmer of light. Nor did anyone answer his
banging.

There was one other place he could go. Madeline
Russell would know where Lillith was.

Not wanting to waste time going to his own house
for a horse, Perth hired a carriage to take him to Nathan and Madeline Russell's small town home. Their
house was lit up and through the windows he could
see people milling. They might not be wealthy, but

they were well liked. Some of the tension that had lent him speed seeped out and his shoulder muscles eased.

Without a qualm, he strode up the steps and knocked. He did not care that he would be arriving uninvited to what appeared to be a small gathering. The butler answered immediately.

'Tell Mrs Russell that the Earl of Perth is here to see her,' Perth said, not bothering to take off his beaver hat or hand over his gold-tipped cane.

No emotion showed on the servant's face. 'If you will come with me, my lord, I will inform Madam of your presence.'

Perth found himself in a charming little room done in pinks and baby blues. It was far from fashionable, but he found that the colours amused him. They were something he could easily imagine Madeline Russell choosing. He did not sit. Time was of the essence.

The door opened and Madeline Russell came in. Her auburn hair was curled around her face and her evening gown was fine white muslin. Unlike her very unconventional room, she was very much in vogue.

Perth forced a smile. 'Mrs Russell, I am sorry to intrude on you like this, but I need to know where Lady de Lisle has gone.'

Madeline's eyes widened. She cast a quick look over her shoulder to see if anyone had heard Perth. Relieved that no one could have, she closed the door behind her.

She looked Perth straight in the eye. 'Why do you want to know?'

Instead of the irritation Lillith's challenges always

caused him, he found Madeline Russell's directness calming. But he was not about to reveal his business to her.

'I did not come here to be questioned, Mrs Russell. I came here for information. The sooner I have it, the sooner I will leave you to return to your guests.'

Her mouth pursed. 'Lillith has had enough of your high-handed ways, Perth, and I quite agree with her. If you cannot be bothered to give me a very good reason why I should betray her confidence, then I won't.' She stood her ground.

The temptation to leave and search for Lillith without any knowledge of her whereabouts was strong. Undoubtedly she was at her Dower House. But he could not be sure.

He gritted his teeth, all calmness at the situation gone. 'You are an impertinent minx. I imagine Russell more than has his hands full with you.'

She nodded and crossed her arms over her chest. 'Flattery will get you nothing,' she replied sweetly.

'Damned if it won't,' Perth muttered under his breath, for he had had more than his share of conquests by using charm. The stubborn look on the woman's face told him it would not work this time. 'Very well, I intend to ask her to marry me.'

Madeline's face softened. 'That is all well and good and something you should do, but I am not sure that is enough.'

He ground his teeth. 'It will have to be enough. I can offer nothing else.'

She studied him, noting the way he stood on the

balls of his feet, ready to pounce. His scar was white. His eyes were hard. He needed Lillith. Perhaps that was enough for now.

'She has gone to her Dower House.'

'I thought as much,' Perth said in disgust. 'And I have wasted well over an hour making sure. Thank you, Mrs Russell, I shall be going now.'

'Tut, tut, Perth. She might just as well have gone to the Continent.' Madeline's eyes clouded. 'And she probably should have.'

Perth stopped on his way to the door. 'What do you mean by that?' But he had a sharp, tight feeling in his gut.

She turned so that she could look him in the eye. 'That is something I don't intend to divulge. If you must know, then it should come from her.'

Perth nodded curtly.

He strode from the room and out of the house. Urgency drove him now more than ever. The sharp twist of his gut intensified. Fierce pride mingled with desire and an urge to protect.

He must get to Lillith.

He stood on the pavement in front of Madeline Russell's house and swung his cane to and fro in irritation. Not one carriage had passed this way in the last fifteen minutes, and it was a long walk to his house in Grosvenor Square. There was nothing else to be done. He set off, his long strides eating up the distance.

Fog swirled around his feet. The cold night air bit through his many-caped greatcoat. Occasionally, the

candle glow from the window of a passing house lit
his way. He increased his pace. There was no time to
lose. Always he was on the lookout for a carriage that
might be for hire. He was sorely tempted to knock on
one of the doors he passed and offer to pay them any
amount they wanted for a horse.

He paused at a likely place. He could smell a stable,
which meant there might be a horse. But there were
no lights.

Footsteps sounded behind him and across the street.
He had been hearing them for some time but had assumed they were someone else out on this night. He
flicked a glance over his shoulder in curiosity.

Three shadows moved in the darkness between two
buildings, but no one came forward. What is going on
here, he thought, finally beginning to think about
where he was and that he was alone. He was a brave
man and not particularly afraid, but hoodlums attacked
in gangs. Even he, with his cane and the sword it hid,
would be hard pressed to fight off a large number of
men.

'Who goes there?' he demanded, forgetting about
the possibility of a horse.

He turned to face the opposite side of the street.
One of the shadows separated from the others and
came forward, empty hands held up in the dim light
provided by the moon and stars. No gas lamps lit the
road here.

'Jus' me, guv. Wonderin' if ye'd have a bit o'
money for a starvin' man?'

Perth watched the man approach. The other two

shadows, men, edged outward on each side of the one coming towards him. Perth flexed his gloved fingers. His leg muscles tightened. The bite of cold air on his face, the tang of soot on his tongue and the chance of danger to his life combined to energise him. This was living for him. This is how he felt with Lillith. The realisation hit him like a blow and took his breath away. No wonder he wanted her so badly. She made him feel alive, as though his life was worth living.

The thugs moved closer, forcing Perth to pay attention to the present. 'I've nothing for you,' he said flatly. 'Take your friends and be gone before something happens that you will regret.'

The man stopped while the other two came forward and edged to either side of Perth. In one smooth slide, Perth pulled the sword from the cane. The steel shone sharply in the dim light. The advancing men paused, then rushed forward as one.

Perth backed up until the building was behind him, then stood his ground. The sword flashed as he countered the attack that had started in earnest. He felt steel hit flesh and one of the men yelped.

'Gor, 'e's got me. The devil take 'im.'

That man staggered and turned aside leaving two men. Perth's mouth twisted into a wicked grin. The odds were getting better.

'Leave now,' he said through clenched teeth, 'and no one else will be hurt.'

The two remaining thugs fell back, but did not depart. He heard them muttering and braced himself for another attack. It came as soon as he had anticipated.

The sword flashed and the one on his right dropped the cudgel that had been raised above his head poised to strike. The heavy wood hit the ground with a thud and the man who had held it whirled away, a stream of filthy language pouring from his mouth like bilge running down a sewer.

Perth watched the second man flee. 'You are by yourself now. Do you think you can do what three of you could not?'

The man slunk back. Perth stepped forward and picked the cudgel up in his left hand.

''Twas suppose ta be easy,' the man growled. 'Nothin' ta worry about. That be w'at the cove said. Damn 'im.'

'Ahh, the light dawns.' He could turn this to his advantage, Perth thought. 'I will double whatever you were offered to harm me if you will take me to the man who hired you.' Even though the light was bad, Perth would swear he could see avarice tighten the other man's face. 'That will give you my money and what the other has already paid you up front. And you will share it with no one.'

The thug rubbed his jaw. 'T'at's a idea. But w'at's to insure you'll pay me? Got the blunt on ye?'

The man was definitely greedy. Perth reached into the inside pocket of his coat and pulled out a leather bag that jangled. He tossed it to the thief. 'My first installment. Tell me when and where you are to collect the second part of your fee for tonight's work and I will meet you there. Then you will get more from me, and I will meet face to face with the man who arranged this attack.'

The scoundrel eyed Perth warily. 'And 'ow do I know you ain't just sayin' this to get away?'

Perth laughed outright; the idea was ludicrous. 'Because I could run you through where you stand without a moment's hesitation.'

The man took several rapid steps back.

'But I want positive proof of who hired you and your word is not enough. Besides which, he probably did not even give you his name. Very likely he did not even hire you himself.'

'Five this mornin',' the man said in a rush and named a place near Nightingale Inn in the East End. A very unsavoury place, but popular with the young bucks. Perth knew the area well.

'I will be there. Now be gone.'

Not until the man was well away did Perth sheath his sword. The cudgel he kept, a grim smile making him look sinister. He would take it with him to the meeting.

By the time he entered his own foyer, it was nearly time to turn around. Fitch, who acted as butler and valet, met Perth at the door.

'My lord,' Fitch said, turning his nose up. 'You are drenched.'

Perth peeled his coat off and then his gloves. His beaver hat was ruined. He handed Fitch his cane. 'This will need cleaning.'

Fitch's eyes widened momentarily, but he said nothing.

Perth grinned. 'Yes, I saw some action.'

'Luckily for you this is the first time. Some of the places you frequent are less than pleasant.'

Perth laughed out right. 'Since I have attempted to take up with Lady de Lisle, my life has been one great adventure.'

'Lady de Lisle? Surely she is not the reason you had to use this sword.' He pulled the weapon from its case and studied the dried blood. 'A good cleaning and oil will make it good as new. Although...' he held it to a candle '...it appears to be nicked. A whetstone will fix that.'

'Make it quick, Fitch. You and I have a meeting in less than an hour in a disreputable part of town and we might find that cane a life-saver.'

Fitch turned and headed to the kitchen while Perth mounted the stairs two at a time, headed for his chambers.

Inside his rooms, he stripped quickly and donned clean, dry clothes with no concern that they were not fashionably tight. 'Twas better to have loose clothing in case he found himself in a dangerous situation again, and he could easily dress himself without Fitch's help. All the time, his mind whirled.

He felt excited and alive. The sense of danger and accomplishment combined to make him aware of everything around him, the heat of the fire, the sound of the wind blowing by his window. This is how he felt with Lillith, ready to take on anything, but he had not recognised the heady delight he took in her company for the same aggressive pursuit of accomplishment he had felt in the army. No wonder he wanted her so badly.

He missed being in the army and the camaraderie along with the knowledge that he did something useful. London and the pursuits of a man of leisure had bored him, and he had not even let himself realise that. Lillith had given him a goal, something to strive for. Now this situation with her brother—for he had no doubt Wentworth was behind the attack on him—gave him another reason to win her.

He had to be right about Wentworth having spent all of Lillith's settlement from de Lisle. There could be no other reason for her brother trying to push her into marriage. But why did the man want him out of the way when he had only recently tried to marry her to him? Very likely because Wentworth knew Perth would not pay the brother's debts as de Lisle had and another man might.

He went to his wardrobe and grabbed a navy greatcoat. The less conspicuous he was the better.

Downstairs, Fitch waited with the cleaned sword replaced in the cane. Perth took the weapon and put a new beaver hat on his head at a rakish angle.

'Like old times, my lord,' Fitch said, a gleam of anticipation lightening his face.

'Have you ordered horses brought around?'

'Of course,' Fitch said, drawing up in affront. 'We might not be in the army now, my lord, but I still know how to prepare.'

*   *   *

The area of London they shortly found themselves in was not a place to leave two thoroughbred horses without having someone stand guard.

'Here, you,' Fitch said, motioning to a youth standing in front of the pubs. 'Watch our mounts and you will be well paid.'

'Better paid than if you steal them,' Perth added, flipping a coin toward the boy who caught the money with alacrity.

The youth bit on the metal. 'The real thing.'

'See you do as we say,' Fitch emphasised, 'or you will be the sorrier for not.'

The boy gave Fitch a scornful look, but he held tight to the reins of the two horses.

Not waiting to hear the final words between his servant and the street urchin, Perth headed to the corner where the thug had said he was to meet the man who had hired him. Along the way, Perth saw several youths he knew in passing. One of them waved at him, but Perth ignored him and kept going. The young man did not follow.

Rather than stand obviously where the meeting was to take place, Perth positioned himself back away and in the shadow. Fitch soon joined him, his hand on the pistol he kept primed in his pocket. The thief arrived shortly after, but the man responsible was late.

Twenty minutes passed. The thief began to fidget, but Perth and Fitch remained steady. Perth decided the tardiness was something Wentworth would do to a lackey he considered unimportant. He would not be surprised if Wentworth did not show. As far as Wentworth was concerned, the deed was done and to meet the thug and pay him the second half of the money would be a waste of blunt Wentworth did not have. The thief would never be able to find Wentworth so the man was safe.

After sixty minutes, Perth stepped forward. ''Tis unlikely that you will ever again see the man who hired you.'

The man had an ugly look on his face. 'Flash cove, 'e'd better 'ope he don't see me again.' His head tilted and a calculating look sharpened his narrow face. ''Ow about the blunt you owe me?'

Perth's face sharpened. 'I have already paid you as much as I intend to. The second half was dependent upon my meeting the man who hired you. That has not happened.'

The man took a menacing step forward.

'I would not do that if I were you,' Fitch said, moving from the shadow where he had remained. 'I have a primed pistol in my pocket, and I won't hesitate to use it.'

The man backed down, but greed still sharpened his features. 'W'at if I finds the cove?'

Perth shook his head. 'Not good enough. I want to confront the bastard myself.'

The thug grunted acknowledgment of Perth's desire, but did not back away.

'We are leaving now,' Perth said. 'Do not follow us.'

The man flashed a crooked grin that showed brown teeth, where he had them. 'Wouldn't think o' it, guv.'

But he watched them collect their horses and he heard one of the flash coves who frequented the nearby pub call the dangerous man Perth. Wouldn't take too much to find his lordship again, for he had no doubt the man was a lord. He was too arrogant not to be.

Perth rode silently home. Fitch followed. Not until they were inside and Perth was unceremoniously throwing clothes into a duffel did either speak.

'My lord,' Fitch said aghast. 'What are you doing?'

'I am packing.' Perth dug in a drawer for a clean shirt. 'Where did you put my shaving kit?'

Fitch fetched it from the shaving stand where it stood in perfect sight. 'Where are you going? And what are you going to do about the person who paid to have you hurt?'

Perth cinched the saddlebag. 'I am going after Lady de Lisle who has gone to the country. As for the person who wanted me hurt, I have a good idea who he is.' A fierce grin creased his cheek. 'I intend to deal with him yet.'

Fitch nodded in satisfaction. 'Wentworth is where I'd put my blunt.'

Perth gave his man a narrowed look. 'How do you know so much?'

'Has to be.' Fitch picked up one of the shirts Perth had discarded in his search for a cravat. 'You are chasing his sister, and he has never wanted you in the family.' He gave Perth a knowing look. 'He has already managed to do harm to you once before.'

Perth's face hardened. 'I was young and stupid then. Ten years have made a vast difference.'

Fitch nodded. 'Now you carry a cane with a sword at all times.'

'Just so.' Perth slung the saddlebag over his shoulder and strode from the room. 'Don't expect me until you see me,' he said.

Chapter Twelve

Lillith stood naked before her mirror. Multi-branched candelabra flanked both sides of the glass and the fire added more illumination as well as warmth. She turned so that her side was reflected and studied her profile.

Was her stomach slightly rounded instead of nearly concave as it had been? She ran her palms over what she perceived to be a slight bulge. She was over three months. Surely she showed. And soon she should feel the babe move. Perth's child. Her child. She felt a quiver of excitement.

The door slammed open.

Lillith crossed her arms over her hips and spun around, intending to severely berate whoever had the effrontery to barge into her private rooms. She gasped. Perth stood framed in the doorway.

'Oh, my lady,' Agatha begged, standing on tiptoe behind the Earl and peering over his shoulder. 'I'm ever so sorry. He barged in the front door and climbed the stairs before anyone knew what he was about. He would not wait.' She wrung her hands and tried to push past the Earl, who effectively blocked the entrance.

Lillith's teeth began to chatter with suppressed anger. She twisted around and grabbed the robe tossed across a nearby settee. She yanked it on.

'Leave us, Agatha,' she said. '*You* did nothing wrong.'

She did not order Perth gone, for she knew by the look on his face that he was not leaving. He moved into the room and carefully shut the door behind himself. That very controlled action told her how furious he really was. His hair glowed damply and water from his greatcoat puddled on the pale green carpet. His Hessians were muddy. He looked as though he had ridden a great distance without regard to the inclement weather.

'You are bold and your lack of manners more than apparent,' she said coldly, hoping to sting his pride.

He stripped off his greatcoat and threw it across the nearest chair. Fleetingly, Lillith thought the water on the garment would stain the finely embroidered upholstery but it could be replaced easily enough.

'You left without a word.'

His eyes bored into hers before his gaze dropped to her belly. He stepped forward and it was all Lillith could do not to edge back and away from his advancement. Clenching her hands in the robe's belt, she stood her ground.

'I don't owe you any explanation of my comings and goings.' She lifted her chin and hoped that the trepidation making her giddy did not show in her voice.

He did not stop advancing until he stood scant inches from her. The tang of cold air and rain mingled with the familiar awareness of him. The urge to sway into him was great, even though anger at his method of entering her house still made her jaw ache from clenching it too much and too tight. She was so weak where he was concerned.

'You are carrying my child.'

His voice was deep and dark and dangerous. His eyes were black pools. Without warning, he gripped her shoulders and pulled the robe down to her waist. Her hands on the belt kept him from stripping the garment completely from her.

'How dare you!' she said, using one hand to futilely try to pull the silk back up to cover her breasts.

'I dare a lot for you and the child you carry,' he said. 'Too much,' he said harshly. 'Too much.'

She stared at him, taken aback by the hunger and need she saw in his face.

'Does that surprise you?' he asked bitterly. 'Well, not as much as it does me. I thought I was over you.'

His gaze ravished her, moving over the mounds of her breasts and making them swell with desire. She longed for his touch, at her bosom and at her loins. But…

'Do you love me?' she finally asked, the words barely a whisper as she forced them through the constriction in her throat.

His gaze came back to her face. 'No.'

'Ah…'

The word tore from her like the moan of a dying creature. Pain ripped through her. She thought he had made her suffer before, but nothing like this final renunciation. She would slap him if she could, but her arms were pinned to her sides by the garment that his large hands still kept at her waist.

'Get out,' she said. 'Get out of my life and do not ever dare to come back.' She pulled in a ragged breath. 'Or I will have you horsewhipped.'

His face turned murderous. 'As your brother did?'

She blanched. 'You lie. Mathias has many faults but he would never do that.'

He sneered. 'You say you would. Why do you suppose he would not do the same?'

'Get out,' she ordered, wrenching from his grasp.

The shrill rip of silk filled the air. She was free from his hold, but stood naked before him.

'Get out,' she said again, forcing air into her labouring lungs. He stared at her, his gaze roving over her like a hot wave of passion.

He swallowed hard and turned on his heel and left.

Lillith watched in disbelief as he walked away. The door swung shut behind him. Silence surrounded her like a suffocating blanket. Cold assaulted her even though the fire blazed and the windows were shut and the curtains drawn. She wrapped her arms around herself and squeezed. Shivering, she picked up the remnants of her robe and tossed it into a corner. The sight of it was too disturbing. She crossed to a wardrobe and drew out another robe and donned it. Only then did she allow herself to collapse on to the settee.

Her eyes were huge as she stared into the leaping orange flames of the fire. How could she have threatened to have him whipped like a common cur? No matter what he had said to her or what he had done, he was a man.

Had Mathias really had him whipped? She cringed at the possibility. But it would explain the scars on his back.

Her head felt as though a vise tightened around it. She huddled deeper into her robe and closed her eyes.

Right now, Perth was somewhere in her house and she would have to confront him. She knew him well enough to know he would not leave until she did so. But she did not think she could bring herself to discuss Mathias horsewhipping him. That was something she was not yet prepared to do.

It was something Mathias would have to answer to, if it were true. And, painful as the knowledge about her brother was, she had no reason to believe that Perth would lie to her about something like that.

She rubbed her hand across her eyes. She still had to face Perth.

Thirty minutes later and fully clothed, she entered the drawing room with as much dignity as her anger with Perth and disillusionment with her brother would allow. Perth should be made to understand that he could not follow her and barge into not just her room, but her life. There was nothing between them. She would not let there be, even if it meant tearing her heart out.

Perth watched her cross the room, her chin high and knew she was more than angry with him. Dressed in a slate grey kerseymere gown that covered her from neck to wrist, she should have been drab. Instead, she glowed. She took his breath away.

He took a step towards her.

'Do not come near me,' she ordered, putting up a hand to ward him off. 'You have no right coming here, and especially barging into my private rooms as you did.' Her voice trembled with fury. 'I want you gone immediately.'

Knowing it would infuriate her more, he sat in one of her overstuffed chairs and crossed one muddy Hessian boot over his thigh. 'In my own good time. I believe we have something to discuss.'

The hectic flush left her face, leaving her looking like the finest porcelain and just as fragile. 'You are in error. We have nothing to discuss.'

The urge to go to her and offer her his name and his protection was great. He resisted. She must marry him on his terms for her conditions were beyond his emotional ability.

He attacked. 'You carry my child. Admit it.'

If he had thought her pale before, he was mistaken. Her skin was nearly as white as her hair. She swayed and put a hand on the back of a nearby chair.

'Ridiculous.'

But her voice was tremulous and her eyes would

not meet his. 'You lie,' he said softly, rising and pacing towards her.

She started to back away, but his hand shot forward and gripped her wrist. Slowly, inexorably, he drew her to him.

'You carry my child and you left London hoping to keep me from finding out.'

Her eyes widened and now she did meet him glare for glare. 'I left London at the same time of year that I always do. You had nothing to do with it.'

'You would sound more defiant if your voice did not shake.' He shifted his hands so that they gripped her shoulders. 'Everything you do is my business.'

'No.'

'Ah, but yes,' he murmured, sliding one hand along her shoulder to the back of her neck. 'Everything.'

He felt her heart beat and the rise and fall of her bosom. Desire, hot and powerful, rushed painfully through his body. Caution and restraint disappeared. He shifted once more, fitting her to him, breast to chest, loin to loin and thigh to thigh.

A soft sigh escaped her parted lips. He took advantage of her vulnerability. His mouth descended and captured hers. Longing flooded his senses. He wanted her, only her.

He sensed her surrender instants before her fingers tangled in his hair. It had always been this way between them. He vowed it always would be.

He drew back. The need to watch her, to see the emotions play over her face as he loved her, were too great to resist. He took one breast in his hand and gently squeezed. Her mouth puckered and a soft sigh escaped her lips. His loins tightened into an ache that demanded release.

He groaned and leaned down to take her other breast into his mouth. Even through the thick wool, he felt her nipple harden. Her hands tangled in his hair and held him tight. Elation surged through him.

He suckled her while both hands slid around her waist to the multitude of tiny buttons that marched down her back. He undid them with skill gained from much practice. Only when he could feel the fine cotton of her chemise did he raise his head and then only long enough to peel the gown down her shoulders to bare her bosom to his gaze and his mouth.

Her nipples pointed rosy and swollen through the gossamer cloth. One thumb tweaked a peak while his tongue laved the other. Her soft sighs drove him on.

With fingers as experienced with chemise ties as they were with buttons, he undid the satin bows and slipped the thin cotton down her chest and waist so that she stood fully exposed to his hungry gaze. The firelight played along her skin like a lover's touch, his touch.

He buried his face in the valley between her breasts and breathed deeply of her. Lilac and woman. Going to his knees, he edged her gown and chemise lower until her belly lay naked beneath his cheek. With a touch light as a feather, he tongued her belly button before slipping lower. Her fingers gripped his hair and held him.

'Please,' she gasped.

'Relax,' he murmured, marvelling at her response to him. Never before had a woman been as wanton with him as she was. And never before had he striven so hard to please a woman. But he found that her ache was his ache, her pleasure his pleasure.

He pulled her clothing the rest of the way over her hips and down her flanks. She stood before him in all her heartbreaking beauty.

Her nearly silver hair hung around her like a silken veil. The light of the candles turned her skin to ivory and left dark hollows that beckoned his hands, his mouth and his lust. She was everything he wanted, everything he needed. She was his.

A groan ripped from his throat as he slid to his haunches and urged her to let him touch her more intimately.

Not until she gasped and trembled in his arms did he stop and then only so that he could slide his face back up to her stomach and rest his cheek against her still-spasming flesh.

More gently than he had ever done before, he ran the tips of his fingers along the soft swell of her belly. He trailed kisses over her flesh. She carried his child and the wonder of it was overwhelming.

He rose to his feet and gathered her close. 'You are mine,' he whispered. 'Now and always.'

She opened eyes still heavy from his lovemaking and gazed up at him as though she had not fully heard his words. A smile tugged at her kiss-stung lips.

This was how he wanted to see her. Always. Drunk from his lovemaking, quiescent in his arms.

He ran his hands possessively down her side and along the curve of her hip and thigh then back up to cup one heavy breast. 'Soon this will suckle our child,' he murmured, awed by the thought.

He stroked the still-erect nipple before bending and taking her swollen flesh into his mouth. Her soft gasps excited him. His loins exploded as he lost control. Surprise caught him and ripped him apart. He gasped.

He had not even entered her and still she wrung him dry of everything he had to give her.

Shaking with a release he had never before experienced, he gathered her into his arms and took her to the couch where he lay her down. With fingers that were no longer sure, he undid the buttons of his pantaloons and freed his flesh. He parted her legs and entered her completely.

She shuddered against him. Her head fell back and her eyes closed. He watched her with shuttered eyes, determined to make her cry out for him. He pulled her closer and began a languid, slow movement that was torture but worth every long, tremulous moment as he saw her begin to shake and then heard a long, low moan of pleasure rip from her.

Driven by more than his own passion, he increased the pace until she screamed and her nails dug viciously into the skin at his shoulders. Still he plunged and still she begged for more. He gave her everything he had and more. He died in her arms and was reborn again, more powerful and more potent. And still he gave her more.

* * *

Later, much later, the fire nothing but glowing embers, they lay a tumble of limbs on the rug.

Perth pushed up on one elbow and looked down at her love-flushed skin. 'I have a special licence,' he murmured, running his palm over the slight mound of her abdomen. 'We can be married immediately. Our child needs a name.'

He was so involved in touching her that it was several minutes before he realised she lay still and unresponsive under his caresses. She caught his wrist in her hand and held him still.

'I am not marrying you.' She took a deep breath. 'I know I am weak where you are concerned, but I am not so weak as to enter a union with you that we will both regret. Not even for the child I am carrying.'

She pushed away from him and rolled to her side and got up with her back to him. She gathered her garments from the floor and pulled the dress over her head.

'Lillith,' he said, 'look at me.'

'No.' She kept her back to him. 'Not until you are clothed and we can speak like adults and not rutting beasts.'

She took a deep, heaving sigh and he was sure she cried. He rose and went to her, totally unconcerned about his nakedness. He put his arms around her and turned her to face him. He had been right.

'Don't cry, Lillith. Everything will be all right. I promise you.' He wiped her tears with his fingertips.

She closed her eyes and pushed against him. 'Don't touch me. Don't come near me. Get dressed.' Her voice rose. 'I will not marry for convenience again.' She opened her eyes and stared hard at him. 'Do you understand? I will not.'

Her continued rejection of him and everything he offered began to simmer deep within him. 'Do you think ours will be a marriage of convenience after the passion we just shared?'

He stepped away and grabbed up his clothes. He yanked on his pantaloons and twisted the buttons closed. Hands on hips, he glared at her.

'Passion,' she spat. 'Passion and nothing more.'

'It is better than what you had with de Lisle.' He leaned forward until his face was nearly in hers. 'Or do you intend to lie to me and tell me he made you feel the way I just did?'

'Why? Why must you make this so difficult?' she demanded, her voice nearly a cry. 'I will not marry you. That is final.'

He stepped back and made her a curt, mocking bow. 'I hear you. But what of our child? Will you condemn it to a life of poverty or, worse yet, a father who is not its true father?' His voice turned cruel. 'I know women of the *ton* regularly have their lovers' bastards and expect their husbands to acknowledge the child as theirs. Some men even allow the child to inherit their titles and honours. Is that what you want?'

'No. And I don't have to settle for that. I am wealthy in my own right.' Her mouth twisted bitterly. 'My marriage to de Lisle insured that.'

'Did it?' he asked softly. 'Are you sure?'

He saw doubt flit across her face before she closed

off the possibility. 'Yes, I am absolutely sure. Mathias is taking care of my estate. De Lisle left it that way. My brother would never pauper me.'

Perth laughed harshly. 'Wentworth? With his inability to stay away from the gaming tables?' He paced close to her. 'Do you know that he lost ten thousand pounds to me a couple of weeks ago? Do you know that he paid me with a draft on your bank?'

She flinched. 'He has money of his own and he keeps it in the Bank of England just as I do.'

'But are you positively sure?' He pushed her with his words and with the closeness of his body. He had to get through to her. 'What if you are wrong and your brother has spent your funds? What if you are no longer a wealthy widow? Then what will become of our child?' He saw fear enter her expressive eyes. 'Can you afford to continue refusing me when you are not sure?'

'I am sure,' she countered, arms crossed protectively across her stomach. 'Yes, I am.' She turned away and moved to the fire where she held her hand out to the embers.

He followed her. 'Check things before you send me away again. A couple of days. That is all it will take. I will wait here.' She flinched. 'Not in your home,' he assured her. 'I will stay at the inn in the village.'

She said nothing, just stared at the smouldering orange coals. She started shivering. The urge to pull her close was strong. He resisted. This was the moment she had to decide.

She angled around, her face a mask of anger and uncertainty. 'I will do as you suggest. But I am sure you are wrong.'

He did not smile. He knew what she would find.

Chapter Thirteen

Lillith made a conscious effort to appear calm as she was ushered into the office of her man of business. Mr Joseph Sinclair had been de Lisle's solicitor and was the solicitor for the current Lord de Lisle. De Lisle had left Lillith's inheritance under Mathias's control with the stipulation that the money be managed by Mr Sinclair. Until now, Lillith had not called on Mr Sinclair, trusting her brother or the solicitor to contact her if there was need.

Mr Sinclair rose when Lillith entered. He was a tall, cadaverous man with sallow skin and wire spectacles. He was a solemn man, his shoulders stooped from carrying the burden of many an aristocrat's financial future. He was very good at what he did if allowed to do as he saw best.

'Lady de Lisle, please have a seat. I am glad you have come to see me.' The pinched V between his bushy grey eyebrows deepened. 'I have sent several letters asking to arrange a meeting with you.'

Her brows rose and the smile she had worn trailed

off. 'Oh. I—' She stopped. Why had she never received those letters? Immediately she thought of Mathias. But, no, that was ridiculous. 'I never received your letters. They must have gone astray.' The solicitor said nothing. The worry she had berated herself for feeling intensified. 'Thank you for receiving me on such short notice.'

Sinclair frowned and his long, thin fingers shuffled papers as though he needed an outlet for nerves. But he was not a nervous man. 'I am glad to see you, Lady de Lisle. I did not arrive on your doorstep because Mr Wentworth said he was keeping you informed of everything and that if you needed my help, you would contact me.' He cleared his throat. 'I now realise that I should have gone around Mr Wentworth.'

Mathias had never said a word to her about her monies or that Mr Sinclair was concerned. Her nerves tightened in a very unpleasant fashion. 'Why have you wanted to see me?'

He answered her gravely. 'I prepared these papers for your brother so that he could deliver them to you.' He shrugged his thin shoulders and handed her the sheaf of papers he had been fiddling with.

Lillith took the packet and set it carefully in her lap, noting as she did that her fingers shook. This did not feel good. 'Perhaps you would tell me what these papers say. It would make things quicker, and I can ask for clarification immediately without having to wait for another appointment.'

He took a deep breath. 'There is no soft or kind way to say this, and believe me I have tried many times. My lady, you are nearly broke.' He paused and the silence grew strained. 'As Mr Wentworth knows.'

She gasped, a tiny painful sound. 'He was right,' she breathed. Despair, regret at her brother's profligacy and fury all combined to make her stomach heave dangerously. She swallowed hard, determined not to give into the urge to cry. 'Is everything gone? De Lisle left me very well off and that was only just over a year ago.'

Sinclair's brown eyes held a hint of pity. 'You have the use of your Dower House until you remarry or die. The house in London was left to you in perpetuity, but Mr Wentworth has taken out a lien on it to pay some of his…more pressing bills.' He spread his hands helplessly. 'That is one of several times I sent you a letter. I wanted to make sure that you knew what was happening.'

'Gambling debts,' Lillith interjected bitterly. 'And your letters never reached me.' Her voice chilled. 'How many have you sent?'

'Three,' he said.

She shut her eyes to block the pity in his. Somehow his notes had gone astray. Or been intercepted. How could Mathias have done that?

Finally, when she was sure she would not crumble, she opened her eyes. Her voice was even calm. 'Please continue.'

'The money in the Funds has been gone for the last six months.' He shrugged and raised his hands palm up in a gesture of defeat. 'I am sorry it is so bad.'

The pain of betrayal constricted her chest. Once

more it seemed that Mathias had used her for his own means without any regard for her best interests. Hurt warred with love. He was all she had left.

'I should have tried harder to reach you,' the solicitor continued. 'You might have been able to talk to Mr Wentworth.'

She shook her head sadly. 'No, I do not think so.'

He bowed his head in acknowledgement of her words. It was normal for a female to have her nearest male relation handle all matters of finance. He had not been surprised by her deceased husband's directive, and would have been very surprised had she managed her monies herself. But he had been saddened when he saw where Mr Wentworth was headed. The man had taken a sizeable fortune and in the space of fifteen months decimated it.

'Can I sell the London house to get funds to live? If I stay in the Dower House I can get along quite frugally.'

Again he had to tell her bad news. 'You will most definitely need to sell it, but the monies realised must go to paying the lien. If there is any left, and I doubt that there will be much, I can invest it in the Funds and hopefully realize you a very modest stipend.'

She looked down at her clenched hands, not wanting him to see the despair in her eyes. No wonder Mathias had been urging her to remarry. He needed another fortune to squander, and to him she was as good as money in the Bank of England. A sigh of despair escaped her before she pulled herself up short.

This was neither the time nor the place to wallow in self-pity.

'Well,' she said, lifting her head and squaring her shoulders, 'that will be better than nothing.' She rose and extended her hand. 'Thank you, Mr Sinclair. This has not been a pleasant meeting, but it has been an educational one. Can you keep my brother from spending whatever monies are realised from the sale of the London house?'

He stood and took her hand. 'I can petition the courts, my lady.'

'A nasty airing of family problems,' she murmured.

'Or I can take the cash in hand and give it directly to you and tell you how to invest it. That would be skirting the letter of the former Lord de Lisle's will, but it could be done.'

She nodded. 'That is much better. Thank you again,' she said, turning and taking her leave.

She walked out of the building with her head high. She was in the centre of London, near the Bank of England and other giants of commerce. Her carriage stood by the paving, the horses pawing the cold cobblestones. At least it was not sleeting. The day was miserable enough without inclement weather.

She picked up her skirts and moved proudly to her carriage. Her servant opened the door and let down the steps. 'Home,' she said, adding under her breath, 'but not home for long.'

She was inside, away from curious eyes just in time. She collapsed back against the cushions and sat in a state of shock. Nothing left. Nearly nine years of marriage to de Lisle for nothing. Everything squandered for Mathias's damnable gaming.

She pounded her fists into the leather seats and wished she were hitting her brother. He had not even had the decency to tell her. Instead he had tried to push her into another marriage of convenience—his convenience. Damn him, damn him, damn him.

The tears flowed freely now as she gave her emotions freedom. Everything she had thought was hers was not. She would have to move out of the London house immediately. She would have to let many servants go. They did not deserve that.

She took a heaving breath and it felt like her chest was on fire. Mathias had much to answer for.

She swiped at the tears still trickling down her cheeks. Enough of this snivelling, she had work to do. Then she would confront Mathias. And then, she licked her lips, then she must go back to the Dower House and Perth.

A grim smile tugged at her lips. She wanted Perth, had always wanted him. But she had known their union would not be good for her. Now, thanks to Mathias, she had very little choice. Without Perth's name, her child would have nothing. She could not do that to the babe.

The despair that weighed so heavily seconds before started to ease. What Mathias had done was beyond excuse, but…

Now she must do as her heart had always urged.

Her reason told her so. There was no other way for her child. For her child.

She must marry Perth.

Four days later, Lillith's carriage pulled into the drive that led to her ancestral home. She had not been here in a number of years. Her father had died shortly after she wed de Lisle, and Mathias had never spent time here.

She watched dispassionately as they drove by the beeches that lined the road. She had never cared for the place of her birth. Her mother had died when Lillith was three. Her father had been distant and uncaring. His first love had been gambling, like his son's. She did not even know if Mathias was here, but he was not in London and with her money gone there were not too many other places he could be.

The coach came to a stop, and she waited for the door to be opened and the stairs to be let down. She was in no hurry for what lay ahead of her.

'Thank you,' she said as she disembarked.

Before her stood a rambling house of indeterminate age. Parts were Elizabethan, some Jacobean and the Palladian front more recent. She did not remember the marble columns. Mathias must have added them in one of his flush times. Her mouth twisted. Very likely after her marriage to de Lisle.

She climbed the steps, wondering if she should knock or if there would even be a servant to let her in. She paused, gathering her anger that had given her the courage to come this far to confront the brother she had always before deferred to. She marched the last distance and pushed open the double doors without hesitation.

She stepped into the foyer she remembered not being allowed in as a child. She had always to enter and leave by the back doors. Children were to be seen, occasionally, and never heard.

There was an air of disuse about the place. The side table where a silver salver should have been was empty and in need of dusting. The black and white marble squares beneath her feet needed polishing. None of the paintings she remembered from her youth hung on the walls. Mathias had probably sold all of them.

Still, no servant arrived and no sound gave hint that anyone but she was in the house.

'Is anyone here?' she called, listening to her voice echo in the enclosed, rounded foyer. She looked up and noted the Waterford chandelier was gone.

For the first time since arriving, she heard a noise. It came from the library. She moved in that direction, wondering if all the books would be gone and the places where family portraits had once hung would now be empty spots of colour against the faded fabric of the wall covering.

'Ah, Lillith,' Mathias said when she opened the heavy oak door and stepped into the room. 'What brings you to the country and without even a note to tell me you were coming?'

He lounged in a leather-covered chair that he had pulled up to a small game table. With casual skill, he shuffled a deck of cards and began laying them out for a game of solitaire.

His nonchalance and the forever-present cards added much-needed fuel to her anger that had begun to flag during her sad perusal of her family home. 'Cards as usual,' she said, sharply. 'One would think that after all the damage they have done you would be heartily sick of them. But that appears not to be the case.'

He looked up at her and lifted one silver brow. 'You are in a nasty mood, Sister. Have a seat and I will ring for refreshment.'

She took the first chair available, a slim Chippendale. 'I am surprised you have servants to bring refreshments. No one met me at the door.'

'You did not knock either,' he riposted. 'Whatever is the matter with you?'

'I don't want refreshment, Mathias. I want satisfaction. I want an explanation.' The angry words tumbled from her. She leaned forward and glared at him. 'And for everything that is sacred, stop playing with those blasted cards.'

He was not a stupid man, just a very selfish one. 'So you have been to see Sinclair, and he has told you the deplorable state of your—our—finances.' He set the ace of spades above the rest. 'I don't suppose I should be surprised, but I am. De Lisle left me as manager of your inheritance. What made you check?'

'Why I checked is none of your business. What matters now is why you lost everything. Everything. You would not even have this...' she waved her arms to indicate the house '…if it were not entailed and impossible for you to gamble away. As it is, it will very likely crumble around you, for you have no money and no inclination to keep it in repair.'

She drew a deep breath and her eyes narrowed. 'Did you intercept Mr Sinclair's letters? For he says that he sent three and I received none.'

Mathias's gaze shifted away before coming back to rest on her. For a second she thought he intended to lie. 'Footmen can always use a little extra blunt.'

'You disgust me.'

'There is no need to raise your voice, Lillith. I can hear you very well.'

His reprimand non-plussed her. She had not realised her voice had risen. She forced herself to unknot her fingers and sit back in her chair. She also pushed aside the knowledge that there was a footman in her service whom she could not trust. It was a small betrayal compared to what Mathias had done.

She tried again. 'I am selling the London house to pay the lien on it.'

He picked up a card and flicked it between his fingers. 'Sinclair mentioned something about that. I did not want to do it. Knew my luck would change.' He shrugged. 'It did not. So the house must go. A debt of honour must be paid.'

She shook her head in disbelief and took a deep breath and the enormous sadness of it all hit her. 'Have you no remorse?' she asked softly.

Mathias shifted in his chair as though he might be

uncomfortable, but nothing showed on his face. ''Tis in m'blood. No help for it.'

Appalled at his callous disregard for all the hurt and damage he had caused and his blithe acceptance of such a destructive habit, she sat motionless and speechless. He continued playing solitaire, his fingers caressing the cards as he flicked through them and laid them out. She might as well not be here.

She took one last look around the library. She had no intention of touring the house and grounds. She was not going to return. Her future lay elsewhere.

She put her hands on the arms of her chair and pushed herself up. She felt weighted down by melancholy and regret.

'I am leaving now,' she said softly. He glanced up. 'I will be staying the night at the inn in town.' She took a deep breath. There was no sense in keeping from him her plan. He was, after all was said and done, her only living relative. 'I will be marrying Perth. It will be a small ceremony in the tiny chapel of my Dower House.' Which would not be hers after the wedding. Another loss.

For the first time since her arrival, real emotion showed on Mathias's face. He surged up, beet-red. 'Perth! I won't have it.'

The anger that had brought her here and slowly seeped from her to be replaced by sadness rushed back. '*You* won't have it? *You* have nothing to say about it. You squandered a fortune of mine on gambling and have not a shred of remorse to show for it.'

He took a menacing step towards her, knocking

over the card table. He ignored the crash. 'I have plans for you to wed Chillings or Carstairs. They are as wealthy as Perth and will be better husbands.'

She glared at him, her muscles tight with fury. 'You can go to Hades, Brother. I married at your direction once. I won't do so again. If you are so desperate to repair your fences, then find yourself an heiress and marry her—if one will have you.'

She cast a critical gaze over his person, seeing for the first time the dissolute man he had become. Once he had been slim and cut a dashing figure. Now he was a caricature of that man. He ran with the Prince of Wales's crowd and a more dissolute, debauched group would be hard to find. She had let her love for him blind her to his faults. She had made excuses for him.

She closed her eyes briefly and tried to calm herself. No matter what he had done or what he had become, he was her brother. When she thought she could speak without losing her temper, she opened her eyes and said, 'I cannot forgive you for what you have done, but you are my brother. My only living relative. At the moment I am very hurt by what you have done, and would prefer that you not visit me. You are, however, invited to the wedding so long as you accept this marriage and do nothing to disrupt it or to cause trouble.'

He stood shaking in his rage with his lips pinched tight but he said nothing. When she realised he did not intend to speak, she turned away, paused and turned back.

'Did you have Perth whipped ten years ago?'

The words left her mouth before she realised that she intended to say them. She had thought she did not want to know and that the past was better left buried. Now this.

Mathias drew himself. 'That is none of your concern. A lady does not get involved.'

Lillith's eyes narrowed. Disappointment ate at her. 'You did.'

She did not bother to stay to hear what he might say. She pivoted and left. There was only so much disillusionment she could take about Mathias, and she had reached that point. She had hoped that Perth had been mistaken.

Her hands shook as she took the hand proffered by her coachman. When she ducked her head to enter the carriage, a tear escaped. She swiped it away.

As she drove off, she took one last look back at the house she had grown up in. It stood, a dim copy of its former glory. She would never be back.

She turned her gaze forward and shivered as though a draught of cold air had rushed over her. Against all her better judgement, her future lay with Perth. She loved him and knew he would care for her and the child they had created. Perhaps in time his desire for her would turn to love. She had to hope for that. For she had no other choices.

Perhaps she could make up for some of the past wrongs done him. If she were strong enough.

Perth sat in the public room of the inn and drank his ale. Outside snow fell in soft waves of white. The village green was covered and the pond had a thin film of ice. Lillith would pass this way on her return to the Dower House.

He had been here nearly a week. Fitch had arrived on his second day with the carriage and a trunk of clothes the batman considered appropriate.

Perth finished the ale and rose. The innkeeper hurried over, wiping his hands on the apron he wore.

'Is there something else I can get your lordship?' He beamed. Perth was a good customer.

'No, thank you,' Perth said.

By now he knew everyone who frequented the pub and many who did not. He was on nodding familiarity with all in the village. He also realised that every man, woman and child in this town liked and respected Lillith. They all watched him to see if he was good enough for her.

'My lord,' a young boy yelled, rushing in from outside, his cheeks red from the cold. 'Her ladyship's carriage just passed.'

'My thanks,' Perth said, tossing the youth a coin. 'You have done a good job of watching for me.'

The child beamed before strutting off proud as a peacock.

Perth turned to his landlord. 'Have my mount brought round.'

Knowing the deed was as good as done, Perth went to his room and donned a coat, hat and gloves. He looked at the cane tossed across one chair. He was not likely to need it here.

Fitch came in from his room at that moment. 'You never know, my lord. It saved your life that one time or at least kept you from a severe beating.'

Perth glanced at his manservant. 'I doubt Wentworth is here or that he has hired thugs again.'

Fitch just looked at him.

'But you are right,' Perth acquiesced. 'There are thieves in the country as well as the city.'

The anxiety that had formed lines around Fitch's mouth eased. 'Lady de Lisle has returned.'

'Yes, and I intend to speak with her before she has a chance to think up another reason to refuse my offer. Although I have no doubt that she has discovered just how dire her situation is.'

'She is proud,' Fitch said. 'As are you, my lord.'

Perth smiled ruefully. 'Yes, and we shall have a hard go of it because of those traits.'

Perth left. Outside his horse waited. He got into the saddle just as another carriage barrelled through the narrow high road. He backed his horse on to the pavement just in time to keep from being run over. The man driving the carriage was hamfisted and in a hurry.

The cane he had decided to take in spite of its awkwardness on horseback lay on the ground where he had dropped it when his horse shied. He looked at it ruefully.

'Fitch,' he said to the batman who had followed him down and witnessed the scene, 'please return that to my room. I will be making greater haste than I had thought and carrying that will only hamper me.'

Fitch frowned, but picked up the cane. 'Be careful if you've a mind to go after that idiot.'

Feeling the self-appointed protector of this little village, Perth considered going after the vehicle and putting the fear of God into the occupant. But the need to see Lillith was greater.

'I have a more important meeting.'

He set off for the Dower House and soon became intrigued when he realised that was where the carriage headed. He slowed his pace to keep just behind the coach for now he had a suspicion of who made such reckless haste in the ice and snow.

He'd be damned if Wentworth would interfere this time.

When they reached Lillith's house, he reined his horse to a stop right behind Wentworth's carriage and dismounted. Activity erupted around them. Grooms came for his horse and to lead Wentworth's carriage to the stables.

Wentworth disembarked, saw Perth and turned white, then scarlet. He halted for a moment before continuing on toward the door. Perth cut off his path.

Perth eyed the other man with disgust. Wentworth's nose was starting to glow red in the cold. His greatcoat with its multitude of fashionable capes made him look like an over-inflated balloon instead of the dashing figure he probably thought he looked.

'What are you doing here?' Perth demanded, hands on hips. He regretted the cane he had left behind when Wentworth's carriage had nearly run him down.

'Out of my way,' Wentworth snarled. 'I need to

speak with my sister. What she plans is folly.' Bold as his words were, he did not move forward.

A hard grin showed Perth's teeth and accentuated his scar even as exultation filled him. Lillith intended to marry him.

'What she plans is the only means open to her after the débâcle you have made of her affairs.' He moved until his face was nearly touching Wentworth's. 'A situation you will never have the opportunity to cause again. Mark my words, Wentworth, I will have none of your importuning. I won't pay a single bill you have now or will have in the future. And if you come around, I will be sorely tempted to horsewhip you myself, instead of taking the coward's way out and hiring someone to do it—as you did.'

His deadly calm words filled the cold, still air. Wentworth's ruddy face blanched. Without a flick of an eye, Perth stepped aside. Wentworth hurried past, pulling on his cape to ensure that it did not touch the Earl.

Perth followed at a leisurely pace. He had no desire to see Lillith's brother again. When he finally entered the foyer, Wentworth was gone.

'My lord,' the normally imperturbable butler said, taking the hat and gloves Perth held out. 'We were not expecting you. Her ladyship is indisposed.'

'Her ladyship is with her brother, and I've no desire to interrupt them.' He strode past the butler. 'Show me to a room where I can wait for her.'

'Um…yes, my lord. This way, my lord.' Simmons set off down the hall.

Perth soon found himself in a small room that looked like Lillith's workroom. There was a desk littered with papers and a basket of mending set beside a large, comfortably overstuffed chair. A fire roared in the grate and the curtains were opened to show a winter garden. He found it a cosy place and made himself at home.

He and Lillith still had to discuss the terms of their wedding. He would wait patiently until she arrived, now that she was his. He did not have long.

She burst into the room, obviously agitated. 'What are you doing here? I sent word to the inn that I accept your offer of marriage.'

He rose and made her a bow. 'Your talk with your brother must not have gone well. I fear he was not in a good mood after the one he and I had in your driveway.'

She made her way to the window, her back to him. She had a slim, elegant back that the thick wool dress did not hide. He thought that perhaps there was just a little bit of widening at her waist, but that might easily be his own desire. He wanted the child she carried. The urge to take her in his arms was strong, but the tilt of her chin told him that that action would only make things more difficult. He could wait now that she was to be his.

'Why are you here?' she finally asked, her voice tired.

'Are you getting enough rest?' he asked, ignoring her question.

Exasperation pinched her brows together. 'I get

enough sleep, but there is not enough rest in the world to compensate for having my brother rant and rave at me over you and then finding out that you are here to do the same over something else.'

Her words gave him pause. He had been ruthless in his pursuit of her. Perhaps it was time to woo her. Theirs was not a love match, but he wanted more than a marriage of convenience.

'I am not here to berate you, Lillith,' he said soothingly. 'I am here to discuss the settlement I intend to make on you and our child. I thought you would not want me to discuss it with your brother, given the circumstances.'

'That is true enough,' she said bitterly. Her hands unclenched and she turned to face him. 'I want provision for our child should it be a boy or girl. I won't have any child of mine being bartered like a piece of goods.' Her mouth drooped just slightly. 'I know too well what that is like. And I want a jointure independent of you. I trust you will not make my brother the executor.'

A hard smile split his lips before he nodded agreement. 'You shall have all of that. I will also arrange for our future children to have financial independence. I also know what it is like to be considered a commodity instead of a person.'

She blushed at his words. He too had paid for her brother's machinations. 'And I will *not* sleep with you.'

He gave her a slow, sensual smile as his gaze roved over her. 'We shall see.'

'I won't.' Her voice rose. 'Agree to that term or I won't marry you.'

He turned away to conceal the anger that her insistence caused. But when he spoke his voice was cool. 'I won't force you.'

'Nor seduce me,' she added.

'I cannot promise that,' he said softly, turning back to her. His eyes held hers. 'But you can always refuse me.'

He heard her sharp intake of breath and had some measure of satisfaction. He'd be damned if he would marry her, live in the same house with her and not sleep with her.

'Well,' she said, her voice raspy, 'that is settled. We will be married tomorrow. Right now, I am tired.'

He stepped in front of her, causing her to stop her steps to the door. 'I am looking forward to our wedding, Lillith. It is long overdue.'

Her eyes widened but she said nothing. She edged around him and he let her go. He could be patient. He would be patient. Tomorrow she would be his.

Chapter Fourteen

Lillith stood in the tiny church connected to her Dower House. She did not normally take services here, preferring to go to the church in the village where she could meet the people who worked the de Lisle land. Only the vicar was present from the congregation.

Now the early part of December, the building was dim inside even though candles were lit. Outside it snowed. She shivered.

Mathias stood behind her on the left. He had stayed the night with her in spite of everything. She had not had the energy or the anger to have her servants throw him out. She was too overwhelmed by this marriage and everything it meant.

Perth stood beside her in morning dress. She would swear she could feel the animosity between the two men as waves rolling over her.

The vicar cleared his throat. Lillith focused on him. The banns had not been called. Perth had a special licence. Everyone in the village still knew they were marrying. There was to be a reception this afternoon for the town folk, hastily arranged but something she wanted to do. It was her parting gift to the people she had taken an interest in and helped where needed for the last ten years. She would miss them like she already missed the servants in London that she had had to let go and the servants here who would not be accompanying her to Perth's property. Simmons, thank goodness, would come with her.

She refused to cry.

There had been no time to have a special gown made even had she wished it. She had found a wool dress in palest pink that she had worn several winters before. It had been tight in the bust, that seeming to be where she had gained weight with the child, so she had spent several hours letting out the seams. Agatha had asked to do the chore, but Lillith had declined. Sewing soothed her. The rhythmic in-and-out of the needle calmed her frayed nerves. Tomorrow she would start on clothes for the baby.

The vicar cleared his throat again, as though something were lodged in it. He began the ceremony.

She said the words required of her and vaguely heard Perth agree to take her as his wife. No one objected.

'The rings.'

She looked at the vicar. 'I have no ring.'

He cleared his throat once more and looked away. Perth was paying him a handsome fee to perform this ceremony so quickly.

'I do,' Perth said, his voice deep and sure.

He took her by surprise.

Fitch reached into a breast pocket and pulled out a ring that flashed in the yellow light of a nearby candle. Opals and diamonds formed an oval larger than the first knuckle of her thumb. She gazed at it. Opals were bad luck if not your birthstone. They were her birthstone.

She put out her left hand so Perth could slip the ring on. It slid on as though it had been made for her finger.

'It was my mother's,' the Earl said quietly. 'I know she would want you to wear it.'

His warmth was not something she had expected. He was marrying—no, had forced her to marry him for the sake of the child they had made. She had agreed for that child's sake. The earldom of Perth was not something a woman could easily give up for her unborn child. Especially now.

'You may kiss the bride,' the vicar said, his voice wavering.

She had not expected this. She felt Perth's hand at her waist like a brand, turning her and pulling her toward him. She heard Mathias snort in irritation. Then she heard nothing as Perth's mouth touched hers and the roaring in her ears drowned out all else.

It was not a light, impersonal kiss of acknowledgement. It seared to her bones. His fingers bit into the small of her back and held her tightly to him so that she could feel his arousal. His lips moved over hers and his tongue slipped inside her. She could taste the whisky he had drunk before coming here. Surely he was not nervous? The scent of cinnamon and musk filled her nostrils. It was a lip-tingling, thigh-melting kiss that left her wanting more.

He released her and she stumbled back so that Mathias had to put out an arm to steady her. 'Your reaction is disgusting,' he hissed in her ear.

She blushed at the truth in his words. It did not help when she glanced at Perth and saw the harsh angle of his jaw and the dark hunger in his eyes. He had said he would not force her, but if just his kiss given in front of witnesses made her want him, she was doomed. He would have her and she would beg him to do so.

Somehow, she pulled her emotions together and edged away from Mathias. She lifted her chin and took the arm Perth extended. Side by side, they left the chapel. The others did not follow.

Safely away from curious eyes, Lillith snatched her hand back. 'I must go and prepare for the festivities later.' He took a step after her and she whirled on him. 'Do not follow me. Remember what I said.'

His look turned hard. 'Your words say one thing, but your body and every move you make say something different.'

'I am in control of my body,' she said, wishing it were so.

He gave her a mocking smile as though he knew how false her boast was. 'Then I will see you later.'

She hurried away, trying to push him from her mind by running down a mental checklist of what needed doing for the party tonight. She needed to talk with Cook about the food, Simmons about the beverages

and Agatha about what she would wear. All her
clothes were uncomfortably tight. Something would
need to be let out.

Her feet kept pace with her thoughts. And still she
could not keep from remembering the feel of Perth's
mouth on hers.

She was doomed.

Perth raised his third glass of champagne in salute
to the innkeeper who whirled past with his wife in his
arms as they nimbly executed a move in the country
reel being played. With sardonic amusement, he saw
that Wentworth consumed as much drink as he and
there was no gambling to be had. The man must be
going crazy.

Seeing Lillith make her way around the crowded
room, studiously ignoring him, he could easily understand what it was like to be crazy. He wanted her in
the worst possible way.

She moved with a grace that few women possessed.
And she was kind to everyone.

His mother had been like that. The daughter of a
wealthy landowner, she had run away with the
younger son of a younger son who was a career army
officer. His parents had married for love and, to the
best of his knowledge, they had never regretted it. He
had been the only child.

Lillith passed in front of him, dancing energetically
with the blacksmith. The man was twice her size
and lumbered. She would be lucky not to have
bruised feet.

She was well liked by the common folk.

Churlishness not being one of Perth's traits, he pushed off from the wall and went to ask one of the town's ladies to dance. He chose an older woman who would enjoy herself but not simper at him. He could not stand simpering.

Meanwhile, he would bide his time until tonight.

An eternity later, or so it seemed to Perth, he stood beside Lillith and said goodbye to the last of their guests. Wentworth had disappeared long before.

'Simmons,' she said, totally ignoring Perth, 'please see that everyone is given extra wages for tonight and before they are let go. I have letters of recommendation for everyone.'

He nodded.

She turned away with a slump to her shoulders that Perth had rarely seen. The last weeks had been hard on her.

As though she sensed his attention, she straightened her shoulders and looked at him. 'I am tired and I am going to bed. Alone.'

He crossed his arms over his chest and returned her stare. 'This is our wedding night.'

'We have a bargain.'

'You have a stipulation. I did not say I would honour it.'

She gasped. 'You most certainly did.'

'No,' he said slowly. 'I said that I would not force you, not that I would not seduce you or sleep with you. We are married.'

'This is my house, and I forbid you to follow me.' She spun on her heel and walked off.

Perth watched her, enjoying the sway of her hips and the elegant curve of her back. But she was very much confused if she thought he was not going to join her. He sauntered behind her, far enough away that she did not bolt.

'My lord—' Simmons materialised '—I will show you to your room.'

Perth glanced at the butler. 'Thank you, but I know where my room is.' He saw Lillith start up the stairs. 'And I am going there.'

He headed off, but not before he heard Simmons sputter. However, the butler was in a difficult situation and there was nothing he could do but stand aside.

Perth sauntered after his wife, arriving at her room shortly after she did. He did not knock, and fortunately Lillith had not locked the door. He could almost think she wanted him to enter, but he knew better. She had thought he would not follow her after being told not to. She had much to learn.

He entered and closed the door behind himself. She sat sprawled on a settee, her feet up and her hair down. She made his blood heat.

She shot bolt upright. 'What are you doing here? I told you not to follow me.'

He moved to a chair and sat down, crossing one leg over the other. His dancing pumps gleamed in the fire-light. 'And I told you that I would.'

'Well, you can just leave.' She pointed imperiously at the door. 'Now!'

'Lillith,' he said quietly and clearly, 'I have already told you. We are married. I intend to have my conjugal rights.'

She huffed and she flushed and she looked away from the desire he made no effort to hide. 'You will have to seduce me then, for I will not walk into your arms.'

He studied her, noting the luminosity of her skin and the sheen of her hair. She held herself proudly. She was intelligent and she had spirit, both traits he valued. And he desired her with an ache that was constant and painful in its intensity.

But he was getting tired of these confrontations and recriminations. Perhaps wanting her was not enough any more. He began to think it would be nice if she would return his interest without him first having to force her into arousal.

'Perhaps you are right,' he said thoughtfully. 'As much as I want to make love to you—and make no doubt losing myself in you is something I desire above all else—I begin to think that your resistance is growing tiring.'

Her mouth dropped. He nearly laughed at her surprise, but he really did not find this situation at all humourous, just her unexpected reaction.

'You are growing tired?'

He nodded. 'A little. You see, I am not used to working so hard for my pleasures.'

'Oh.' She picked at her skirts. 'I did not think you did. That is all part of why I insist that our marriage remain one of convenience.'

'A marriage of convenience usually gives the husband the right to enjoy his wife's charms,' he said softly.

'You already have,' she retorted. 'And I am carrying your child. That is the focus of a marriage of convenience. We have fulfilled it.'

'I see,' he said quietly. 'As far as you are concerned, if you bear my son then you have fulfilled your obligation.'

She nodded.

He stood abruptly, suddenly wearied beyond bearing. 'Much as I want you, I find that perhaps it is time I spared you my unwanted attentions. After a while, even the most unobservant man realizes when his presence is not only not wanted, but dreaded.'

He had never thought he would reach the point where he would not do anything to have her. But he had.

He made her a curt bow and left.

Lillith did a slow turn, studying her suite of rooms in Perth's London town house. Rich greens and golds and browns made the large area seem warm and inviting. Heavy furniture from another era filled the space and provided comfort. In all, it was not a very feminine room but she liked it. What Perth's chambers looked like, she did not know and did not want to know.

Except that curiosity moved her towards the connecting door. She had heard him leave immediately after bringing her here, so there would be no one inside. She told herself it was not like she was invading his privacy. He would be more than willing to have her in his bedchamber.

Taking a deep breath, she turned the knob and pushed open the door. The room was dim with the curtains pulled and no fire or lit candles. Still, she could see that it was as spacious as her own and done in the same colours and style of furniture. The two rooms were mirrors of one another. How strange.

Quickly, she stepped back and closed the door. She would never know why they were decorated the same since she could not let Perth know she had been in his room while he was gone, and she had no intention of going into his room while he was in it. Perhaps the person who had decorated the rooms was a man. It was a mystery she would never solve.

Agatha chose that moment to enter Lillith's room, her arms full of gowns. 'My lady, I am glad you are here. Mr Fitch just told me that the Earl is engaged to Lord Ranvensford this evening for dinner and dancing. You will need to choose your gown and we will have to let the seams out of the bosom.'

Not only was Lillith's stomach growing, but her breasts were swollen and sore. Her nipples were constantly erect and rubbing against her chemise. Being in the family way was very disconcerting.

Lillith sank into the nearest chair. The last thing she wanted to do was face London Society. But she must. The sooner done, the sooner the talk of their rushed marriage would become yesterday's old news. And there was only a week or two left before Parliament adjourned for the winter.

'The white muslin with the pink overlay,' she told Agatha. 'While you are enlarging it, I will nap.' She still barely showed her pregnancy, but she tired more easily and was more emotional. There was no other explanation for the way she had railed at Perth on their wedding night.

She took off her dress and put on a wrapper. But before climbing on to the high four-poster bed, she wrote a quick note to Madeline and asked Agatha to have it delivered. Nothing would perk her up like a visit from her friend. That done, she fell into a deep sleep.

Lillith woke to the sounds of someone moving around. She levered onto one elbow and looked around. The room was lit only by the fire, and it took several minutes for her eyes to become adjusted.

Perth stood by the mantel, gazing down at the flames. He was dressed for evening in black breeches, stockings and pumps. A white shirt glowed in stark relief against the darker colours. He held a box in his hand.

She sat fully up and pulled her wrapper up to her neck and clenched it shut. 'What are you doing in here?'

He turned and gave her a sardonic smile. 'The last I checked, this was my house.'

Her eyes narrowed, but she did not let loose the

harsh words that sprang to her lips. 'We have an agreement. We are not sleeping with each other.'

He sauntered toward her, his gaze lowering. 'Just because I am in your bedchamber does not mean that I intend to seduce you. Although—' he stopped at the foot of the bed '—the idea does have appeal.'

The heat he could so easily arouse in her flared. She jumped out of bed, rather than lie prone. 'Then why are you in here?'

'I have brought you something,' he said, holding out the box.

She eyed it as one might eye a bomb. 'What is it?'

'A gift, Lillith. Nothing more,' he said with the tone of one sorely tried. 'It will not hurt you nor is it a bribe for your favours. It is freely given because I thought it would become you.'

'Oh,' she said, feeling ashamed of her suspicions. What made them worse was knowing that she wanted him to try and seduce her. No matter what she said, her body craved him.

She took the box, opened it and gasped. A parure of diamonds and opals flashed in the meagre light.

'Do you like them?' he asked, a note of hesitation in his voice.

This was the first time she had ever heard him sound uncertain. She looked up at him. 'They are beautiful.'

It seemed to her that his body relaxed, although until that instant she had not realised that he was tense.

'I had them made to go with the ring.'

'But why? I have plenty of jewellery. You do not need to give me more.' She spoke thoughtlessly, thinking only of the money these must have cost him. She had already cost him so much.

His voice hardened and he stepped away, putting his back to her. 'Everything you have is from de Lisle. These are from me. I expect to see them on you this evening.'

Before she could think of something to say that would compensate for her previous words, he left. The door closed behind him with a definite click. She sighed. She could follow him, but she did not think that would solve the issue over the jewellery. And it would only precipitate another situation.

Instead she set the box on the bed and lit the candles in a candelabrum so she could see the jewellery better. A necklace, earrings, two bracelets and a brooch glowed in the yellow light. The opals were multi-hued and full of fire. The diamonds that surrounded the opal cabochons were white and clean. They were truly beautiful pieces. He must have taken time and consideration over this gift.

She set the candles on the table and lifted the necklace out. It cascaded over her fingers, heavy and seductive. She took it with her to the mirror and held it to her neck. The piece flashed, a perfect foil for her pale skin and silver hair. Yes, Perth had chosen well.

She whirled when the door opened, expecting it to be Perth. Relief, followed rapidly by disappointment, swamped her when she saw Agatha.

'My lady,' the maid said, 'I have done the best I can with this bodice. I hope it will be enough.' She glanced up from the gown in her hand and her mouth dropped. 'My lady…did the Earl give you those? They are finer than anything you have.'

She gave her maid a rueful smile. 'Yes, he did and wants me to wear them tonight.'

Agatha moved closer, her gaze riveted to the necklace. 'It will be magnificent with your dress. Are they…pardon my asking, but are they because of your condition?'

She had not thought of that. 'Perhaps. He did not say.' She glanced at the delicate little porcelain clock by the bed, a feminine piece that seemed out of place in the room. 'But we must hurry.'

An hour later, Lillith stood before the mirror in all her finery. Agatha had attached the bracelets, one on each arm over her gloves, and she had put on the earrings. The necklace still lay in the velvet box. She considered seeing if Perth would come and put it on her as an amends for her earlier words.

'My lady, you will be late if we linger,' Agatha said, picking the necklace up and moving to drape it around Lillith's neck.

Lillith sighed as her maid hooked the piece. 'Twas just as well. Agatha's impersonal touch was just that. Perth's fingers at the nape of her neck, and his warm breath caressing her skin, would have only caused trouble.

Agatha draped a fine paisley shawl over Lillith's shoulders and stepped back. 'Perfect, my lady.'

Lillith eyed her finished toilet. She turned from side to side. She did look good and no one would know she was pregnant. That would come later when she bore the child five months after the wedding. Well, that was not unheard of either.

Perth waited downstairs in the foyer. When she joined him, he cast a quick glance over her.

'The jewels become you,' he said, taking his hat and cane from Simmons.

'Thank you,' Lillith replied, wondering why she felt as though something was missing. She did not want compliments from him, but she had to admit that she had expected more.

She preceded him outside and allowed the footman to help her into the carriage. Again she was disappointed. Much as she railed at Perth and at her reaction to him, it felt strange and incomplete to have someone else hold her hand as she got in the coach.

On their wedding night he had desired her above all else. Since they reached London, he had been, with a few exceptions, distant. He behaved as though they really did have a marriage of convenience. And then he gave her the magnificent jewellery. She shook her head in confusion.

'What is wrong?' he asked, sitting opposite her with his back to the horses.

She cocked her head to one side and studied him in the pale yellow light from the interior lamps. His expression was saturnine, his scar pronounced. He looked dangerous, and distant and distinctly bored.

'You have changed since we got to Town.' She spoke openly, not wanting to further complicate their relationship with lies and subterfuge.

'I have tired of pursuing you and having to wear down your resistance. Our wedding night showed me that there is no pleasure in forcing you.'

'You always did before and seemed none the less excited.' Ridiculous as it was, she could not keep a tiny hitch of hurt from her voice. She was fickle.

He looked away from her to gaze out of the window. 'That was before we married. I still want you.' He turned back to her and his dark eyes pierced her. 'But I am tired of fighting. When you are ready for more than a cold bed at night, let me know.'

His words hurt, which surprised her. This is what she had demanded. Unfortunately for her, she had never really thought he would give in to her demands. Now he had and she did not like it. But it was for the best. If he did not pursue her, she would not be tempted by him and give in.

Yes, this was definitely for the best.

Chapter Fifteen

Thankfully, they arrived at Ravensford's house shortly afterwards. The gathering was larger than Lillith had anticipated. Fifty to sixty people milled about the Earl's ballroom: some danced, some talked, and still others played cards in the alcoves.

Perth kept a light touch at her waist as he steered her towards their host and hostess. Even knowing he did not touch her with the intent to seduce her, the feel of his fingers was comforting. No matter what their marriage was, he would protect her and their child.

'Ah, Perth,' Ravensford said, breaking away from the small knot of people he had been with and coming toward them. 'And the lovely Lady de Lisle.'

'Lady Perth,' her husband said firmly.

Ravensford's green eyes widened before he smiled. 'You finally did it. Leg-shackling becomes you, Perth.' His smile turned wry as Perth grimaced. 'And you, Lady Perth,' he added, taking Lillith's hand and raising it to his lips. 'Congratulations to both of you.'

Lillith blushed under Ravensford's scrutiny. 'Thank you, my lord.'

He released her hand and stepped back. 'Make yourself scarce, Perth, I wish to speak with your wife.'

Lillith thought that a fleeting look of concern marred Perth's otherwise imperturbable countenance, but it was gone before she could be sure.

'Then I shall go and pay my respects to your wife,' Perth countered, sauntering towards Lady Ravensford and her court of admirers.

Lillith turned an inquiring look on Ravensford. He took her fingers and put them on his arm.

'A walk around the perimeter will keep us away from all but the most curious.' He guided her to the wall with the least people. 'I see he gave you the opals. I was with him the day he ordered them. He was very concerned that they be good enough for you.'

'Perth?' she asked, incredulous that her husband could be so insecure. That was not the man she knew.

'Opals were his mother's favourite gem, but the family did not have the money to buy her many. The ring he very likely gave you for the wedding was all she had, and his father spent an entire year's salary on it. A hardship for an army officer. Perth's parents were long dead by the time he inherited the earldom.'

This was a window into her husband's past that she had not expected. 'I did not know any of that.'

'You would not. He would not tell you, but I will.' He stopped her and held her gaze with his. 'He will not tell you this either, but I will. He loves you, but does not yet realise it. Give him time.'

She stared, nonplussed. 'This is too private, Lord Ravensford. Please say no more.'

He shrugged. 'I had thought you a stronger person than this. I also thought you would like to know.' His voice turned cold. 'I see that I was mistaken. Shall we return to the rest of my guests?'

He did not wait for her response, but guided her back to Perth and left her with a curt bow. Perth frowned.

'What has got into Ravensford? That is no way for him to treat you.' He took a step after his friend, but Lillith grabbed his arm. 'What are you doing?'

'I am keeping you from making a mistake, Perth. I provoked Ravensford. He is justifiably upset with me. Let it be.'

He studied her carefully for long moments. Lillith felt other gazes on them. She heard a susurration of voices. Word of their hasty wedding was spreading.

He eased and she released his arm. 'See the older woman over there by the column,' he said, his voice closer to normal.

She looked where he indicated to see a strikingly handsome woman with silver hair cut fashionably short, an ideal foil for the oval perfection of her creamy complexion. She wore Lillith's favourite colour of lavender.

'She is beautiful. Who is she?'

'The Dowager Countess of Ravensford.'

'But I thought she was against Ravensford's marriage. I would not expect her to be here.' She took a closer look. On second glance the Countess did not appear as happy as she might.

'She was against the union and is still unhappy about it, but Ravensford made it plain that he would cut her from his life before he gave up Mary Margaret. He is an only child and was the delight of both his parents. He still is paramount in his mother's affections, and she does what she must.'

Lillith felt a twinge of envy. She had never known her own mother and her father had never cared. So she had given all her love and devotion to Mathias and been betrayed.

'He is fortunate.'

Perth looked down at her. 'Our child will have that love and devotion, I swear it.'

She blinked in an effort to stop the sudden and inexplicable tears his words caused. She could not trust herself to say something in response without crying, so she turned away. She felt him move away and instantly felt bereft, but could not make herself call him back. Things were happening that she had never expected, and she was having difficulty absorbing them.

Lost in her thoughts, she wandered into one of the rooms where cards were being played. One table had four for whist. Another had a faro game. The woman who was bank smiled, the others either frowned or groaned. In faro, the odds were in the favour of the person who was bank.

She watched vouchers and coins change hands. In her mind, she saw fortunes being tossed away and futures being ruined. A hand touched her shoulder and she jumped. Only then did she realise that her shoulders had hunched and her fingers had fisted.

'Lillith,' Perth said quietly for her ears only, 'not everyone who gambles loses a fortune. Most of the people play for fun. Not one of the people here tonight is in debt or has lost his or her inheritance.'

The comfort his words brought, silly as it might seem, allowed her to relax. She leaned back into the solidity of his chest and was glad for his support and warmth.

'You are right,' she whispered. 'I just let myself get caught up in my own experience with Mathias.'

'I know,' he said softly, bringing his hand to the nape of her neck and gently massaging the stiff muscles there.

'Here are the lovebirds,' a bright voice said.

Lillith started and would have jumped away from Perth but his fingers tightened. She turned to see Madeline Russell with Nathan in tow. Lillith smiled in delight.

'I did not know you were coming,' she said, extending her hands to take Madeline's.

'I did not tell you because I knew that as Perth's wife you would be here, and I wanted to surprise you.' She grabbed Lillith's hands and pulled her into an embrace. 'I am so glad to see you looking so good,' she murmured. 'Marriage becomes you.'

Lillith looked swiftly at Perth from the corner of her eye to see if he had heard, but he and Nathan had moved off. 'Thank you for the compliment, and you are as outspoken as ever.'

Instead of looking chagrined, Madeline looked supremely satisfied. 'Now that I see you, I am glad I told Perth where you had gone.'

'So you are the one. I thought so.' But her words held no censure. Things had turned out for the best.

Madeline shrugged shoulders covered in very fashionable gauze thin muslin and spangled netting. 'He was desperate to find you. I think he knew,' she finished on a whisper.

Lillith nodded. 'A lot has happened since I last saw you.' She drew Madeline to an alcove where they stood with their back to the wall so they could see anyone approaching. 'Mathias has gambled away my settlement from de Lisle.'

'That snake,' Madeline said. At Lillith's frown, she added quietly, 'I know he is your brother, but he is lower than a snake. He is…he is…I cannot think of anything that is worse than him.'

Lillith sighed and once more felt close to tears. She took a deep breath. 'Perth would completely agree with you.' She must have sounded weepy for Madeline put her arm around Lillith's waist.

'Oh, Lillith, I am sorry to upset you.'

Lillith blinked. 'You are right about Mathias. I know that and should be beyond this. I do not know what is wrong with me, but everything upsets me more than usual. This is just one more incident.'

'Well, smile,' Madeline said firmly. 'We are being watched.' She flashed a blinding grin at two dowagers. 'As for the moods, 'tis your condition. I swear, I cried from sun up to sun down.' She laughed. 'Nathan threatened to leave me for nine months.'

Lillith laughed. 'Surely not. Nathan is besotted with you.'

'True,' Madeline said complacently, 'but even he was sorely tried.'

Feeling much better for the laugh and for having told Madeline the worst that Mathias had done, Lillith allowed her friend to lead her to where Perth and Nathan stood speaking with Carstairs, Chillings and Lady Annabelle. Noting that Perth stood beside Lady Annabelle, Lillith could not stop a twinge of jealousy.

She told herself that it was her condition that made her overreact. Then, always honest with herself, she admitted that it was not. She would be jealous of Perth's interest in any other woman—Lady Annabelle was worse because the woman was so intriguing.

'Nathan, darling,' Madeline said cajolingly as she took her husband's arm, 'be a dear and go get Lillith and me something to drink.' She cast an arch look at Perth. 'Unless you would like to do so.'

Perth glanced from Madeline to Lillith and bowed. 'I would be delighted.'

From the look on his face, Lillith knew he was far from delighted. But she was glad of Madeline's manoeuvring. The errand separated Perth from Lady Annabelle.

'Congratulations,' Lady Annabelle said, moving closer to Lillith. 'I understand that you and Perth are recently wed.'

'Thank you,' Lillith murmured.

'My congratulations as well,' Chillings said.

'And mine,' Carstairs added a trifle slowly. 'His good fortune is our loss.'

'Thank you again,' Lillith said.

Perth returned with their drinks. He handed Madeline hers with a flourish. 'Next time, I will let Russell do the honours.'

'I normally do,' Nathan said good-naturedly.

Madeline laughed.

'Would you care to dance, Lady Perth?' Carstairs asked.

Lillith flicked a glance at her husband who looked ready to step between her and the other man. Hastily, she said, 'Please.'

Carstairs extended his arm and she accompanied him to where the dancing was taking place. It was a country reel. To Lillith the music went on too long and by the time they were finished, she was winded.

'Would you care to go on the terrace for some fresh air?' Carstairs asked.

She was sorely tempted, but thought better of it. 'No, thank you, Mr Carstairs. I had best return to my husband.'

He nodded. 'As you wish. I had hoped that you would like respite.'

She paused at the tone of his voice and looked up at him. 'Why would you think that?'

His tanned skin turned a burnt red. 'I should not have said anything. My apologies.'

'No,' she said quietly. 'I truly do want to know why you think that.'

He angled her away from the direction they had
been going so that they walked in enough privacy to
speak. 'I overstepped the bounds of propriety, but your
brother said that this marriage was not to your liking.'
He stopped and waited as though trying to decide what
else to say. 'At one time, he intimated that you might
be open to receiving an offer from me.'

Lillith stiffened.

'I am truly sorry,' Carstairs said, his deep voice full
of chagrin. 'I see now that Mr Wentworth was mistaken.'

Still more to put at Mathias's feet, Lillith thought
bitterly. She kept her tone low and easy. 'I am the one
who is truly sorry, Mr Carstairs. My brother can be
overbearing at times when he believes that what he
does is in my best interests.' She had to stop for a
moment to let the lie settle. She did not like telling
untruths, but in this case she could not tell the truth.
'I agreed freely to this wedding.'

'I see,' Carstairs said, his voice circumspect. 'I
should return you to Perth.'

'There is no need,' Perth's deep baritone said from
nearly right behind them. 'I have come to fetch my
wife. It is time we were gone. She needs all the rest
she can get.'

Carstairs lifted one dark brown eyebrow. He looked
as though he would say something, but nodded instead. 'I hope to see you around town.'

Lillith smiled at him before allowing Perth to escort
her to the foyer where he bundled her into her heavy
cape and then out into the street where the carriage

waited. Instead of allowing the footman to help her, Perth handed her inside.

She had no sooner settled herself than Perth demanded, 'Was Carstairs importuning you?'

His question took her by surprise. She could never tell him the truth. He would challenge Carstairs and then Mathias.

'No, he was merely allowing me to catch my breath before returning me to you. The dance was more strenuous than I had thought.' She smiled softly. 'It would seem that dancing requires more effort right now than normally.'

'I am sure there is more to it than you are saying, but I will let it drop.'

'There was nothing to it,' she said coolly. 'And if there was, so what? I am carrying *your* child.'

She had not meant to goad him. The less interest he took in the intrigues Mathias insisted on creating, the better for everyone. Mathias had much to answer for, but she did not want him hurt or killed and particularly not by her husband. But Perth's lack of interest in her lately had piqued her. Against her better judgement, she wanted him to desire her. No sooner had she realised that, than she berated herself. She was totally unreasonable! It had to be her condition.

'True, the child you are carrying is mine. As the rest will be.' He made a flat statement that brooked no contradiction.

'Well, they certainly will not be another man's,' she retorted.

He grinned at that, his teeth a white slash against

his swarthy complexion. But instead of replying, he banged his cane on the carriage roof. The vehicle stopped and without a backward glance, Perth leaped to the ground and set off walking.

Nonplussed and not a little bit angry at his desertion, Lillith fought the inclination to follow him. The urge to yell at him like a fishwife was strong. She was crazy. He was only treating her the way she had demanded. He was treating her as a man would treat a woman whom he had married for convenience. After all, she already carried his child.

Still, her hands shook uncontrollably and tears were near the surface. Things were going horribly close to the way she had dreaded they would.

The next morning, Lillith sat in the breakfast room drinking hot chocolate when Perth joined her. She could not help the frown she greeted him with. He had not come back last night, or, if he had, she had not heard him even though she had lain awake until daybreak.

'Good morning to you, too,' he said, helping himself to a large slice of ham and ale and sitting across from her. 'I am glad I caught you before you left today.' He took a bite of ham. 'I have something for you.'

'Really?' She sipped her hot chocolate and nibbled on her toast. 'More jewellery?' she asked, not really thinking so or wanting any, but wanting to needle him.

He gave her a considering look. 'If that is what you want, then I shall get you more. I have already taken the Perth family jewels into Gerrard's to be cleaned and reset. There are rubies and sapphires and some South Sea pearls.'

Exasperated at herself and at him, her reply was tart. 'Nothing of the sort. I was merely curious.'

He finished his ham and drank down the ale. 'Then perhaps you will be more pleased with today's gift than you were with the opals.' He stood and went to the door where he stopped and waited for her.

Lillith's scowl intensified. She had wanted a marriage of convenience and that was exactly what he was giving her—except for the lavish presents. She sipped the last of her chocolate and rose, moving at her own leisure in spite of his haste.

Whatever he had for her, it was outside and he was excited. Watching him practically dance from foot to foot finally eased her unhappiness with him. He swept her out the front door and stopped.

In the street, a prancing pair of grey horses were harnessed to a silver cabriolet with black trim and a black top pulled up. The door was emblazoned with the Perth coat of arms.

'This is for you,' he said softly.

She gasped. 'Me? It is fabulous. I mean, it is beautiful. Surely it is for both of us.'

'No,' he said firmly, taking her by the arm and directing her down the steps and to the coach. 'It is for you alone.'

'But…thank you,' she said, remembering how he had wondered if she would like this gift more than the last. 'It is truly a magnificent present.' She turned to him, perplexed. 'But why? I already have a carriage, and I have already had so much from you as my settlement.'

He scowled at her. 'Your other carriage was de Lisle's and it has his coat of arms. You are no longer the Dowager Lady de Lisle. You are Lillith, Countess of Perth. This cabriolet reflects that.'

'Ah,' she breathed as though she understood, but she did not. 'This is to show the world that I am your property.'

'That you are my wife,' he corrected. 'I thought you might take it to your meeting with Mr Sinclair. See how you like it or if there is something you want changed.'

She shook her head in amazement. He was showering her with very expensive things. It was disconcerting.

'That is a good idea. I must go get my pelisse and a cape,' she finally said. 'The day is cold and a drizzle starting.'

He nodded and let her go.

Lillith rushed up the stairs more to escape him and the situation than because she needed to hurry. There was still plenty of time before she needed to leave. However, the horses pulling her carriage would need to keep moving. She could take a ride around London, possibly Hyde Park, before going to Mr Sinclair's. It truly was a beautiful vehicle.

An hour later, Lillith exited her new carriage. Her appointment with Mr Sinclair was in five minutes. Parliament would be over in several days, and she wanted to get an update on her affairs before she and Perth left for the country.

She entered the outer office and was quickly ushered into his private room. He rose and offered her a seat close to the fire. She sat with alacrity.

'It is getting colder by the hour,' she said.

'Winter. I should imagine you and the Earl will be leaving for the country soon.'

She nodded. 'As soon as Parliament ends. The Earl has some concerns he is attempting to get Parliament to address.'

Mr Sinclair nodded. 'Yes. His bill for the returning soldiers. Many people are in favour of it, but I doubt that he will get it passed. 'Tis a shame.'

Lillith was momentarily taken aback. She knew that most of the people in their circles were aware of Perth's endeavours, but she had not realised that his name and cause were so well known that people outside of their sphere were also aware of what he did. Pride in her husband's efforts brought a lump to her throat.

'My husband has many fine qualities,' she finally managed to say around the tightness that made swallowing difficult.

'Many,' Sinclair agreed. 'And he is very generous.'

Lillith coloured and wondered if news of her magnificent jewels and new carriage had managed to travel this far. 'He is.'

Mr Sinclair smiled. 'I have the marriage settlement

papers here for you to read and sign. You will see that the Earl has agreed to far more than we asked for.'

'What?' She reached for the papers.

'He has bought your London house that was on the market and it will go to the second child you have if the first is a boy. If the first child is girl, then the house will be hers. He has also given you a very large join-ture that will continue in the event of his death whether you remarry or not. And he has settled ten thousand pounds on each of your children who will not inherit the earldom. Most generous indeed.'

She gaped, only just managing to keep her eyes from widening. 'Most generous indeed,' she repeated, too stunned to think of something different.

Mr Sinclair cleared his throat. 'There is one stipulation to everything. Mr Wentworth must never be in charge of handling any of this.'

'That is a wise course,' Lillith said, instantly relieved.

The good news and the bad news in the open, she signed the papers with relish and rose. 'Thank you so much, Mr Sinclair. I know that the past months have been difficult on you, but I think you will find the future ones much more pleasant.'

He bowed over the hand she extended. 'As I hope you will, my lady.'

She left his offices with a lightness of step that she had not experienced for a very long time. And it was all because of Perth. The journey home was much more pleasant than the journey to Mr Sinclair's.

She delighted in the well-sprung comfort of her cabriolet. The soft wine leather squabs beckoned her fingers and she took off her gloves to stroke her bare skin over the fine leather.

And there was Perth's generosity to her and to their children. This might be a marriage of convenience, and Perth might be acting toward her in some ways as though it was, but his behaviour was that of a man determined to show his new wife that she was valued. He was behaving as though theirs was a love match, and he was trying to show her how greatly he cared for her security and sense of worth. Which she knew was not the case. Nor could she let herself be so weak as to think it was.

'Twas very unsettling.

Chapter Sixteen

Lillith reined her mare in. She and Perth were leaving London tomorrow and she had been busy packing; she had not wanted to come here. But Mathias had sent a note asking her to meet him in Hyde Park. He had not been to see her since her wedding and she found that she missed him, and this would be her last chance to see her brother for some time.

It was late afternoon and the sun would soon be gone. She wished he had picked a warmer spot, preferably inside. But he had said he did not want her coming to his rented rooms. None of her friends, not even Madeline, would have him in their home and his friends were mostly unmarried men.

A biting wind whipped the bare tree branches around and caused little wavelets to crest white on the surface of the Serpentine. The ducks that swam on the pond in summer were gone.

She heard the sound of horse's hooves on the hard ground, and angled her mount to face that direction. Instead of seeing her brother, she saw her husband. He rode quickly and drew his horse to a halt just as she thought he would ride her down. She knew in an instant that he was furious.

'What in blazes do you think you are doing? In the park at this time of day with the sun nearly down and no groom?' he thundered. 'Anything might have happened to you. And if you have not a care for yourself, consider our child.'

On the defensive and knowing she should have brought a groom, she shot back, 'I came here to meet Mathias, who will not come to the house—as you very well know. He is still my brother, and I do still want to stay in touch with him.'

'Then meet him somewhere warmer and safer than Hyde Park in the late afternoon in the winter when nearly no one is around.'

He turned his horse and started off as though he expected her to automatically follow. Her hackles immediately rose and she stayed put. He glanced back at her, his brows drawn.

'Come along.'

'I told you, I am waiting for Mathias.'

'And I am waiting for you,' he said coldly.

She drew herself up, prepared to resist him.

A shot rang out. Her horse reared and she slid off onto the ground, hitting it with a force that knocked the wind from her.

'Lillith!'

She heard Perth's anguished cry, but could not sit up just yet and tell him she was fine. Her lungs burned and would not seem to fill with air. He was beside her before she recovered.

'Lillith, my God, are you all right?'

He lifted her into his arms just as another shot rang out. Instantly he dropped, covering her body with his. His hands shielded her face and head. She heard the horses neighing.

'We have got to get out of here,' he muttered. 'Can you run?'

Realisation of their peril hit her like a runaway carriage. 'Yes, I think so,' she managed. 'I will have to.'

He nodded. 'That's my Lillith. Now.'

He stood and pulled her to her feet. He swung her in front of him and propelled her forward. Another shot rang out. She felt his hand slip from the small of her back but return almost immediately.

She grabbed her riding skirts in both hands, cursing their bulkiness, and ran for her life. Her lungs laboured. She heard Perth's boots pounding on the ground and felt his breath hot on her neck. They made it to a copse of trees where Perth shoved her behind the largest trunk and pushed her into a crouch.

'You make a smaller target,' he explained, kneeling beside her and shielding the part of her body the tree did not protect.

She gasped for breath and pushed her hand hard against the stitch in her side. Frantic to know what was happening, she angled so that she could look around the trunk.

'Damnation,' Perth said, yanking her arm so that her

head was no longer exposed. 'What are you trying to do, give them the perfect target?'

Instantly chagrined, she said, 'You are right. I did not think.'

He let out a long, frustrated breath. 'The best thing that could happen to us right now would be for your brother to come along. Whoever is shooting at us is bound to disappear if too many get involved.'

'But why would anyone shoot at us?'

He shrugged. 'Who knows? It has been a hard winter. Perhaps someone is desperate beyond words and willing to risk the very great possibility of getting caught.' He slanted her a dark look. 'Maybe someone was waiting here on purpose.'

His words fell between them like stones.

'Surely not,' she finally managed to get out between shaking teeth.

He shrugged again and this time he winced. She ran her gaze over him and saw the red stain on his back right shoulder that was slowly spreading.

'You have been hit,' she said, suddenly frantic with worry. 'We have got to get you to a doctor.'

'Hush,' he said, his tone gentle. 'First we have got to get away from here. Everything else can wait.'

She knew he was right, but that did not stop the icy fear that clutched her heart. 'We must at least stop the bleeding.'

She lifted her skirts and ripped at her petticoats. Another shot rang out.

'Stop it,' he said. 'The trunk of this tree is not large and all your twisting around makes you the perfect target. I would rather bleed to death than have you get hurt. Now stop.'

A shot hit the tree, sending pieces of bark ricocheting. A sliver caught her cheek. She yelped and reached up to see if the piece had stuck. It had not, but her gloves came away with a dab of blood.

Perth vowed, 'Whoever is behind this will pay dearly.'

Fierce pride filled her for she knew he meant it, and right now she wanted nothing more than revenge on the person who had shot him. No matter how he felt about her, she loved him.

It was fast becoming dark.

'We will try to escape again. They will not be able to see any better in the dark than we will. That is, if someone does not come looking for us very soon. The horses will have returned to the house and the groom will immediately tell Fitch.' He had no sooner said the words than the sounds of approaching hoofbeats came to them. 'Ah, I knew I could depend on Fitch,' he said with great satisfaction.

To Lillith's relief, it seemed that Fitch had brought a small army. Several riders held flambeaux to light the scene. Every one of them carried pistols which they had out.

'Fitch,' Perth yelled. 'Over here.'

Lillith heard Fitch tell several of the riders to fan out and look for the attackers. Men and flambeaux moved into the dusk, trailing smoke and the scent of pitch. She marvelled at Fitch's efficiency.

Quickly the remaining men surrounded her and

Perth. The orange and yellow flames from the flambeaux shot into the sky and cast the men's shadows
behind them in elongated parodies.

'I knew something was wrong,' Fitch said, dis-
mounting. 'A good thing you mentioned something
about coming here.' He cast a quick, involuntary
glance at Lillith.

She caught him looking at her, however briefly, and
knew this whole débâcle was her fault. But surely her
brother had not planned *this*! Someone must have
known he had sent her a note or had seen her leave
the house and followed her, thinking she would be
easy prey. Mathias had his faults, as she knew only
too well, but this went beyond gambling away and
inheritance—or even a horsewhipping. *Surely…*

'Take Lady Perth home,' the Earl said, thrusting her
forward into the arms of a nearby rider. 'She was
thrown from her horse and I want her examined immediately by a doctor.'

In a jumble of limbs, Lillith found herself sitting in
front of the head groom. 'You are hurt as well, Perth.
You need the doctor more than I. Come home.'

Fitch jerked and spun around. He took a step towards the Earl, but when he spoke his voice was calm.
'She is right, my lord.'

Perth grunted. 'I will live. I have taken worse. Right
now, we must look for those scoundrels or any trace
they left.' His hands fisted. 'They are not going to get
away with this.'

She shivered involuntarily, the cold and his chilling
words finally penetrating the numbness that had de-

scended on her. 'Then do not lay more at their feet by
staying and letting your wound worsen.'

'Take her home, Thomas,' Perth ordered the groom.
To ease the harshness of that order, he crossed over
and took Lillith's hand. 'I would not stay here if I
thought it was endangering my life. Trust me that I
know these things.'

She gazed down at him and saw that he meant what
he said. It would not be so bad if she had not seen
Fitch turn away in disgust. Still, there was nothing she
could do.

'Take care, then,' she said, leaning down and kissing him lightly. He stepped back in surprise. 'I will
have a doctor in to make sure that neither the babe
nor I have taken harm. And I will have him stay to
examine you.'

He stared up at her, and she knew that her sponta-
neous show of affection had startled him. Never before
had she kissed him unless it was in passion and after
he had already aroused her.

He stepped back. 'I won't be long.'

Perth turned away and motioned for Fitch to follow
him. 'The shots came from this direction,' he said,
striding off. As occupied as he was on finding some
trace of their attackers, he still listened for the sounds
that would tell him Lillith had left.

'Her ladyship will be all right,' Fitch said gruffly.
'She is a strong one.'

Perth moved into a copse of trees and squatted.
'Bring the light over here.'

Fitch arrived and crouched beside the Earl. He

grumbled in disgust. 'Nothing here but a bunch of dirt that's been scuffed up.' He shifted some of the earth through his fingers. 'And some powder. You will never find them from this.'

Perth stood, frustration in every line of his taut body. 'I know, but I had to try.' He pivoted on his heel and grunted in pain. 'I guess I had better get home and have you look at this.'

'You should have done that instead of chasing after evidence you won't find,' Fitch said sourly.

Perth eased up his pace enough to lessen the pain in his shoulder. 'I hoped for something.' He cast a sideways glance at Fitch. 'Her brother sent her a message asking her to meet him here.'

Fitch's intake of breath was loud in the cold, silent air. 'Why would he do a fool thing like that?'

'We can only guess,' Perth said, moving more slowly than he liked.

Thirty minutes later, he sat in a chair in his bedroom in front of a roaring fire with just his breeches and stockings on and cursed the doctor examining him. 'Blast it, man, do you have to prod so deep?' He ran the fingers of his free hand through his hair. 'How is my wife? Is the babe all right?'

Doctor Johnson, a young man with sandy brown hair and piercing brown eyes, kept on doing his examination. 'Your wife is fine and so is the child she carries. They are both resting. She is in better shape than you are. If you had sent for me immediately, I might not have to dig so deeply, but the ball is lodged solidly in muscle, maybe even bone. Fortunately for you, I was a surgeon before becoming a doctor. Still, you will be lucky if you don't come down with a fever.'

'I shall be lucky if I am not arrested for your murder,' Perth muttered. But the relief he felt over Lillith went a long way to making him feel more charitable towards the doctor.

From his position on the other side of the Earl, Fitch said, 'He has never been a good patient.'

'That I can believe,' the doctor muttered. 'Almost. Now hold still.'

Hold still. Perth saw lights in front of his eyes and bit down hard on the piece of leather Fitch had given him to chew. Then an excruciating wrench and the doctor held the forceps high. Between the tongs was the ball.

'Whisky,' Perth demanded.

'After I am through,' the doctor said, pouring the contents of a decanter liberally along the wound.

Perth sucked in his breath. 'You could have told me you were going to do that.'

'It would not have made it hurt less.' The doctor handed him the decanter.

Perth took a long swig. 'No, it would not.' He sank into the chair.

'You have an interesting pallor that should rival Byron's in the drawing room,' the doctor said drily. 'I suggest that you stay in bed for quite some time.'

Perth closed his eyes and took another long drink.

'Thank you, doctor. Please see to my wife before you go.'

The doctor looked over Perth's head to Fitch.

Fitch shrugged. 'Best do as he says. Knowing that her ladyship is well cared for will ease him more than anything else.' He carefully took the decanter from the Earl's slack fingers. 'I will watch over his lordship.'

The doctor nodded and left through the door connecting to Lady Perth's chamber. He had given her a light dose of laudanum to calm her nerves, and she lay quietly on the bed. But he noted that her eyes were open.

'How is my husband?' she asked softly before he had taken two steps into the room.

He closed the door behind himself and went to the bed. 'Your colour is back, and your husband has a strong constitution. I understand he has suffered wounds like this several times. That accounts for the scars on his body.' He did not mention the scars that criss-crossed the Earl's back.

She gave him a wan smile. 'Is that your way of telling me that he will be all right?'

'That is my way of telling you that he is a fool, but hopefully will take no lasting harm. Although I warned him that he might run a fever. His man says he knows what to do.' He reached the bed and took her wrist to feel her pulse. 'Your husband is more concerned about your well-being than his own, and his man says to care for you and the Earl will do fine.'

Her smile widened. Even hurt, Perth was stubborn to a fault.

Shortly after, the doctor pronounced, 'You are as well as can be expected after what you have been through. I will give you the same advice I gave his lordship: get some rest.' He frowned at her. 'I trust you will follow my orders better than he, for you have a child to consider.'

She had intended to defy him and go to sit beside Perth and watch over him, but the doctor's words chastised her. Today she had not thought much of the life she carried and had consequently endangered the babe.

She nodded. 'I will do my best, doctor. And thank you.'

'Thank me by taking care of yourself.' He packed up his bag and went to the door. 'I will be back tomorrow to see how you and the Earl are doing. I expect to see improvement.'

She waited until the door closed behind him before getting up. She would rest in a chair beside Perth's bed. The doctor had said her husband was strong, but she had also seen the anger in the doctor's eyes. She knew the emotion had been caused by Perth's disregard for his own safety.

She slipped from the bed and on bare feet went to Perth's room. She did not knock, not wanting to disturb him if he slept. To her relief he was in bed, but the light of a single candle showed his extreme paleness. Worry quickened her pace.

'He is sleeping more from the whisky than the wound,' Fitch said softly.

She had not seen him and his voice surprised her.

She whirled around. He sat in a chair by the smouldering fire.

'You startled me,' she whispered. She looked back at Perth. 'The doctor was not happy with him.'

'Neither was I,' Fitch said, getting up and coming to the bed. 'But you know how he is.'

'Yes. Stubborn and arrogant.' Tentatively, very conscious of the servant beside her, she laid her palm on Perth's forehead. 'He feels cool.'

'Right now,' Fitch agreed. 'If he gets a fever it will come later.'

'Oh. I do not have any experience nursing someone with a wound.' She took her hand back. 'My times in the sickroom have been childbirthing and illnesses.'

'Not much difference when all is said and done,' Fitch said. 'I will ring for some tea and biscuits. If you intend to stay, you will need to keep your strength up.'

She was not hungry, but knew he was right. 'I will be right back.' She hurried from the room to hers where she grabbed a thick, wool robe and belted it around her waist. She returned in time to see Fitch open the door and a footman carry in a laden tray.

She poured Fitch tea and then herself. She added biscuits. 'You are undoubtedly tired,' she said. 'I can watch him by myself.'

Fitch took a drink before answering. 'Thank you, my lady, but you have been through nearly as much today as the Earl. It would be better if I watched tonight while you rest. In the morning you can take my place.'

He made sense and she was tired, but she could not bring herself to leave. 'I am not tired.'

He frowned at her. 'You are as stubborn as he and for no good reason. If he gets worse, it won't be for some hours. You will be far more use to him then if you are rested.'

He was irritated with her and rightly so. His words made sense. With as much graciousness as she could muster, she agreed. But before she could leave, she had to check on Perth one last time.

He lay as still as before and just as pale. Unmindful of Fitch who stood behind her now, she gently smoothed the hair from her husband's face. Then she ran a soft touch over his scar. Even with the white line down his cheek, he looked somehow vulnerable.

She realised with a start that she had never seen him like this before. Every other time she had seen him in bed, he had been awake and making love to her. Now he lay here hurt, and all because of her. She had no illusions. He had taken the bullet when they had run, when his hand had briefly fallen from her back. He had taken a bullet that would have hit her squarely between the shoulder blades.

She squeezed her eyes shut. Please let the wound not fester. *Please let him not die.* He might not love her, but he cared enough to risk his life for her. That meant a great deal.

More devastating was the certainty that she could not live without him.

The next morning she woke to Agatha moving around the room. 'My lady, your brother is here to see you.'

'My brother,' Lillith murmured, sitting up in bed.

'He has been here for nigh on an hour, my lady,' Agatha said, putting down the tray with Lillith's morning chocolate and toast.

Lillith dragged herself out of bed. She had not slept well with worrying about Perth. But at least she was past the morning sickness. She ate the toast first to insure that her stomach stayed settled, then drank the hot chocolate. Afterwards, Agatha helped her into a loose-fitting morning dress of pale blue kerseymere that was several seasons out of date.

Only then did she go to meet her brother. Even so, she was uncomfortable. Tell herself as she might that he was not involved with what had happened yesterday, she could not get past the fact that he had asked her to meet him in the place where she and Perth were attacked.

Mathias sat in the breakfast room drinking coffee and eating a beefsteak. He appeared perfectly at home. He looked up when she came in. 'Ordered some food when it became obvious you were not coming down soon.' He took another bite.

She eased into a chair across the table from him and waved away a footman who offered her more chocolate. 'Perth is hurt.'

'That is what the man—Simmons, is it?—mentioned. Dreadful when Hyde Park ain't safe. And in broad daylight.' He continued eating.

Lillith watched him. 'It was not exactly full daylight. The time you set for our meeting was a scant thirty or forty minutes before dusk. Perth came after me…and you never arrived.'

He waved his fork, a piece of meat hanging precariously from the prongs. 'Got waylaid. Prinny needed my advice on a waistcoat. Could not refuse the Prince of Wales.'

Lillith's eyes narrowed, but the tale was not far fetched. The Prince of Wales was a notorious dandy, and he was possessive of his friends. He could very easily have commanded her brother's presence for nothing better than to comment on the fashion of a piece of clothing.

'So, did you come today to talk to me about what you could not speak about yesterday? Although I find it unusual that you come to our house for the first time after Perth is hurt and confined to his bed.'

Mathias's mouth thinned. 'Are you trying to imply something, Lillith? Because if you are, and if it is what I think, then you are beyond the pale. I came because I knew I had been insufferably rude not to have sent a lackey to meet you and tell you that I would not be coming. It slipped my mind.'

She accepted his apology, but did not completely accept his reason. 'Why did you want to meet with me in the first place?'

'I want to stay in your town house that de Lisle left you. Rumour says Perth bought it for you and, as his wife, you can well afford to let me use it.' His blue eyes took on an ugly glint. 'The man gives you everything and will do nothing for me. 'Tis the least he can do, through you, of course.'

She could hardly believe what he had said. Even for Mathias, the idea was outrageous. Still, he was her brother. Telling him no would be hard. Perhaps too hard.

'Why do you want to stay in town? Everyone is leaving.'

He finished his beefsteak. 'The Prince will not be leaving town for several days. He wants me around and I don't want to stay in rented rooms any longer.' He wiped his mouth with the napkin. 'I find myself unable to afford them.'

Lillith's hands clenched into white fists under cover of the table and her eyes narrowed ever so slightly. He was insufferable. But he was her brother. Much as she wanted to tell him no, absolutely no, the words stuck in her throat.

She took a slow breath and hoped her voice would not show her fury. 'You may stay there for the present. Perth is sure to find out and he will want you out.'

Mathias stood and an ugly look settled on his face. 'He has made the house over to you.'

She rose so that he would not be towering over her and shook her head. 'That is not true. It is in my keeping for our second child or first girl.'

'The same thing,' he said pointedly.

She shrugged. 'Not exactly. And if Perth wants you out when he finds out, then I will be obligated to ask you to leave.'

His mouth thinned and his face reddened. 'Already he is more important to you than your own flesh and blood. And I thought yours was a marriage of convenience. I see I was mistaken.' He sneered. 'He is giving you more gifts than a man gives his mistress.'

She stiffened. 'I think our conversation has gone on long enough, Mathias. I had hoped for something different from you, but I see it is to be the same as always.'

'Not quite,' he said. 'Normally you pay more regard to what I have to say.'

He pivoted on his heel and left. Lillith watched him, sadness replacing the anger of minutes before. He was still her only living relative. That meant a great deal to her. It hurt greatly that her brother did not have the same feelings of love and commitment. Hard as it was on her, she had to admit that she was nothing but a means to a fortune for Mathias.

She sat back down and rested her head on her hand. She was very tired this morning and Mathias's visit and the ugly confrontation between them had only exhausted her further. That was the reason tears were so close. Nor did his absence ease the ugly feelings that seemed to permeate the room.

For the first time in her life, she began to truly despair of ever having a loving relationship with her brother. All the time before she had been the one to be conciliatory and to do whatever it took to maintain their relationship. Now for the first time, she was not so accommodating and the rift between them widened with every encounter while her relationship with Perth was doing just the opposite.

She took a deep breath and stood back up. It was past time she went to check on her husband. Before coming down to breakfast she had looked in and both he and Fitch had been sleeping, Perth in bed and Fitch in a chair pulled up to the bed. She had left them to come and eat. Now she needed to go and relieve Fitch and she wanted to care for her husband.

Chapter Seventeen

Lillith entered Perth's room as quietly as possible, not wanting to wake her husband. She realised immediately that she could have entered on a horse and not woken him. Fitch sprawled in a chair not two feet from the bed and snored loudly enough to wake up the dead.

She shook her head in amusement and crossed to the batman. Gently so as not to startle him, she shook one of his shoulders.

'Wha—?' He started awake.

'Shh,' she said. 'I have come to relieve you. There are eggs and kidneys downstairs hot from the kitchen. You will feel the better for having them.'

Once awake, wide awake, Fitch stood and stretched. 'Right, my lady. I will just have some and return.'

She shook her head and put her fists on her hips. 'You will do more than that. You will eat until you can eat no more and then you will get some rest.' When his mouth set in a stubborn line, she firmed hers.

'That was our agreement last night. I kept to my part and went to bed. Now you must keep to your half.'

He looked as though he would argue, and Lillith straightened her shoulders and prepared for battle. He shrank a little bit and a huge yawn caught him.

'You are right, my lady. I did agree to that and you did do what you said you would do.' Another yawn took him. 'And I am tired.' He gave her a rueful grin. 'Two hours in a chair don't do much.'

She returned his grin. 'And you were snoring loudly enough to wake Perth.'

Fitch shook his head. 'No. His lordship can sleep through cannon fire when he is tired enough or wounded. My snoring is not enough to rouse him. Trust me on that.'

'I suppose I must,' Lillith said, believing him, having already seen the proof. 'Now go. The doctor should be here soon.'

'Call me if you need help,' Fitch said, casting one last glance at the Earl who still lay fast asleep.

'I will,' Lillith promised.

No sooner had the door closed behind Fitch than Lillith strode to the bed and looked down at Perth. His thick black hair fell in several waving hanks over his broad forehead, making him look young and vulnerable. Not even the silver wings at his temples could detract from the image. Ebony lashes lay fanned across his high cheekbones. Even his scar seemed relaxed.

Softly, so as not to wake him, she brushed the hair back. The backs of her fingers grazed his skin. She stopped. He was hot. She cupped his face in her palm. He was very hot. Worry puckered her brow.

She stepped back and looked for water. She knew from her own experiences that cool water could help bring down a fever. She found what she sought on his shaving table. She poured the liquid from the pitcher and dipped a convenient cloth in. She wrung the excess moisture from the fabric and went back to Perth.

His eyes were open and he watched her.

'You are awake,' she said inanely.

'What are you doing?' he asked, his voice barely a rasp.

'I am going to sponge you. You have a fever,' she said calmly, not wanting to upset him with her concern.

'I am thirsty,' he said. 'Is there water to drink?'

She laid the cloth on his forehead before returning to the pitcher and pouring a glass full of water. She took it to him and held his head while he finished the entire thing.

'Thank you,' he murmured, his voice a little less harsh. 'I needed that very much.'

'You are welcome,' she said, setting the glass on a nearby table. 'Now lie still and let me sponge you. You will feel much better for it.'

He gave her a smile that was almost, but not quite, lecherous. 'I am sure that I will.'

She eyed him narrowly, wondering if he felt better than she had thought. When he closed his eyes, she decided that he did not. She stroked the damp cloth over his face until the material felt warm, which was not long. At this rate, she would need to move the pitcher and bowl closer to the bed. She did so, but not without some difficulty. When she was finished and once more looked at her patient, he was watching her with a grin.

'Very diverting,' he said. 'Why did you not call Fitch to help?'

'Because he spent the night watching you. It is my turn now while he gets some much-needed sleep.'

'The two of you are trading off duty?' he asked, an unreadable look in his eyes.

She nodded. 'The doctor should be here soon to check on you.'

'And you,' he added firmly. 'How are you doing? And the babe?'

She stopped wringing the cloth out and looked at him. She saw concern. 'We are both fine. Doctor Johnson said we were doing better than you.'

'That young man was very opinionated. Fitch could have done as well.'

She turned to him, hands on hips in exasperation. 'Then why did you even bother sending for a doctor if you did not value his opinion?'

He looked as though the answer were obvious. 'Because Fitch could have cared for me, but he has no experience with pregnant women.'

'Ah,' she said sharply.

She turned abruptly away to dip the previously forgotten cloth back in the water and to hide her reaction to his words. Everything he had done yesterday had been for her and their child. First he had come after her in Hyde Park. Then he had taken a bullet in the shoulder to protect her. And lastly, he had ordered a doctor he did not think he needed so that she and the child she carried would be cared for. His concern took her breath away.

She went back to his side with the damp cloth just as someone knocked on the door. 'Come in,' she said, laying the cloth once more on his forehead.

'My lady,' Simmons said from the doorway, his nose held fastidiously high, 'there is a…person…here who says he knows the Earl.'

Lillith smiled. Her butler was a snob. 'What type of person is he?'

From the bed Perth asked, 'Is he a ruffian with several teeth missing?'

'Yes, my lord,' Simmons said barely repressing a shudder. 'And filthy.'

Lillith heard Perth chuckle, which was followed by a sharp intake of breath. She whirled around and marched back to his side. 'You are to be more careful.'

'I know what I am supposed to be,' he said, throwing the cover off and swinging his legs over the side of the bed. 'And I know what I intend to be.'

His face turned as white as the sheet riding low on his lean hips and he swayed to the side. Lillith grabbed him and held him to her.

'You may go, Simmons,' she said, not wanting the butler to see what would shortly be happening between her and her husband.

'Tell the man to wait,' Perth ordered just before the door closed. 'Or I will have your hide,' he said loudly.

On a quieter note, he said, 'That ruffian is important. He knows who attacked me several weeks ago and he might be able to find out who shot at us yesterday.'

Her brows rose. 'That is quite a responsibility for a man that Simmons would just as soon throw out the door.' She eased him to a sitting position against the pillows. 'But that is unimportant. You do not feel well and should not be out of bed.'

'Well,' he said, pushing up, 'I intend to stand on my own two feet shortly.'

She bent over him and put her palms on his chest to gently push him back. Heat emanated from his flesh even through the fine lawn nightshirt he wore. He swore as he fell backwards.

'You are going nowhere. You have a fever.' She kept her hands on him for fear that he would try and rise as soon as she removed them. 'Perhaps after Dr Johnson has examined you.'

'I will damn well do as I please, Lillith. This is not the first time I have had a fever, nor is it the first time I have been wounded. I never stay coddled in bed, and I have no intention of doing so now.' His gaze ran seductively down her. 'Unless you have something entertaining in mind that we might do?'

She flushed and her bosom ached. 'No,' she snapped.

'A pity,' he said, but with no real sound of regret. 'Now you can help me or I will do it in spite of you.'

She met his challenging gaze without blinking. She knew by the tightness of his jaw and the glint in his eyes that he meant what he said.

With a sigh of resignation she ungraciously acquiesced. 'As you demand. But let me check your bandage for bleeding first.'

He nodded. She unbuttoned his shirt and slid it off his shoulder. He leant forward enough for her to see the back. The wound was well wrapped.

'Fitch changed it during the night,' Perth said.

'Ah, that explains why there is no blood.'

'Or none that can be seen,' Perth finished. 'Now are you satisfied? I will even tell you how to tie a sling so that my arm does not pull down on the muscle.'

She moved back. 'You obviously know much more about this than I.'

'As I said,' he said with seeming patience, 'I have been through this before.'

He once more swung his legs over the edge of the bed. Again he swayed and his face blanched, but he remained upright.

'Stay put long enough for me to get Fitch,' she finally said, irritated with his stubbornness, but not wanting him to hurt himself further.

'No,' he ordered. 'Fitch needs his rest. You can help me; by the time we are done with our visitor, the doctor will be here. After he leaves, we can wake Fitch.'

'That is less than ideal,' she muttered.

For the first time in days, he gave her a genuine smile. 'It is the best I can offer you. Now, I will make do with a dressing robe over my nightshirt. That will be much easier than dressing me.'

She eyed him from the corner of her eye, wondering if the tone of his voice was meant to be seductive or teasing or both. The sharp angles of his face and the tension that emanated from him decided her that he meant both.

'Where is your robe?' she asked, backing away from the attraction he had suddenly become. Even wounded he was the most virile man she had ever encountered. She shook her head in wonder and chagrin at her physical weakness where he was concerned.

'Behind that door,' he said, indicating a door she had not noticed before.

She entered his dressing room. A small trundle bed was tucked against one corner for Fitch if he felt the need although Lillith knew the batman had his own suite of rooms, unusual as that was, on the third floor. As she had always known, Fitch was not a servant.

An array of dressing gowns hung from pegs. 'Which one do you want?' she called.

'The one you like best,' he answered, which was no help.

Quickly, so as not to test his patience which she knew to be short, she grabbed the nearest one that looked like it would be warm. It was finest black cashmere embroidered in silver silk dragons. It would be warm and regal. Whoever the person was who waited for them would be suitably impressed.

She came out of the room and went to him. He stood with the help of the bed on which he had the hand of his good arm propped for support.

'I would have helped you,' she said in exasperation.

'I am not a cripple, Lillith,' he said with an edge to his words.

She stared at him. 'Of course you are not, but you did not need to risk hurting yourself when I am perfectly capable of supporting you while you try to stand and get your bearings.'

He scowled. 'I don't like being dependent.'

'No one does,' she retorted, exasperated by his determined independence regardless of whether what he did was best.

'Some more than others,' he stated flatly, holding out his hand for the robe.

She was so disgusted with him that she threw the garment at him. He caught it with his good hand and proceeded to don it. It was small satisfaction when he pulled the sleeve up his bad arm and winced.

'I might have saved you that pain,' she said acidly. 'Let us just hope that you did not start your wound bleeding again.'

'It does not feel like it,' he said, belting the sash.

She noted that he moved with increased confidence. 'Some tea and food will help.'

He nodded. 'And I am sure that our guest would like some.' He glanced up at her after getting his slippers on. 'You could order Simmons to set the breakfast table.'

She closed her mouth on a sharp retort.

'Where is my cane?' he muttered.

Minutes later she found it in the dressing room and brought it out to him. He took it and started slowly towards the door. She followed behind, wondering if she was strong enough to break his fall should he lose his balance. In the hall, she rushed ahead to order the food and find a footman to help Perth down the stairs. Her husband had already started down when she got back.

'Let Robert help you, Perth,' she ordered.

Perth stared pointedly at her. 'Do you remember someone else using this very cane on these stairs, refusing to be helped? I do.'

'Well, I did not climb all the way. Fitch helped me.'

'I am going down, I think I can manage on my own. It is my shoulder, madam, not my leg.' He took another step down. 'You may go, Robert.'

The hapless footman looked from one of them to the other. Fuming, but knowing that Perth would do it his way, much as she had insisted on her way, Lillith said, 'Yes, Robert, go and tell Simmons we will be down shortly.'

The footman bowed himself away.

Perth continued down the stairs and Lillith followed.

The smells of ham, beefsteak, coffee, hot chocolate and toast assailed her senses as she entered the breakfast room she had left barely an hour before. She watched Perth take his usual seat. She noted beads of perspiration on his forehead, but he moved with deliberation. Once she was assured that he would do, she studied their guest.

The man was a ruffian and everything Simmons had said about him was true. At the moment, he stuffed his mouth with beefsteak and gammon at the same time. One hand curled around a mug of ale, which he slurped with a full mouth.

Perth watched him with grim satisfaction, the lines around his mouth more pronounced than normal. Simmons entered and served the Earl his favourite gammon steak and kidneys. Eggs sat on a side dish with toast. Strong black coffee steamed in a mug. Perth ate slowly, careful of his wounded shoulder when he cut his food and lifted his fork since he was right-handed, the same side that was hurt.

Lillith sat down beside Perth, their guest having taken her normal place. She took tea and a piece of toast, sipping on one and nibbling on the other. She was not hungry, but she was extremely curious.

The man took his last bite and drank his last gulp, belched and grinned in satisfaction. 'Thanks for the food,' he said, his look anything but grateful. 'I got the name you want, guv.'

Perth carefully set his fork and knife down. 'Of the man who hired you to assault me?'

'Assault? Oh, attack you. Yes.' His grin widened. 'Got more information I think you'll be wantin'. Somethin' about an attack in 'yde Park.'

Lillith jerked in surprise and her tea sloshed over the side of the cup to stain the white linen tablecloth. She noted that her husband took the extra news calmly, almost as though he had expected it.

'They were ordered by the same man,' Perth said flatly.

'That's right,' the other man said, much as one might praise a child that has guessed the correct answer. ''Ow much is the flash cove's name worth to you?'

'I already know the man's name,' Perth said quietly, his voice sending shivers down Lillith's back. 'What I want from you is to tell my wife.' He glanced at Lillith and then back to the man. 'I will pay you well.'

The ruffian named a sum that made Lillith choke. She expected Perth to say no.

'Simmons,' Perth said, 'go to the library and open the middle drawer of my desk. You will find a sheaf of bills. Bring them to me.' Simmons left. 'Now, the name.'

'First the money.'

'The name.'

''Ow do I know you'll keep your word? The other one didn't.'

Perth leaned forward, his left hand a fist on the table. 'I am not the other man.' His voice was cold. 'You will do well to remember that.'

The ruffian edged back in his chair. 'Right, guv. Right. No insult. Just can't always trust a swell cove. They got the blunt, but they don't always pay.'

Perth's eyes blazed. 'The name.'

'Right. Wentworth.' The man's grin returned. 'Rumour says 'e 'ired the men what shot at you yesterday, too. Me pal, Mike, says 'e 'eard it.'

Perth frowned in disbelief. ''Tis more likely your friend Mike was the one who shot me.'

'No, guv. No,' the other man said.

Through this Lillith sat frozen. Feeling rushed back like needles. 'No,' she murmured. 'No, you are wrong. Your friend is wrong.' But even as she said the words, doubt swamped her. It fitted. It fitted too well. 'Oh, no,' she whispered, sinking back into her chair and closing her eyes to close out the faces of the two men.

The ruffian's eyes widened and he snickered. 'Know the cove? 'E's a nasty one, 'e is. Nivver paid me what he owed me for attacking the guvnor 'ere.'

Lillith opened her eyes and stared the man down. Whether he was right or not, he did not need to gloat. The urge to reach out and slap the grin from the man's face was strong. She gripped the edge of the table instead. Her knuckles turned white and her nails dug into the cloth.

'Are you sure?' she asked.

Even as she asked, she knew his answer would not change. Mathias had done too much. But why? It made no sense.

The man's face darkened. 'I ain't uppity like the likes o' you, but I keeps me word. All I got.' He stood. 'I don't lie.'

'Do you have proof?' she demanded. 'Or are we to take your word?'

The ruffian bristled. 'Me word is me bond.'

Lillith looked away. All she was doing was taking her hurt and anger out on this man. If Mathias really had done this, then so be it, but until they had proof, she had to give her brother the benefit of the doubt.

Perth rose as well, careful not to move his right arm any more than necessary. 'I believe you,' he said quietly. 'My wife is upset. You shall have your money.'

Simmons returned then with the bills. The pile was an inch thick. Perth took it from Simmons, fanned through it and handed it over.

Surprise made the ruffian's mouth drop. 'This is more than we agreed to.'

'Take it,' Perth said. 'For your honour—and your discretion. I don't expect to hear another word of yesterday's incident or this conversation from anyone. Do I make myself clear?'

The man shot him a hard look but he kept the money. 'Yes. Thanks. I gotta go,' he added, moving around the table, careful to keep a wide berth between him and Lillith.

'Please show our guest to the door, Simmons,' Perth said.

Simmons bowed and hurried after the man who was scurrying out. Lillith watched them without conscious thought.

'He was lying,' she whispered. 'He had to be. Mathias is many things, but he is not a murderer.' She sank back into the chair and her hands dropped to her lap. Her gaze lifted. 'But I understand that you must know for sure.'

Perth watched her find excuses for her brother—again, and the anger that he felt boiled to near-explosion point. 'Why do you find it so hard to believe?' he asked harshly.

'He is my brother,' she said as though that explained everything. 'And that man just wanted money. He would have said any name. He just came up with Wentworth. He might have even known that was my brother's name. How do I know?'

'He is the brother who sold you to de Lisle, gambled away your marriage settlement and tried to sell you a

second time. He had me horsewhipped while he
looked on. Why should he not stoop to attacking me
and nearly killing us?' he asked, his words nearly a
snarl. 'Blood does not always mean love.'

She glared at him. 'He might have you attacked.'
She drew a deep breath. 'I can believe that. I do not
doubt that he had you whipped years ago, but he was
young. He would never do that now.'

Perth's voice turned deadly quiet. 'If you believe
that, then you won't mind confronting him with this
man's accusations. Your brother will deny everything
and you will be further assured of his innocence.'

Alerted by his ominous tone Lillith looked at him
closely. 'You really hate my brother, don't you?'

'Yes. He has used you and done everything in his
power to physically hurt me.'

She took a deep breath and stood. 'All right. I will
send a note to Mathias, asking him to call. That way
you will not have to travel. I will ask him with you in
the room so you can see his reaction too.' She turned
away from him and went to the door. She paused before leaving. 'Will that satisfy you?'

'Yes,' Perth said.

She did not rise when he left the room. She did not
think she could lift her hand, let alone get to her feet.
This felt like a nightmare with no happy ending. She
had argued for Mathias, but a tiny kernel of pain and
doubt made her chest ache.

Mathias had done so many despicable things. But,
God, she did not want to believe him capable of this.

Chapter Eighteen

Lillith sat rigidly in a heavy oak chair. Perth lounged on a green-and-gold upholstered settee. Doctor Johnson had just left, having pronounced his patient to be doing well but having a mild fever. He had recommended bed.

They were in the front drawing room. A gold carpet covered the wooden floors and green-flocked gold curtains framed large windows that looked out on to the street. The light was good and she would be able to see every nuance on her brother's face when she told him about that man's accusations.

Neither she nor Perth said a word to each other. They had not spoken since he left her in the breakfast room. She had sent word to him about the meeting through Simmons, and Simmons had brought back Doctor Johnson's diagnosis.

She had not been capable of hearing anymore about Mathias.

The door opened and Simmons announced, 'Mr Wentworth.'

Mathias saw Lillith first and headed to her. 'I came as soon as I got your note,' he said. He saw Perth when it was too late to sit further away. 'Perth,' he managed through gritted teeth.

Perth nodded. 'It has been a while, Wentworth. Had any big wins lately?'

Lillith frowned at Perth. 'Stop that,' she ordered. He gave her a bland look, his face completely unreadable. 'Please have a seat, Mathias,' she said, turning back to her brother.

She waved to the chair closer to her than to Perth. A large, heavy table laden with books, pictures and candlesticks provided a type of barrier between the two men. She did not think that in his current condition Perth could come over the table if something went wrong. She instantly pushed the idea aside. Nothing was going to go wrong because Mathias was innocent of that awful man's charges.

Mathias crossed one elegantly shod leg over the other. 'I hope you are doing well,' he said to the air in Perth's direction.

'I have been worse,' Perth drawled. 'In fact, ten years ago I found myself bedridden for nearly a month.'

'So I heard,' Wentworth said.

Lillith looked from one to the other. They were talking about the time Perth had been whipped. It made her uneasy to see her brother talk so cavalierly about an injury he had been responsible for causing. The callousness showed a side of Mathias that she was seeing more and more of. It hurt. She took a deep, shuddering breath.

'Mathias,' she started, her voice too loud. 'Mathias,' she began again more quietly, 'I have asked you here to tell you this horrible thing an awful man, of no account, has told us about you.' She gripped her fingers tight and told herself not to worry. It was all lies. 'I know everything he said is a lie, but...'

Mathias's gaze flicked from one to the other. His jaw twitched, a nervous habit that Lillith knew only surfaced when he was wary.

'Go on,' he said.

In a rush, she told him everything.

Perth stared at Mathias. His voice was cold and so deadly soft that it was barely audible. 'This time you went too far, Wentworth. This time you endangered Lillith. No matter what answer you give here, I will see that you are ruined.'

Mathias's gaze flicked to Perth before he looked away. The only evidence that he had even heard her was the continued tick. Wentworth, debauched libertine and addicted gambler and coward, carefully picked a scrap of non-existent lint from his sleeve and made no eye contact. 'Perth knows the truth, Lillith.'

Lillith's mouth dropped. She felt as though she had been sucked dry of everything. She sank deeper into the leather cushions. All she could do was stare in dismay at her brother.

Perth watched Lillith's face blanch and her shoulders slump. Wentworth never once looked at his sister. For that alone, Perth wanted to beat the man insensate.

Still, he did nothing and said nothing. What happened next depended on Lillith. He thought she would defend her brother's indefensible actions. She had so many times in the past that he had no doubt she would do so again, no matter how much worse these last were.

Lillith's eyes shone with tears but none spilled. 'You did have those thugs attack Perth. And you did have someone shoot at us,' she finally said, her voice barely audible. 'Why?'

As though he merely spoke of the weather, Wentworth said, 'The imbeciles were to beat Perth up, hopefully warn him away from you. It had worked once before. As to the shooting, they were supposed to follow Perth and get him. They were stupid enough to shoot when he was with you. That was not supposed to happen. I truly did intend to meet you.'

She shrank further into her chair, her face pinched by pain and disillusionment. Perth nearly rose and went to her. Now, more than any time since he had known her, she needed his support. He hardened his resolve. She also needed to see her brother for what he really was.

'As to why,' Wentworth continued, gazing out the open windows now, 'I told you not to marry Perth. He was not, is not the man for you.' He looked at the Earl. 'I told you to leave her alone.'

Perth returned his look. 'I do as I please.'

'You left her alone before.'

'That was because she was married before I could do anything, and when I challenged de Lisle to an *honourable* duel that might have made her a widow, he beat me. I had no other choices.'

Outside snow began to fall. The wood on the fire cracked, sending a minor explosion of sparks into the room to die harmlessly on the carpet.

'How could you?' Lillith demanded, beginning to get some of her colour back. 'How could you do such despicable things?'

Wentworth looked uncomfortable for the first time. 'I had to. Perth has refused to help me financially. I am facing ruin and ostracism from the *ton*. De Lisle saved me before. I needed you to marry another man who would pay my debts or give you the money to do so.'

'Gambling,' she spat. 'I should have known. We have already had this discussion. I just did not realise how far you would go to support your habit.' She looked at him and disgust marred her features. 'You are despicable, Mathias.' She rose and went to stand over him. 'You are worse than despicable. You are dishonourable. Even by your warped standards, you should know that.' She sucked in air, her chest rising and falling.

'I did what I had to,' he said softly, never showing by expression or tone that he felt remorse.

The tears that had glistened before started falling. Her hands shook and she made no effort to stop them. 'Leave my home. Leave England. Not even you, my brother, a friend of the Prince of Wales, can do the things you have done and get away with them.'

Mathias managed to stand by leaning away from her

and angling behind the chair that now separated them. 'I won't go to the Continent. No one but you and Perth knows.'

'You will,' she nearly shouted. 'You had my husband attacked and then shot. He might have been badly injured. He might have been killed. You did all of that because of your gambling debts. You will go to the Continent or I will tell everyone in the *ton* what you have done. I will ruin you.'

'You are hysterical,' he said haughtily. 'You will do nothing of the sort. If you ruin me, you ruin yourself. Not even Perth's rank will save you.'

'I don't care,' she retorted. 'You *will* go. I don't want you near us where you might decide to do something else. Next time—' she took a deep breath '—next time you might kill him. Go now. Today. Or I swear I will do everything I have threatened.'

Perth rose and took a step towards them. He had never seen Lillith like this where her brother was concerned. He had never expected to. The most he had thought would happen was that she would rant and rave at him and tell him to stay away. Never had he thought she would banish him to the Continent. And especially not for him.

Wentworth stood his ground for long minutes as he and Lillith stared at each other. 'What happened to loving me because I am your brother?' he finally asked.

She swiped at her tears. 'You have gone beyond what I can accept. You nearly killed my husband and all because you wanted me to marry another man who would pay your gaming debts. Now it is my shame to be your sister.' She dropped her hands to her sides and clenched them. Her face turned stony. 'Get out of my house and do not come back. Do not go to my London house either. You are no longer welcome in any place where I am. And…if you are not on your way to Dover by tomorrow morning, I swear to you that I will tell the world what you have done.'

For the first time since Perth had known Wentworth, he thought the man felt something besides self-interest. He almost looked deflated.

'You leave me no choice,' Wentworth finally said in a voice gone dead.

She glared at him, saying nothing. After what seemed an eternity to Perth, Wentworth left. Simmons met him at the door, and Perth knew the butler would escort Wentworth to the door. Only then did Perth go to Lillith.

He went to put his arms around her, but she shoved him away and moved to the window where she could watch her brother leave. Perth heard the sounds of wheels on cobbles and knew that Wentworth drove away. Only then did she turn to him.

'Are you satisfied?' she asked bitterly.

'Yes.' There was nothing else he could say to her that was not a lie.

'Good. Then please go away so I can be miserable in private.' She turned from him again and stared resolutely out of the window, even though he saw her shiver from the cold he knew to be coming through the glass.

He took a step towards her. The long, elegant length of her back begged for his touch, his comfort. His heart begged him to touch and comfort her. Closing the distance between them was hard, but not as hard as what had to follow.

'Lillith,' he murmured when only inches separated them. 'Please look at me. I have things to tell you.'

Her shoulders hunched and she crossed her arms on her chest and still refused to look at him. 'There is nothing you can say to ease the pain of what you just forced me to acknowledge.'

He sighed. 'Did you want to remain ignorant of what your brother is willing to do? I had thought you stronger than that.'

She took a hiccuping sob and he could not help himself. He gripped her shoulders and drew her back against his chest. The need to comfort her was paramount. It was an emotion that he had thought cut out of him ten years before.

'Lillith,' he crooned, 'I am sorry for what has happened, but I cannot be sorry that you finally know. I cannot, no matter how much it hurts you.'

She stiffened under his fingers, a reaction he would have thought hard for her to do since she had already been cold as ice. 'I think I must go away for a while,' she said. 'I need time to accept what I have learned today. Perhaps I will stay here in London, in my house, while you go to the country. Yes,' she said with increasing determination, 'that is what I will do. It will be for the best.'

'No,' he said, the word a shot. 'I won't allow it.'

The patience he had hoped to have with her evaporated. He twisted her around and caught her chin in his hand. The old anger flashed in her eyes, but it brought him no familiar excitement.

He was too scared.

Sweat broke out on his brow. He knew that if he did not tell her now that he loved her, if he did not open himself up to possibly be hurt by her again, that he would lose her. She had been through too much and he had offered her too little. What he had to do, open himself to her, was the hardest thing he had ever done. It made taking a pistol shot in the shoulder seem a mere bagatelle.

Still he took a deep breath. 'Lillith, my wife. My love.' The ultimate words stuck in his throat.

Surprise, shock, wonderment moved over her face as she looked at him. The tears that had flowed for her brother stopped as she cried out softly, 'Perth. Jason, what are you saying?'

He felt her trembling in his arms. The hurt and anger of seconds before might never have existed to look at her eyes now. It humbled him to know the power he had over her happiness. It humbled him and made him very grateful.

'I…' he faltered again. 'It is easier to go into battle than to say I love you.' He smiled down at her, drinking in the love that shone in her face. 'I love you, Lillith, Countess of Perth, mother of my children. I love you more than life itself and I always have.'

'But why now?' She shook her head just a little, perplexed by what to her was a sudden change.

He shrugged. 'I have always loved you. I just re-fused to believe it after what happened before. But I knew I wanted you more than life itself, and when I knew you carried my child I had to have you. But...' he paused, hoping his next words would not cause a rift '...I could not allow myself to trust you as long as I knew that your brother was first in your affections. I knew he did not want you married to me and would do anything to separate us. As long as that possibility was there, I could not, would not, did not even let myself realise—that I love you.'

The flash of irritation that had entered her eyes dis-sipated to melting blue love. 'Oh, Jason. I am truly sorry. I never knew. Before now, I could not have abandoned Mathias. But I can promise you this: no matter what might have happened, he would have never separated us.'

He raised one brow in doubt.

'It is true,' she said. 'For I have loved you from the beginning. That is why I did not want to marry you. I did not want to see you every day, knowing you did not love me when I loved you above all else. I did not think I could stand it and stay sane. But the child changed everything.'

'For you, not for me,' he said softly. 'The child gave you a reason to marry me. I have always wanted you, but I had to get beyond my own hurt to discover that I had never stopped loving you.'

He bent down to kiss her; before he did so, he asked gently, 'Lillith, will you marry me again, for real?'

She wound her arms around his neck and pulled his mouth to hers. 'Yes, my love. Yes.'

Epilogue

Lillith gazed around at the small party gathered here at Ravensford's country seat for the Christmas season. The Duke of Brabourne and his bride were back from the Continent. She had taken a liking to the Duke and his wife almost instantly. There was something about a reformed rake that greatly appealed to her feminine side. He also treated his wife as though she were his most cherished possession. For her part, Juliet, Duchess of Brabourne, melted every time her husband so much as glanced at her.

She watched the men casually talking by the fireplace. It was obvious that they knew each other well and liked and respected each other.

'A toast to our newest newlyweds,' Brabourne said, lifting his glass of whisky, the drink of preference for all three. 'May they live long and be fruitful.'

'May we all live long and be fruitful,' Perth said with a loving look at Lillith as he drank.

'Which we are all doing our best to fulfil,' Mary Margaret said meaningfully.

Lillith laughed. All three women were in the first stages of pregnancy.

'Ahem.' Perth cleared his throat. 'I might as well make a clean breast of everything.' He gave his two friends a sly grin. 'You particularly will be interested in what I have to say,' he said to Ravensford.

Ravensford's green eyes narrowed.

'I could almost be embarrassed except that what I did turned out for the best—as all of you will agree,' Perth continued.

'What did you do, Perth, write those appalling bets about us in Brook's Betting Book?' Ravensford demanded. 'That would explain why none was ever written about you and Lillith.'

Perth gave a deprecating shrug, then burst into laughter. 'Who other? I could tell it was the only way you and Brabourne would come to the sticking point. And you would have been miserable for the rest of your lives if you had let Juliet and Mary Margaret get away.' He raised his glass again. 'I did it for the best.'

'You rogue,' Ravensford said, laughter bubbling in his voice. 'I should have known.'

Lillith marvelled at her husband. He was an arrogant, domineering man who liked his own way, but he was also perceptive enough to know that his friends had been in love and unwilling or unable to admit it to themselves. Much as Perth had been.

She rose and went to his side. 'Jason, you are incorrigible,' she murmured.

He looked down at her with enough love in his eyes to last a lifetime. 'I do what I must, madam.'

'That you do,' she murmured. She tilted her head up so that she could kiss him lightly on his scar. 'Oh!' she exclaimed. 'Oh, my goodness.'

'What is wrong,' he asked, his arm instantly around her. 'Are you sick?'

She smiled. 'I…I am wonderful.' She took his hand and pulled it tighter around her waist so that his palm rested on the slight swell of her belly. 'But our child is restless.'

A look of startled wonder transformed his features. 'Our child,' he murmured. 'Yes, I…I feel a kick.'

'Another toast,' Ravensford announced. 'To the future Earl of Perth.'

Lillith smiled. Perth beamed.

'Or the future Lady Amelia Beaumair, for that is what we will name a girl,' Perth said.

'To our child,' Lillith said simply.

'To our love,' Perth replied, kissing her.

* * * * *

Harlequin Historicals®
Historical Romantic Adventure!

*From rugged lawmen and
valiant knights to defiant heiresses
and spirited frontierswomen,
Harlequin Historicals will
capture your imagination with
their dramatic scope, passion
and adventure.*

*Harlequin Historicals...
they're too good to miss!*

HARLEQUIN®
Presents

The world's bestselling romance series...
The series that brings you your favorite authors,
month after month:

Helen Bianchin...Emma Darcy
Lynne Graham...Penny Jordan
Miranda Lee...Sandra Marton
Anne Mather...Carole Mortimer
Susan Napier...Michelle Reid

and many more uniquely talented authors!

Wealthy, powerful, gorgeous men...
Women who have feelings just like your own...
The stories you love, set in exotic, glamorous locations...

HARLEQUIN®
Presents

Seduction and Passion Guaranteed!

HPDIR104